Call Of Passion

AF103295

Orangebooks Publication

Smriti Nagar, Bhilai, Chhattisgarh - 490020

Website: **www.orangebooks.in**

© Copyright, 2022, Author

All rights reserved. No part of this book may be reproduced, stored in a retrieval system, or transmitted, in any form by any means, electronic, mechanical, magnetic, optical, chemical, manual, photocopying, recording or otherwise, without the prior written consent of its writer.

First Edition, 2022
ISBN: 978-93-92878-03-9

The opinions/ contents expressed in this book are solely of the author and do not represent the opinions/ standings/ thoughts of OrangeBooks.

Call of Passion

Duriya Kasubhai

OrangeBooks Publication
www.orangebooks.in

Acknowledgements

I would like to thank my daughters – Karishma & Rukhsar, for supporting me in getting this book out. A big thank you and appreciation to Zainab Pacha, for all the support and help in editing my book from scratch. My three beautiful girls have played a very important role in planning the publication of my second book.

From the first draft to the final draft, and the final look of the book, they have worked really hard to help my book get the treatment it deserves. This would have been impossible without you.

Thank You.

Lots of Love,

Duriya Kasubhai / Mom

Chapter 1

Delilah Redford looked around her, rather disinterestedly. She was back in London after a lapse of three years that she had spent in Switzerland, where she had been enrolled in a finishing school. She was a transformed young woman now, and she knew it. She looked enchanting in a dress of lettuce green linen. She lifted her hand to tuck the straying thick, dark brown tresses behind her ear, as they kept teasing her lips and eyes which served as a great source of irritation, especially when she had to wait for long tedious hours in a queue to pass through the immigration and customs at the airport. The routine was inevitable, but Delilah felt understandably annoyed. She felt the dampness of her hair and let out an exasperated sigh.

Her eyes were the most incredible – green, sparkling like emeralds, with ridiculously long eyelashes, and, furthermore, thickened by the aid of mascara. Her gaze darted into the direction of the glass partition, where she could clearly discern the eager public waving out to the new arrivals. Anxiously she searched amongst the crowd for a tall, dark, imposing figure, but her eyes met no one by that description.

Heathrow airport hadn't changed much in those past three years, she reflected irrelevantly, while her eyes pricked with suppressed tears and her head seemed heavy like her heart. So, he hadn't come after all to receive her and she felt like bursting into tears.

After passing through the customs and immigration clearance, she hastened towards the lounge and ordered a glass of sugared lime juice. Immersed in the thoughts of her step-brother, Dominic Redford, she was unaware of the masculine attention she was attracting by her overall attractiveness, not to mention her exceeding good looks.

She was not tall, but neither was she short; her slim proportions were beautifully curved and softly rounded with the tiniest waistline; and small yet, beautifully formed breasts. Her dress reaching up to her slim, rounded thighs revealed the graceful lines of her calves and delicate fair ankles. Her legs were long and slender; and her feet with pink-tipped nails were diminutive like their owner, who closely resembled a small, exquisite model of perfection.

But this particular young woman had a volcanic temper, that only one person by the name of Dominic Redford could control without so much as raising his voice. One quelling look from those deep, blue eyes would usually prove sufficient to silence her. But, alas, things would not be quite the same hereafter.

He had not been able to subjugate her, though that had never been his intention. She was far too spirited for one thing, and also easily offended. Dominic would never admit it, but he had a soft spot for his aggressive step-sister, hence he often endeavoured never to bruise her sensitivity.

One amorous young man approached Delilah's table and smiled at the beautiful girl rather amicably, hoping to create an impression.

She gazed up at him and her forehead creased into a frown. The young man's smile widened, not in the least ruffled by the look of disapproval aimed at him.

'May I join you at your table?'

'Sorry...no. I'm expecting someone,' she inserted coldly.

The man, however, refused to be snubbed. He settled himself into a chair standing opposite her.

After that she did not pay much attention to him, merely continued to look around her for some sign of a tall, familiar figure. Restlessly she began to tap her fingers on the table.

'Shall I order something for you?'

She looked at him then, but with a total lack of interest.

'No thanks,' she said carelessly, obviously not bothered by his presence. This only served to intensify the young man's interest in her. He was accustomed to a different, and a more positive reaction from the opposite sex, but he found Delilah's indifference intriguing and challenging. He smiled good-humouredly and ordered two cups of tea for both of them.

'By the way, my name is Russel Dexter. What's yours?'

'Delilah...' And suddenly her eyes caught sight of the man who had been all this while in her thoughts, even throughout her journey from Switzerland to London, and it had persisted till this very moment.

Upon seeing him striding towards her in his long, brisk strides, her heart missed a beat. His features were sharp with penetrating blue eyes and those compressed lips, that looked so sensuous when twisted into a smile. She stood up and fixed her gaze upon him, forgetting all else. He now stood by the table and subjected her to an intense and disturbing scrutiny. Her gaze for a moment wavered before his, for she had been caught off guard and a flush suffused her cheeks.

'I'm sorry if I'm late. The traffic detained me.' He glanced across at Russel with mild interest. 'Won't you introduce me to your friend, Delilah?' And the way he said her name was in itself disturbing. The inflection in his voice had been slow and caressing, but without the hard expression changing.

'This is er – Russel Dexter.'

The young man stood up to shake hands with the older man.

'Russel, meet my cousin Dominic Redford.' The "cousin" had been a reluctant inclusion. She couldn't bring herself to address him as a step-brother, let alone brother, as they shared no blood ties, whatsoever.

Russel's eyebrows lifted fractionally.

'Dominic Redford, the well-known business tycoon? It's you, isn't it, who's started a revolution in wool and exclusive fabrics? And if I'm not mistaken, you also own a coal mine in the United States?' his brow wrinkled up in some confusion and deep contemplation. He was trying to conjure up some more details about the well-known personality now standing before him, and viewing him quizzically. 'Ah, yes, I had also read in the papers about your large estates and vineyards in Spain. It's often reported that you visit your properties there running in acres and acres... and to... to meet you this way, in person, is an unusual experience after only having read about you in the papers and magazines. Never anticipated that I'd meet you this way though.' He seemed visibly impressed by the man's quiet, overpowering personality and that distinctive aura of affluence and aristocracy.

Dominic appeared to be slightly bored but waited patiently for Russel to end his conjectures; not that they were incorrect, but he resented the publicity that came with them; such exposure he took great pains to avoid, as he then became quite frequently the subject of speculation that his reserved temperament found intolerable; a liability he could do without.

'You are well-informed, Mr Dexter. I won't be surprised if you should provide me with the narrative of my personal affairs, er...essentially speaking, my multiple affairs with women. I have earned considerable fame in that particular direction,' he quipped sardonically, and Delilah observed that years had lent maturity to his striking good looks.

The light tropical suit that he wore fitted him perfectly and subtly revealed the hard litheness of his athletic physique. Not an ounce of extra flesh was in evidence in the perfectly formed body of the man. He smelled faintly of expensive tobacco and aftershave lotion. Russel appeared perturbed by the older man's tone.

'It is not my intention to pry into your private affairs, Mr Redford,' he spoke affably, yet managed to retain his self-respect.

There was now the slightest gleam of appreciation in Dominic's eyes. 'For that, you must either be a good gossiper or a conscientious reporter. What are you, Russel?' he asked in his deep, profound voice, carrying a note of faint amusement.

'I'm neither, Mr Redford,' he smiled expansively upon being put at ease.

He soon took leave of them both and extracted a promise from Delilah that they would soon meet. She had merely nodded, her mind once more returning to the man standing beside her. Suddenly he turned to face her and regarded her with some interest.

'You look beautiful, Delilah,' he remarked quietly.

Just then the waiter came with the tea that Russel had ordered, and it was Dominic who paid the bill and gestured for the waiter to take the cups away. Soon after they were leisurely walking towards the exit door. The luggage had been already collected and deposited in Dominic's car. Again, glancing at her sideways he remarked with some emphasis, 'You have changed and for the better. Never thought you'd look so...attractive.'

She lifted her eyes to his for assurance, but he had averted his gaze and began looking straight ahead of him, as they walked to his waiting car.

'Come.... Mother and Father are waiting for us. The girls have gone to an exhibition.'

'Is Mother still suffering from the migraine?' she asked concernedly. She loved her mother very dearly. Two hours to go before they would reach Cambridge; a long wait, she reflected.

'Nothing has changed much, since you were last here – in England,' there was a subtle irony in his words, as he broke into her thoughts.

'H...How is Papa?' her voice shook nervously.

This was one question that she had dreaded to ask. She had to admit in all honesty that she simply adored her step-father. Also, were anything to happen to him, she knew she would be deprived of a best friend who understood her temperament so well and was always able to bring out only the best in her. On the other hand, his son from his first wife had the opposite effect on her; a look of dismay had entered her face.

She had never known her own father, as he had died succumbing to a deadly fever, while she was still in her mother's womb. It was then when Sampson Redford had proposed marriage to her mother, promising to provide her with a home and security, and all he had wanted in return was that she would look after his son and two daughters from his previous marriage. Selena Berkely had accepted his proposal because she occasionally fell sick and decided that she alone would not be able to bring up her child, and grant the child a perfect upbringing with her keeping mostly unwell and indisposed. But she was and had been an extremely loving woman with a charming and a gentle disposition, the latter part which could hardly be applied to her daughter who was high-spirited and quick-tempered.

Way back in the past, when Delilah had still been in Selena's womb, her mother had been working for Sampson Redford as his private secretary. But because she would often remain absent and irregular on account of her failing health, she had then decided to relinquish her job, even though she had known that she would not be having sufficient income to support herself and her baby. The little that she received from her husband's pension could hardly be described as sufficient, but Sampson had insisted that she continue to work.

He had been most patient and had shown much understanding by allowing her to keep her job, despite the fact that she remained absent for a major part of the month. But soon she had begun to feel guilty about taking undue advantage of his magnanimity, and besides, the staff was beginning to put an entirely wrong interpretation to Sampson's innocent display of understanding, obviously suspecting his motives for practising such patience and understanding with Selena. His being extra nice to her and showing her such kindness was misconstrued by all in the office.

Finally, Selena, unable to tolerate the injustice meted out to Sampson, had promptly handed over her resignation letter, but again understanding her reasons for making such a sacrifice, he in turn had proposed to her in his straight-forward manner. She had accepted, although, there had been some hesitation. They both came from two radically different backgrounds. He had aristocratic blood in his veins, and she hailed from a middle-class family. She had had her doubts about whether the marriage would work. But it had, and ever since she had never regretted that instantaneous decision that she had taken over twenty years ago.

She had lovingly brought up Dominic, then a twelve-year-old lad, Joan only a year old and Anna two years her senior; when Selena had given birth to Delilah. As Delilah grew up, she also developed affectionate feelings for her new family; particularly her step-sisters, but with Dominic, it had been a strained relationship from the very beginning.

Delilah's eyes were now shaded with pain and a stronger emotion, something akin to a violent frenzy that she had no control over, every time she thought of the young Dominic, who had in the past constantly tormented her in more ways than one. Each time her feelings had undergone a change that she found difficult to comprehend, but of late she had noticed a tremendous change coming over Dominic. He was quieter and more saturnine.

In retrospect, it seemed like he would mostly keep to himself and his actions, which had in the past been thoughtless and uninhibited were now more controlled and expertly schooled. He scarcely spoke, but the little that he spoke, was more likely to be imprinted in the minds of those who came in touch with him. Yes, he had definitely changed, Delilah smiled reminiscently.

She climbed into the waiting black Mercedes and Dominic quietly slipped beside her, behind the wheel. He motioned the car towards the highway and with smooth dexterity, he accelerated down the well-constructed road but took care to maintain the permitted speed. Indeed, Dominic had changed a lot.

'You never answered my question, Dominic.' She glanced sideways to study his hard, handsome profile; something that had always fascinated her.

'You never gave me that opportunity,' he said quietly, his long fingers resting lightly upon the wheel.

She looked at him enquiringly.

'What do you mean?'

'You appeared to be preoccupied.'

She sank back against the leather upholstery and shut her eyes.

'That shouldn't have stopped you from answering my question,' she said in a tight voice.

His eyes for a moment ran over her meaningfully, before he once more started focusing on his driving.

'Everything about you has developed so beautifully except for your brains. Father is a heart patient. He suffers from periodical attacks, but thankfully they are never very serious. You should know that, as I have been keeping you well informed, and besides, a heart patient is never really healthy and vigorous for that matter, so why the stupid question? Your concern sounds almost too…factitious.'

She flinched from that cruel remark.

'H…How can you say such a thing when you know very well how much I love Papa?' she felt a prick of tears somewhere behind her eyes.

'I'm sorry,' he apologised quietly. 'That remark I admit was uncalled for.'

'Could we change the subject, please?' she said in a tearful voice, her fingers playing around restlessly with her kerchief.

She blushed crimson when suddenly she remembered how he had looked at her while waiting to collect her luggage. That look had been almost primitive in its intensity, and then she sighed inaudibly. He had reverted to his cold, formal ways. Now, left to her private thoughts she dreamily visualised the massive brick mansion they were presently residing in; her beloved home in Cambridge. The journey to Cambridge was altogether too tedious an affair, although the prospect of returning home after a stretch of three years was simply delightful.

In Switzerland when she had seen the love and harmony in the family that she had stayed with, it had often made her feel nostalgic, and several times she had longed for her own family. And now that she was on her way to her own home, she knew she would not have wanted anything more than that, for the moment at least.

The silence between them was suspended in the strained atmosphere like a threatening cloud. She turned to look out of the window, watching the passing view, but with vague interest. It was mid-noon and by the time they would reach home, she thought vaguely, it would probably be two to three in the early evening. She was already beginning to feel the effects of the long journey that she had had. Her eyes became heavy with sleep and she felt fatigued. So confidently resting her head against his shoulder, she shut her eyes.

She had shifted closer to him, but she was not aware that he had gone taut when the tip of her breast came into contact with his arm. She was too tired to realise that her proximity could affect him, just as strongly as his nearness had a way of disturbing her, and her breathing.

'You don't mind, do you?' she asked drowsily. She was too tired and sleepy to care.

'What?' he queried in a strange voice.

'That I should lay my head on your shoulder?' she glanced up to meet his indomitable expression.

'Not if you can keep quiet,' he said in a voice that had turned slightly hoarse. His sinewy fingers had involuntarily tightened round the wheel, and his knuckles showed white.

She laughed huskily.

'All right, if you say so,' she complied in a whispering tone, her eyes partly closed and her mouth too had parted, though quite unconsciously.

He just then happened to glance in her direction, and the picture that she presented was enough to boil any man's blood, and Dominic muttered an angry oath under his breath. He resolutely turned away from the cause of that momentary distraction and concentrated on his driving instead.

Minutes ticked by and after some fifteen minutes or so Delilah lifted her eyes to meet those that were looking straight ahead of them both, studying the road the car was moving over. Her lovely face was upturned, her lips smiling tantalisingly, and her eyes gleaming with lazy laughter.

'May I talk now?' she asked softly, gently digging her long nails into his hard, muscular arm, and causing him to catch his breath. 'Did it hurt?' she queried provocatively.

She then inched closer to him and whispered into his ear.

'Tell me, Dominic, did it hurt?' By drawing closer to him, her breast was pressed lightly to his arm that stiffened beneath the gentle impact of her tantalising curves.

Her soft, curvy thigh was resting against his hard one, and quite unintentionally she allowed her hand to rest on his thigh, her fingers caressing the expensive material of his slim-fitting trousers beneath which his flesh seemed to ache for further contact with the beautiful, young woman sitting so close to him.

'No to both your questions. Now move,' he said in a hoarse voice. 'There is plenty of space in the front seat. Get back to your corner, will you?'

She watched him enquiringly.

'Why, do you not fancy it?' she asked tentatively. She could see that he was moved.

'Oh, shut up!' he whispered in a violent tone. He changed his gear. He did not see the tears welling up in her eyes. She instantly moved to her side of the seat.

'Either you are still innocent or damn it...you are deliberately being provocative!'

The rest of their journey was spent in silence. Delilah quietly observed through tear-filled eyes the row of cottages standing against a scenic background with rugged mountains, so fierce and outstanding, and contrasting well with the widespread, deep blue of the sky; like it were enveloping the gigantic mountains in its cool cloak of security, shading it from the unpredictable weather or so it seemed. The stars taking their positions in the sky would still have been a welcoming sight, had they not been veiled. But, for such a merry sight she would have to wait for the advancing night. Her eyes for a second focused on Dominic before they once more raced with the moving scenery, that provided her with a vague diversion taking her away from disturbing thoughts.

Delilah felt relieved when a new view took over. There were now tall, graceful-looking buildings forming a row of similar constructions and with a few elegant-looking shops thrown in for effect with wonderfully-decked showrooms displaying various items and goods; in some shops and boutiques, wax models greeting passers-by with their smiling countenance; set and immobile but attractive, nevertheless.

People were scurrying in and out of the shops with their purchases; a look of satisfaction about them. Some walked in, encouraged by the eager crowds collected in and dazzling lights and the irresistible display of goods artistically arranged in the glass windows; drawing the public's attention to it.

The car sped past a few elegant banks followed by a vast roadway specially reserved for smooth traffic, and closely followed by some more buildings and prettily sketched out restaurants, and some more shops, each more opulent than the other, displaying tempting merchandise. Delilah longed to see the familiar sights to her left, but she quickly decided against it.

Their ultimate destination was getting closer. She was aching for the sight of the edifice, which was her home, and the estate rich in fertility and fruit trees stretching for miles into vast acres. She felt nostalgic for the proportionate garden which was her favourite spot whenever she needed to be on her own, with the songs of the birds and awareness of the enchanting music floating in the air; her only companions that she could afford to welcome, as otherwise, she preferred to be alone.

When they finally reached home, the whole family was waiting outside at the gates to receive her. The moment she emerged from the car; she was gathered into her mother's arms. In her happiness, she cried on her mother's shoulder like a child and was soon after enfolded in her father's arms. A hard businessman he was, but that did not stop him from being sentimental about the return of his favourite daughter. He had tears in his eyes. He bent down to kiss her on her forehead.

'Welcome home, my little beauty.'

Both the girls kissed her affectionately and were genuinely glad to have their youngest family member back in their midst again. Delilah turned and was just in time to see Dominic disappear through the open, tall, iron gates, and into the direction of the estate. This was her first day at home and already he was avoiding her, as though he couldn't stand the sight of her. Couldn't he at least make a pretence of having an interest in her, if just for the benefit of the family? She wondered bitterly, for how long would this continue? But she ought to have known that Dominic was the last person to practice diplomacy if he should resent being civil to a particular person. But, was being discreet and polite an act of hypocrisy? She doubted it. So, the least he could do was to be polite and considerate to her. It was her personal reflection and she pondered over it with some misgiving.

The whole family had collected in the drawing-room for the evening tea, except for Dominic, who was still out on the estate.

'How did you find Switzerland?' Joan asked excitedly.

Delilah turned to her with a smile.

'It is a beautiful city, but, still, I say, there is nothing in the world like home. I missed England and you all so much that several times I wished I were back with you all, though now, I have no reason to complain,' she smiled contentedly, 'now that I'm here in your midst.'

Sampson and Selena exchanged warm glances.

'Yes, it is indeed wonderful to have you back with us again.' Sampson pulled her over his lap and Selena looked on with visible admiration at her husband and daughter. The girls observed the love between the father and the daughter with twinkling eyes.

'Hey, Dad, do you think we could fit on your lap… seems like it's fully occupied. I think we deserve a little pampering too.'

And with a burst of hearty laughter, Sampson gestured for them to join Delilah on his lap. They rushed to his side and occupied the remaining space with yet another merry laugh.

'Mom,' they chorused in a trio, 'fancy joining us?'

Selena blushed and refused to meet her husband's teasing glance. 'My generous proportions will not allow me that privilege.'

Sampson threw back his head and laughed.

'How right you are, dear.' But when he saw his wife's black frown, he immediately changed his tune, 'But be rest assured, dearest, I prefer you exactly the way you are now.'

Selena nodded satisfactorily.

'Okay, girls...one of you had better go out and inform Dominic that his father wants him here.'

Sampson looked at his wife enquiringly.

'What for, dear?

'You have an appointment with the doctor today. Remember?' She put aside her knitting and came to sit beside her husband. 'You know, darling, you can't possibly go alone. Dominic's presence would prove helpful. Please, darling, now don't argue.'

The two girls got up one after the other, kissing their father as they quickly left his side and taking care to avoid their mother's eyes as they hurriedly began fleeing out of the room.

Selena smiled at the girls knowingly, well aware they were wanting to avoid her, as she was sure to ask them for some favours.

'Anna, go get your brother,' Selena requested her eldest daughter, knowing what the answer would be.

'Sorry, Mother, but I will be late for my music class,' and she had rushed out of the room.

'Joan, you go then ... no excuses, please,' Selena appealed to her, as it was already getting late and the doctor's appointment was for six.

'Mother, you must forgive me, but I have a date with Bernard. Sorry, but I must hurry.' And she quickly followed Anna out of the room after throwing Selena a kiss with a soft twinkle in her eyes.

Delilah too decided to follow Anna's example and hastened out of the room, for it was an ordeal for her to go up to Dominic to convey the message to him.

'Delilah... just a moment...'

'Sorry, Mama, but er...' she faltered, looking for a plausible excuse to avoid meeting Dominic again and so soon.

'Oh no... you won't, my dear. You are going out there at once and kindly remind Dominic that he has to keep the appointment with the doctor. Tell him Sampson is ready and waiting for him. Now go. Sorry, indeed!' She murmured exasperatedly.

Sampson laughed quietly.

'You could control a whole regiment if you put your mind to it, Selena.'

'Yes, I think I could if it wouldn't have been for this infernal problem.'

She smiled faintly, pointing to her head. Then her eyes went to Delilah standing by the window-side with her back to her parents.

'Now, what is it? What are you waiting for? Go, child,' Selena said, exasperatedly.

Sampson looked on quietly, but he knew something was amiss. The daughter he loved so much was a grown-up woman now, and her reasons for refusing to obey her mother's command had to be a good one. He had sensed something between his own son and foster daughter Delilah, but it would take some time to completely understand what it could be. He was himself a worldly man. He too had in his heydays sown a few wild oats and recognised awareness in the eyes of women when in a particular man's presence, and though Delilah's face was now averted, he could sense it as though she had herself expressed it to him; the turmoil within the recesses of her tender heart.

But if this was so, then for how long would she avoid the inevitable... was what worried him now. That wouldn't solve any problems. In fact, by facing such a problem, which was a part of growing up, she would be able to adjust well to the difficult stages of growing up. She was still so young and extremely emotional.

'Do as your mama says, dear.'

And Delilah obeyed him almost instantly, though her legs felt like jelly, as she crossed the vast estate to reach Dominic's side, who was standing on the furthest end and supervising the labourers. He seemed extremely busy, and she for a moment hesitated before crossing to where he was standing. He was instructing his men when Delilah intervened, her breath coming faster through her lips.

'Dominic.... I... Mother, er, Father has an appointment with the doctor.'

'What the....,' He turned on her angrily. His hands were resting on his slim, tapering hips, and beads of sweat had formed on his forehead.

'Well, aren't you going?' she looked straight ahead of her, refusing to meet those all-seeing eyes of the man.

'Of course, I am, woman. Er, thanks for the reminder. I had almost forgotten. Now, run along. I'll follow you in a minute.' He then abruptly summoned a few of his men to his side and instructed them to take over until his return. But, when he turned to Delilah back again, he saw her glaring up at him with fiercely beautiful eyes.

'How dare you ask me to...to run along as though I were a child!' her words were a mere whisper but her voice was a hiss.

She looked irresistible at that moment in a fit of anger, and even he couldn't deny it to himself. He deliberately put his arms around her shoulder and firmly led her away from the curious eyes of the labourers.

'You must try controlling that confounded temper of yours. It tends to get out of hand,' he warned her tersely, his fingers biting into the soft, rounded flesh of her upper arm, 'Or would you rather I did something about it?'

With a violent movement, she shrugged his arm away and took him by surprise.

She was facing him now like some enraged, wounded tigress. 'You are utterly despicable! If you dare touch me again, I swear I will kick you hard in your shin,' she warned, sparks shooting from her beautiful eyes.

He stood there looking down into her furious eyes interestedly for a moment. He had a half-smile playing about his lips.

'Did they also teach you to swear and kick in the finishing school? And, don't ever try those stunts with me in full view of my men. You can do it in the privacy of our home. This way I'll feel unconstrained to retaliate in a…very effective way. You understand I am sure…?' he grinned down at her furious expression; his eyes gleaming with wry amusement. 'Come on, we had better move along,' he said with a lazy indulgence. But she refused to budge a step further. He turned sideways, watching her with icy-blue eyes. 'You were not always so obstinate. Now, are you coming or do I have to carry you back to the house?'

'Damn you, I don't like being mocked at…you brute! I'll walk on my own. I don't need you to carry me like I were some invalid.'

His smile was crooked and infinitely attractive.

'Or a beauty in distress, perhaps,' he added in a mildly teasing tone. She threw him a haughty look and marched ahead of him. He soon caught up with her. They were now walking side by side.

'I sometimes wonder from whom could you have inherited such an explosive temper. Some man someday is going to find staying with you a sore trial. And, your children…if they are going to be anything like you, then the poor man will be better off in the graveyard. And, if it does happen to drive him mad before sending him on his final journey, then the lunatic asylum would be the best suitable place for him. All this would surely follow if I know your dumb taste in men.' His eyes gleamed teasingly, as he deliberately threw her a glance.

She was trembling with an inexplicable fury. She turned on him like some beautiful, wild creature, provoked and then raised her hand to strike him a blow on his face, but he had foreseen her reaction and was faster. He caught her hand in mid-air and pressed her clenched fists to his chest. 'Not here, Miss Firebrand.' He carelessly stroked her flushed cheeks. 'And not just yet. I'm getting late for the appointment, though believe me,' he said with a mock, apologetic look in his attractive deep blue eyes, 'it would be a pleasure to draw swords with you. It would be like dealing with a…spirited horse.' And she knew he meant it as an insult.

She had detected a note of faint derision in his tone and with an angry snort, she ran the rest of the way to the house, but she missed the look of deep concern entering into those worldly eyes. In many ways, he thought, Delilah had yet not changed. She was strong-headed, fiercely temperamental, forever quick to retort and looking even more beautiful with the advancing years, but for all her hot-headedness, he knew that deep down she was extremely vulnerable, loving and kind at heart. It was a rare combination but a dangerous one. Many people were taken in by her rebellious temperament when in all truth, it was a facade concealing a kind and gentle disposition. Consequently, people whom she came in touch with treated her with careless disdain, imagining her to be thick-skinned and invulnerable, thinking that she probably deserved such harsh treatment. She was the kind of woman who, although being extremely susceptible to any kind of pain inflicted upon her had the determination to hide it from the world, taking pains to evince no emotion on the surface, her fighting spirit never deserting her.

With a thoughtful expression on his face, he strode across the open gates and leisurely made his way into the hallway, where his father was patiently waiting for him, all dressed. Selena had retired to her room as her head was giving her trouble once again and the pain had heightened. Dominic casually looked around for Delilah, his lips compressed and expelling a sigh. His father knew only too well it was an indication of impatience. He followed his son's eyes that were scanning the large hallway, and every nook and corner of it with growing impatience, then those eyes settled on the curved staircase, and finally journeyed to rest on Sampson's amused expression.

'Looking for my favourite girl, Dominic?'

'Huh, favourite girl, did you say?' he bit his lower lip in contemplation, nodding at his father's teasing enquiry, while vaguely his hands stayed rooted to his lean hips as was his custom, and his eyes reflected a restlessness that did not fool his father.

'Delilah has gone up to her room, son. Come, we'll be late for our appointment.'

He absently followed his father out through the front door and together they approached the car at the gate. Quickly they both got inside the car. Soon they were on their way to Harley Street to keep the appointment with the heart specialist; also, a family friend.

'Dominic, do you know what happened that made Delilah so angry when she came running into the house? She appeared to be in a foul mood.'

Dominic's lips tightened. He stiffened under his father's subtle insinuation, that it was he who was in all truth responsible for annoying Delilah.

'That girl needs to be taken in hand, and as for that temper of hers, it will certainly have to be harnessed or I'll never have peace of mind. Her first day at home and already she has succeeded in trying my endurance. Very soon she will exhaust it and then I'll not be held responsible for the consequences, Father…I repeat, someone had better teach her a lesson in discipline.' He navigated a left turn, and reduced the speed, as the traffic grew denser and the movement of many vehicles standing in parallel rows made his movement restricted, and as the time for the scheduled appointment was getting closer, a sigh of exasperation escaped his lips.

'But, son, you only need to use the word "harness" with horses more often than not. One can endeavour to curb the young woman's temper and not harness it, and I love the child too much to be able to be stern with her and train her in... discipline.' His eyes shone with affection for his foster daughter. When he smiled to himself, it looked like he was smiling reminiscently.

'You are being over-indulgent with her, so much that you have spoiled her,' said Dominic airily.

'Well,' his father laughed amusedly. 'Someone must spoil her. She deserves an indulgent father. Her mother is rather too strict with her. You are intolerant and impatient with her. You never have a kind word to say to her, and the girls are too involved in their own affairs to be bothered about the youngest member of the family. No one seems to realise that she is no longer a child, but a woman with a woman's feelings, her desire to be wanted and loved with a craving for attention and deserves appreciation for her finer qualities, that may not be perhaps visible owing to a strong feeling of inadequacy that often makes her behave in the way she does,' he tried to explain with some feelings; a man not much prone to excitation.

'You're defending her,' pointed out his son discouragingly.

'Not at all,' Sampson contradicted firmly, decisively.

'Then what is it?'

'Look, son, she has reached a point in her life where she wants to be acknowledged as an individual with a mind of her own. She has too much spirit for one thing, that I admit, but to destroy her spirit in the name of discipline would be cruelty, doing injustice to that girl's vital, bubbling personality.' His eyes suddenly twinkled merrily. 'Besides, that girl presents quite a challenge. If that reputed finishing school could do nothing to tutor her spirited nature, monitor her uninhibited behaviour and turn her into a refined young woman, then I can't think of anyone who'd have the strength, courage and er, the stamina to curb her wild and uninhibited disposition. Any comments?' he glanced sideways at his son rather significantly.

'I get the message, Father. You want me to volunteer for that particular assignment. But I'm afraid I'm not prepared to prove obliging in this particular matter. You can start looking elsewhere for some unfortunate man with that crazy job planted in your mind,' he concluded firmly.

The look on his father's face was deliberately jeering.

'Naturally, I will have to look elsewhere if you fear she may slay you alive.'

Momentarily their eyes met and Dominic saw the challenge in his father's eyes and began to laugh softly.

He was aware he was swallowing a bait, but that was better than being called a coward to your face.

'I think we are giving too much importance to Delilah. I accept the challenge, Father, and now let's change the subject.'

'I'm glad you accepted the challenge. Rather you than me, any day,' and both father and son broke into laughter. Sampson's frank admission for once was accepted with a humorous laugh.

'Before I forget, have you contacted Ted in Spain? It appears to me he is losing interest in the job,' Sampson remarked in a faintly exasperated tone.

'Do you know, I personally think we shouldn't have appointed him as our estate manager, especially a man like him who can't stay away from his young wife for even a minute. If he had his way, he would bring her to his workplace with him and carry her round like some Christmas gift,' Dominic said with a hint of satire, as he continued, 'You're worrying unnecessarily. The post can sometimes be delayed. There is a possibility that we might receive his letter tomorrow or the day after,' he reassured his father and was relieved when Sampson did not mention anything regarding Ted after that.

Back at the clinic, the doctor watched both the father and son walk toward him and he frowned darkly. The smile in his blue eyes belied his frown.

'Dominic, you are two minutes late. I understand it's the traffic again.'

Samson's eyes were twinkling with mischief.

'Now, how did you guess that, my dear fellow?'

'Doctor Cromwell is a man of unusual perception, Father,' Dominic intervened in a lazy, amused tone and the doctor smiled.

'So, even powerful men like you can't dodge the sluggish traffic motion…you were helpless, weren't you?' the doctor teased.

'No wealth or influence would be able to work wonders here. I guess every man, however wealthy and powerful, at the end of it, is a man like any other,' Dominic replied with an easy smile.

'Such reasoning cannot be ruled out,' the doctor agreed after some serious thought.

Sampson intervened jovially.

'Hence, Doctor, an impediment that could not be prevented and the result; we are two minutes late, so forgive this very brief procrastination, and start counting my heartbeats,' Sampson concluded with a humorous laugh, and the doctor soon joined him, sharing his good humour, and indulgently did as he was bid with his ready stethoscope.

'For how many more years will I live? Don't just add years blindly,' Sampson remarked with a wry grin.

'I'll give you another decade, Sampson. Perhaps even longer than that, and no jokes,' and he meant it.

Dominic hitched his leg on one of the low tables lying about in the consulting room and coolly surveyed the two friends discussing matters of health.

'You better advise Father to take his medications regularly. I've heard complaints from Mother lately. At this rate, I doubt, if he will even survive for five more years,' Dominic broke into the middle of their conversation with startling frankness.

'Ah, complaints!' Sampson explained softly 'That is about the only thing I get from my wife, nowadays,' he said with a resigned nod of his head.

'From what I've heard, you still dote on your wife, and it couldn't be unless she satisfies your every whim, and so, my dear man, your remark hardly justifies this truth that I constantly hear about.'

'So, you listen to gossip, eh, Doctor?' Sampson looked disapproving, but his blue eyes were twinkling with amusement.

Soon after a complete check-up, Sampson then took leave of his friend, followed by Dominic at a much slower pace.

'Let's just hope Father will listen to reason,' Dominic had said as a parting shot.

'Oh, he most certainly will. Remember, Dominic, your father is not an automaton. He has a mind... a well-balanced mind and a reasoning power. So, he is not likely to fall apart. He hasn't reached that age and even then, he won't lag behind. As I said, he is strong.'

'Hmm, that I agree wholeheartedly, Doctor. So long.' And with a half-grin, he strode out of the room, walking a few more paces till he fell into step with his father.

'He is a grand chap,' Sampson remarked appreciatively.

'Oh yes!' Dominic agreed absently, his mind a distance away.

They were soon on their way home, talking away animatedly. Dominic had always got along excellently with his father. They shared a compatibility that made it so much easier for them to be on informal terms with each other, almost as though they were two friends enjoying a long-standing friendship of many years.

It was twenty past eight by the time they reached home. Selena was waiting for them in the hallway. The girls were nowhere to be seen. They had probably escaped, keeping some appointment or the other as was their custom, thought Sampson absently.

'What did the doctor say?' Selena asked with some anxiety; a question that was to her of the utmost importance.

'Ah, that...my dear, you now need not worry. The doctor says my heart will not stop beating for...let's say, some two more decades. Now, isn't that the news that calls for celebration?' he laughed jovially, putting his arms around his wife's shoulder.

After a while, Dominic strode off in the direction of the barroom where he helped himself to a glass of cognac, leaning indolently against the bar counter and sipping his drink thoughtfully.

Delilah returned from a party her friends had given in her honour. She went straight to her room without waiting to stop to talk to her father, who, it appeared, was as usual, too anxious to have her by his side again.

'I won't be a minute, Papa.' And she ran up to her room, quietly changing into a simple dress of light blue with sprinkles of pink and white embroidered flowers all over the border and cap sleeves with a square neckline. She hurriedly splashed cold water on her face and hastily applied gloss over her lips of a deep pink shade. Even in simplicity, she managed to look enchanting.

She joined her parents in the drawing-room. Her mother was applying varnish to an antique piece, and she watched the produced effect with some satisfaction. Sampson was relaxed in a recliner, smoking his pipe and watching his daughter's entry into the room with an indulgent smile.

'Did you enjoy the party?' he enquired indulgently.

'Hmm, yes,' she answered, lightly picking up a magazine and ostensibly scanning the small prints in it. She appeared to be extremely restless on the surface, though.

Her sisters, she knew would be coming home late. But she hadn't encountered Dominic, yet. Perhaps he too had disappeared somewhere on his own, taking his car with him. Such was his custom, she thought vaguely, this being whenever he felt tensed and weighed down with problems. But, when the man in her thoughts casually strode into the room, she received a mild shock and discovered that she was pleased to see him, though she made a pretence at indifference. He came straight towards her, his smile mildly mocking.

'The magazine must be pretty enthralling to hold your interest,' he jibed softly.

She frowned up at him.

'Where were you? I didn't see you when I came minutes ago.' She resumed her study of the magazine, not willing to show him that she was strongly affected by his presence.

And, even though Sampson made a pretence of reading his newspaper, he was watching his son and Delilah with a calculative mind. He came to the conclusion that their relationship would soon blossom into a very passionate affair, and perhaps even someday would progress into love, but that right now it was strained and both were uncomfortable with each other, though neither made it known to the other what extraordinary effect they had on each other. At that moment, he felt his heart reach out to them.

'Had you taken a peek in the barroom, you would have found me there. I might have even invited you to join me for a drink,' his tone carried mild sarcasm.

'Indulging in intoxicating drinks is not one of my vices.' She raised her eyes to his and looked beautiful and arrogant.

He met her eyes with a hint of mockery in his.

'I'm glad that you have vices after all, and are normal as the rest of us mortals, I was beginning to suspect you were an angel dropped from the mighty skies by mistake into this hell of a place they call earth,' he remarked with open mockery and fully succeeding in antagonising her.

'I assure you my entry into this particular hell, as you call it, was no phenomenon,' she countered sweetly, 'and also that I'm no angel, but if given a pair of fangs I would gladly tear you apart. Does that prospect frighten you…make you nervous?' she asked provocatively.

'No, it excites me,' he returned with a grin, watching her with a devilish gleam in his eyes.

Just then Selena came and stood outside, watching them with some amusement and not without affection. Her eyes were lit up with quiet laughter.

'Dominic, do me a favour, and take this girl out somewhere, anywhere, as long as she stays away from home. She dislikes staying indoors, and if she is compelled to stay in the confines of the house for too long, her mood becomes a shade too dark for comfort, and she is likely to bring the roof down over our heads.'

Hands on his hips, he subjected Delilah to deep scrutiny that carried a disturbing quality about it.

'I can't say I disapprove of the idea, Mother,' he commented quietly.

'Well, then,' Delilah demanded, shutting the magazine and standing up. 'What are we waiting for? Where do you propose to take me?' she looked up at him expectantly.

'I said I don't disapprove of the idea, but I hardly think it is worth the effort, and I don't recall making any proposition to you.'

With her lips firmly pressed together, she decided to leave the room, her eyes blazing quietly, but Dominic had caught her wrist in an iron grip and pulled her to him roughly, 'Where do you think you are going?' he said tersely.

'Out. What is it to you where I go and what I do with my free time?' she whispered back in a fierce tone.

'Must you always fly off the handle on such trivial matters? When are you going to learn to talk like a lady?' his grip on her wrist tightened.

'Let go of me, damn you!' she bit out fiercely, her eyes staring daggers at him.

After a brief silence, however, he said quietly, 'Apologise at once.' His eyes a hard blue reflected a fury that rose from within him, but what he was endeavouring to control.

'Leave her alone, Dominic,' came his father's soft entreaty.

Selena did not interfere, merely watched the scene unconcernedly, and with complete disregard for her daughter's feelings.

'You will apologise instantly, Delilah or I'll not be responsible for what should follow later.' Dominic had turned a deaf ear to his father's entreaty.

'Oh, go to blazes!' she shouted furiously, struggling to extricate herself from his steely grip. But when she received a resounding slap across her face, she was effectively silenced.

There was a momentary silence after which Sampson stood up and confronted his son with a reproving look.

'I'm beginning to regret asking you to take charge of Delilah.'

'Papa! You said that?' Delilah came back to life, and though her eyes were dry of tears, they looked like the eyes of a wounded deer. Her palm was unconsciously resting against her cheek.

'I regret too, Father,' Dominic returned as if Delilah hadn't spoken then, ignoring her completely. Then turning to Selena; a rather quiet and subdued Selena. 'I apologise, Mother, I shouldn't have done that.'

With a muffled cry Delilah ran out of the room, and into the garden, but even she had not anticipated Dominic following her out there. She was resting her head against the trunk of the tree, standing isolated in the far corner of the garden, crying softly and feeling utterly alone and dejected. He stood there from across the lawn, looking very tall and grim and severely handsome. He let her cry. He never came forward, merely stood there watching the small, forlorn figure with mixed feelings.

Only when she turned to confront him with accusing eyes, did he step forward, and crossing to her side in a few long strides he grabbed her by her shoulders. She was shaking uncontrollably. He couldn't decide whether she was trembling with fury or it was because her sensitivity had been bruised. 'I... I'm getting out of here. Y... you'll never ever see me again. Even Mama does not care for me, and Papa too has turned against me, and...and you, oh, y... you are horrible!' silent tears rolled incessantly down her cheeks.

With a soft muffled exclamation, Dominic buried his face suddenly in the curve of her long, slender throat, his sensuous lips passionately caressing the smooth flesh of her throat, while those lips murmured incoherently... words that set her heart racing. She let out an unrestrained gasp at the touch of his lips against her arched throat, where a pulse was beating erratically.

His lips leisurely wandered down to travel over the soft curve of her full breasts and luxuriantly lingered there until another gasp escaped her lips. His fingers bit into the soft, gently rounded flesh of her upper arm. He lifted his head then and noticed her astonished expression, mingled with yet another expression of awakened ecstasy. The tears stood still in her eyes, which were now filled with a shy wonder, an emotion that he recognised as fear and nervous anticipation. Fear? That he couldn't understand, but he understood the nervous anticipation.

'Don't be afraid, Delilah,' he murmured softly against her quivering lips 'this is all a part of growing up. In my company, you must not hesitate to show what you feel and react accordingly. God! But you're such an amateur in most respects! And you need to be taught so many things. Your lips, lovely one,' he touched them gently with his own, 'are so innocent and untouched.' He murmured against her arched throat where a tiny pulse was throbbing crazily.

Her hands involuntarily went around his neck shyly, hesitantly pulling his head in level with hers and lifting her lips to meet his in a far more mature and searching kiss that he had delivered, and which almost took her breath away. When her hand accidentally touched his thigh, she felt him shudder slightly and she experienced a strange pleasure at the knowledge that she had the power to move him too, sexually.

For the first time, she became aware of her irresistible femininity. She felt a small quiver go through her when he softly bit into the lobe of her right ear, his lips then caressing the behind of her ear lobe, and his hand slowly and deliberately explored every curve of her enticing body till every fibre of her being began responding to his expert manipulation. She discovered then that she was no longer an adolescent, but a woman capable of passionate feelings and giving an equally passionate response in the absolute sense.

'Young women, don't ever use such language. It sounds more or less like an abuse,' he whispered into her ear, pulling her yet closer to him, 'and that is why I struck at you. I'm sorry if the slap was too hard.' His eyes were laughing into hers.

'I...I'm sorry too.' She lifted her head which had been resting on his chest. 'But I can't help being what I am. It is innate...er, my temperament that you always regard with censure. Can't you accept me as I am, Dominic?' she met his eyes, and while hers were wide and questioning; his were serious and contemplative.

'When you know that something already belongs to you, then where is the question of accepting it, however easy or difficult the acceptability of it may be then. You understand?' he took her shoulders in a firm grip.

'Do I belong to you?' she looked at him, wide-eyed.

'You belong to everyone in the family, just as everybody in the family belongs to you,' he explained quietly, releasing her shoulders, and going to stand a little further away from her, with his broad, straight back now facing her. She slowly walked to his side.

'You mean that Dominic?' There was a renewed hope in her voice.

'I mean it,' he said gently, almost patiently, like talking to a small child. 'And when you belong to someone, they then have the right to check you when you should be in the wrong, also take stronger measures should you get out of hand, but such steps can only be ensured if you happen to care for that person, very dearly, or your actions could be easily misinterpreted.'

'Papa asked you to take charge of me, but I'm not a child to be taken in hand this way,' she remonstrated softly, looking at him enquiringly.

'You are most certainly not a child. You are merely a trifle untamed, therefore you need to be taken in hand. And, because you are extremely recusant, he is positive that I am the man who will be able to smoothen the er…rough edges and make that unyielding quality that you possess more flexible. Get the point?' his eyes were twinkling with quiet laughter as he turned to meet her frown.

'You are being exceptionally diplomatic today,' she remarked testily, not being able to help her annoyance from surfacing.

'Perhaps,' he observed quietly, his hands folded across his chest. He continued to watch her now quizzically.

'You think you can do it?' she asked scornfully.

'Do what, Delilah?' he queried patiently, consulting his wristwatch, the gesture indicating that he was getting late for the appointment that he was to keep with his estate agent, who had arrived from Spain that morning.

'Correct my temperament that you seem to dislike so much?' Her lips curved into a derisive smile, her hands resting on her beautifully curved hips, her long nails carelessly tapping her hip bone.

'This is what I mean,' he said in a still quiet, patient tone. 'You think that you're beyond redemption.'

'I just don't think it is so. I'm dead certain, and that is why I believe it's a waste of time and energy reforming me into a more subdued person,' she shrugged gracefully; her air of cool confidence served as a mild form of instigation.

Dominic's lips were tightly compressed for just a second, before he said in a voice as uncompromising as his glassy blue eyes that had lost their lustre and just then seemed hard. 'It's a matter of opinion. I'll prove you wrong.' He had a certain look that she found disconcerting. Both their eyes strayed to the two girls who had just then returned home.

'Discussing the weather, eh, Delilah?' Joan grinned like a mischievous imp.

'Were we, Delilah? Discussing the weather?' Dominic asked in a soft, mocking tone.

'Hardly,' she answered in a monosyllable.

The two girls had subsided into the canvas chairs lying about in the garden.

'Oh, that was some party! The wildest I've ever been to,' Joan expelled an exhausted sigh.

'I'm glad,' Anna said with some relief, 'I had taken the car or God knows what with packed buses and trams, I would have never been able to reach my office on time.'

'You'll excuse me, girls, I have an appointment to keep,' Dominic said in a light tone, throwing them a parting wink as he abruptly took leave of them.

'Hey, why go so soon? There is never a moment when we can have you to ourselves,' Joan complained to her brother. 'It's always work for you. Work...work and work.'

'Ask Delilah, she'll be able to tell you differently,' he grinned roguishly, and with this last jibe he strode off into the house to fetch his car keys.

Delilah was seething inside with fury but maintained her outward calm. She felt like going after him and delivering him a hard kick on his shin and a piece of her mind for good measure.

'Delilah, stop scowling, dear, and come and join us here.' Joan patted the chair next to hers.

Delilah came forward and subsided into it silently but her restlessness increased with every passing minute, though she appeared beautifully serene on the surface and contrived to speak to the girls without any trace of impatience.

Anna pressed the bell for a light drink and almost immediately one of the housemaids served them a full jar of coke on a silver tray, with squashed lemon. Joan poured into three glasses the refreshing beverage and offered it to the other two, while putting her glass to her lips, sipping the iced beverage leisurely.

The roar of the Cadillac was enough to make them realise that Dominic was on his way to keep his appointment with his estate agent.

'And to think I was going to ask him to take me on a round to the estate,' Joan complained helplessly, putting down her glass on the table.

'What for, for Pete's sake?' Anna asked irritably, sipping her coke and visibly enjoying the touch of squashed lemon in it.

'I am intending to take up agriculture, that's why,' Joan answered stiffly.

'You seriously wanted him to take you round the estate at this time of the night? It's past eight, dearest,' Anna laughed scornfully.

'If you mean it's dark outside, then let me tell you that lights are blazing out there along the border of our land in quick succession, and you can see every bit of the land as clearly as though it were daylight.' Joan had a triumphant look in her eyes. Then turning to Delilah, she addressed her in an eager tone, 'I have some news for you. One particular man is interested in meeting you. He is quite a stunner! Would you be interested, Delilah?' she watched Delilah expectantly.

Delilah smiled with some amusement.

'What is his name?'

'Dean Fobster. He said he heard about you returning to England and wanted to meet you this very day, but he couldn't as he had to leave suddenly for Australia. But he has asked me to inform you that he would be back next week. My, if only he would transfer his attention to me,' she groaned regretfully, but her eyes were twinkling mischievously.

Delilah expelled a sigh.

'Now come to think of it, I have known Dean since high school. We were great pals then, but perhaps, we may not be able to enjoy the same rapport we shared in the past. It has been quite some time since we drifted away from each other, purely unintentionally though,' she sighed again, her mind drifting into the past. 'I still have his phone number. I will reach him on his return from his trip. Er, thanks for passing on the message to me. Say, how do you know him so well?' Delilah asked casually, her expression still one of amusement.

'Oh, he happens to be the head manager of the firm I am presently working for,' Joan shrugged carelessly.

Anna stood up and suppressed a yawn with her open palm.

'I think I'll retire to bed, girls. Good night! Why don't the two of you follow my example too? It is past ten.' And in light steps, she crossed the garden to enter the palatial house.

'I wonder what she has against men. When anybody mentions a man in her presence, she reacts to it as though unpleasant weather was mentioned,' Joan reflected concernedly.

'Has it ever occurred to you that she may be feeling bitter towards men in general? Who knows...perhaps she's suffering from a severe attack of disillusionment? She may have in all probability suffered at the hands of many men, and each time her affair must have proved a complete product of disillusionment, and mere cause for misery and further heartache. And, whoever has said: "To love is a divine experience" must have been a guaranteed idiot!' Delilah added contemptuously.

'Yes, it is feasible,' Joan reflected with a frown.

'What? That he must have been some idiot who said that?' Delilah put in scoffingly.

'No, silly!' Joan laughed. 'I had Anna in mind when I said that, that she may be bitter towards men in general.'

'But she seems so hard-boiled on the surface,' Delilah contradicted her own conjectures. She continued, 'Never go by appearance, I guess. They are generally deceptive,' she remarked quietly.

'So are some of the men I know,' Joan smiled bitterly.

Delilah's eyebrows shot up in a question mark.

'Since when have you turned cynical?'

'Ever since that beast Roger took me out for a ride and married my closest friend Sylvia, instead. Nowadays you can hardly count anyone as truly trustworthy?'

'I hope I never undergo such an experience, if only for the man's sake. Why... I would tear him to shreds if he so much as looks in another woman's direction.'

When in a state of fury, Delilah's eyes closely resembled the eyes of a beautiful cheetah.

Joan laughed. 'Heavens! I do believe you mean what you say.'

Delilah stood up and languidly stretched her hands above her head; an unconscious gesture as naturally provocative as her lovely slim curves.

'I am going to sleep, dearie. Good night.'

'Hmm, It's pretty late. Mom will come looking for us...look, there she is,' Joan pointed out to Selena, who was standing inside the glass-panelled doorway.

'Do you intend to stay up the whole night?' Selena smiled indulgently.

'Oh, Mama...we were just going inside when you came along,' Delilah said in a voice heavy with sleep. With a shrug, Selena returned to the house, leaving the door open.

Once in her room Delilah changed into her nightdress and slipped inside her bedsheet, sighing heavily. No sooner had her head touched the pillow did she go off to sleep. In her state of slumber, she remained completely impervious to the roar of the Cadillac. The abrupt shutting of the car door went unheard, brisk firm footsteps continued striding up the stairs, walking along the elongated corridor, although the sound of footfalls was deadened as the corridor was richly carpeted.

Dominic was home. The sharp click of the door of a room indicated that he had locked the door to his room, to change for the night. The lights went off after several minutes and the house was once more covered with silence.

CHAPTER 2

'Delilah... come down this instant!' Dominic commanded in a harsh voice, as he stood there at the landing of the stairways and appeared quite furious.

Tightening the cord of her housecoat around her waist, Delilah emerged from her room. She stood on the first step of the staircase and watched him now standing outside the library and seething with a controlled rage. She stared in mute admiration at his extraordinary good looks, enhanced by the inexplicable fury that was reflected on his incredibly handsome features and the tautness of his body muscles.

'Did you go to the library last night?' he asked in a deep controlled voice, though his hard blue eyes were blazing quietly.

'Yes, why?' she answered nonchalantly. She took another step and paused with her hand resting upon the bannister, while the other was lifted to suppress a yawn.

'I thought as much. Now you shall explain what you did with those documents I had left on the desk.'

'What are you talking about?' She leisurely descended the stairs with her eyes fixed questioningly on Dominic, her heart in her mouth. She knew exactly what he was talking about. He was evidently referring to the documents she was quite familiar with.

'Don't pretend like you know nothing about it. You know damn well what I'm talking about; the documents of your father's property, which you had signed, agreeing to hand it over to me. If you had any complaints about the price I had quoted for the property, I would have increased the rate. For God's sake, you did not have to monopolise it. You know very well you could not have afforded its maintenance. You give it back to me quickly. I have to visit the lawyer for the transfer of the property documents.'

She had reached the landing. She stood there silently watching him. 'I can afford its maintenance now. I have an extremely substantial allowance. I have no intention of parting with my property now.'

Those blue eyes narrowed suspiciously and looked icy blue in the morning light.

'You sound very confident,' Dominic remarked caustically.

She smiled tauntingly.

'Naturally, as those papers will never come in your possession. I have destroyed them,' her eyes gleamed triumphantly.

In long, swift strides he reached her side and grabbed her by her shoulders. He shook her till she cried out to be released.

'Should I describe you as perfidious, even that won't be sufficient, but you will not be allowed to go scot-free for committing such a...a stratagem.' He released her abruptly and strode out of the house, and the sound of the entrance door being banged echoed in the whole house, and in doing so awakening the entire household.

For a whole minute, she stared at the shut door. Her shoulders were aching from the rough treatment they had received, and the brutal pressure of his fingers around her arms that had affected her blood circulation. Faint red marks were imprinted on her upper arms. But for that moment, she wasn't aware of it. When she turned to climb up the stairs again, her eyes met Sampson's warm enquiring eyes, and in them she read an infinitely comforting understanding.

Without another word she followed Sampson to the breakfast room. He subsided into a chair and patted the chair beside him. She thankfully accepted the seat offered to her.

'Now,' he began gently, 'what was all that commotion about?'

'I destroyed the document which I had signed earlier, agreeing to hand over to him my property.' Her hands were neatly folded over her lap and her eyes downcast.

'What induced you to take such an action? You know how he detests such defiance wrongly placed,' he reprimanded her gently, though.

'I wanted to prove to him that I am an individual with a mind of my own and that I am entitled to correct the decision I had taken when I was too young to understand its true significance.'

'But, child,' he remonstrated, still in a patient tone. 'To dissolve certain written and endorsed agreements you require a sanction. You cannot take the law into your hands every time you feel like it and not suffer the... consequences.'

'Am I in trouble then?' she looked up at him, her lips set in a firm line of an impossible rebel.

'Not unless Dominic should choose to file a suit against you for breach of promise, but that is out of the question,' he shrugged away the thought as unthinkable.

'I doubt your conviction.' Selena had come so quietly, that they hadn't sensed her presence in the room. 'If Delilah wishes to be acknowledged as an adult, then she must behave like one. As a child or a mere girl, she would have been excused for mistakes committed, but for an adult to behave so irrationally is inexcusable, hence it is very likely that Dominic will see to it my way, and take strong measures to correct the wrong that

Delilah is responsible for.' She then coolly began to pour for herself the tea that the maid had just then brought in. She poured the tea for her husband as well.

Delilah quickly gulped down her tea and excused herself from the room. She went straight to her room and undressed to take a brief shower, after which she slipped into a blue cotton dress with short sleeves.

Back in the kitchen Sampson absorbed his wife's words with disapproval clearly written on his face.

'You are being too hard on the girl, Selena. Why?'

'She is too strong-headed. If I were to go soft on her, she would soon forget even the meaning of discipline,' she stated firmly, delicately sipping her hot tea.

But Sampson knew just how much his wife loved her only child; only she did not believe in pampering Delilah, although she was confusing "understanding" with "pampering".

'Have you tried understanding Delilah?'

Selena nodded. 'It would take me a century to understand that baggage of complexity.' But she smiled indulgently, her serene features softened by that enchanting smile that had captured Sampson's heart over twenty years ago.

'When you love someone then it is imperative to understand them, even if it should take you a century to accomplish the realisation of certain complex characteristics of the individual. Look, Selena, Delilah is no longer a child, although you might think differently,' he sighed. 'If she is rebellious at times that's because she believes everyone has turned against her. She is a spirited girl and strong-headed like you pointed out, but those qualities are not exactly unaccommodating as you would have me believe.'

'I think the understanding you show her is more than sufficient,' she stated lightly, refusing to give the matter much importance.

'Still, if you should decide to be less stern with her, you would then discover that she is capable of responding to a few kind and loving words beautifully. Give it a try, Selena, you will then realise I was right.'

Selena looked into her husband's eyes and smiled warmly. 'You love my daughter as though she were your very own.'

'Yes, I love Delilah and she is ours. Our daughter. Not just yours,' he stated quietly.

Anna and Joan just then entered the room. Anna yawning, greeted her parents mildly almost absently, 'Good morning, Father. Morning, Mother. Where is everybody?' she looked around her curiously, eyes searching for Dominic and Delilah.

'Dominic was in a hurry to leave. I guess he skipped his breakfast. And, Delilah has probably gone up to her room,' Selena said in a casual tone.

'Was I dreaming or did I hear a heated conversation and a sharp bang of the door? Wow!' Anna joined her parents and sister for breakfast.

'Oh, it was nothing serious. Dominic and Delilah had their slight differences, that's all,' Sampson said evasively.

'Ah! those two are at it again,' Joan said insinuatingly.

'What do you mean?' Anna asked her curiously.

'Have you seen the movie, "The Taming of the Shrew"? An old movie I confess but relevant with the present situation,' Joan added for good measure.

'Are you being sarcastic?' Anna asked in a disapproving voice. By nature, she was more like her father; quiet and reserved with a gentler disposition.

Joan quickly responded, 'I was only joking...Forget it, but to see a woman being subjugated by a man can be a humiliating experience, only that's what is happening in this very house. Well,' she trailed off resignedly. 'Men often think they can afford to be masterful. I wonder if Delilah will like the idea of being dominated by big brother. Something is brewing between these two, so watch out,' she shrugged.

'You are being fanciful,' Anna interjected quietly. 'In the movie, the hero hasn't exactly brought the heroine to heel as you would have me believe. He merely trained her to behave less like a shrew and more like a woman, prepared to show due respect to her husband, and accept his terms to maintain peace and discipline in the house. What's wrong with that, pray?' she insisted.

'Nothing that you would understand, anyway. He was domineering, nevertheless,' Joan said obstinately.

'And, that is what a man should be, to some extent if he expects harmony in his home,' Selena suddenly interrupted, having caught bits of their conversation and looking at her husband significantly. 'Your father is kind and loving but he is no less a man when it comes to asserting his authority to maintain law and order in the house.'

Sampson smiled amusedly. 'As long as a man isn't a bully, he can rule the world if he so wishes with confidence, patience and strength of mind,' he had intervened.

Because they were all talking at cross purposes, never stepping to the main point, Sampson tried to change the subject.

'Your mother and I are deciding to visit the Opera. Are you young ladies planning to stay home on a Sunday?' he mused, helping himself to another cup of tea.

'Certainly not!' Joan retorted. 'Philip is coming to pick me up at eleven. We are to attend a dance session and from there we might go to see a movie...the latest that's running in town,' she informed quickly

'What about you, Anna?' Sampson asked.

'I haven't decided yet,' she replied briefly, biting into her buttered toast.

Later, when Sampson and Selena had driven off to the Opera, Joan's current boyfriend, Philip Robinson came to pick her up from their house. She was ready and waiting for him. She promptly jumped on his motorbike and Philip followed her example with a burst of hearty laughter.

'That's my girl! Always ready to enjoy life to its fullest.' He bent to kiss her on her smiling lips. 'Do you know that you look lovely when you smile this way, and when you are grouchy, you decidedly look like a lost monkey?' he laughed when she sharply poked him in his ribs.

'Hey, watch out! We will both fall if you don't behave,' he warned cheerfully.

'Well then, stop calling me a monkey,' she retorted sharply.

And with yet another burst of youthful laughter, he proceeded to dodge a car with the recklessness that is so typical of youth.

When finally, Delilah descended the staircase and walked into the drawing-room, she found Anna engaged in reading a novel. She looked up from the book that she was reading and met Delilah's glance that held a question.

Anna threw Delilah a half-smile that was strangely compassionate in quality. 'What were you doing all morning locked up in your room?' her voice now softly enquiring.

'Oh,' Delilah made a slight gesture with her hands. 'It was the case of preferring one's own company, once in a while. I was beginning to feel crowded. Almost oppressive. Don't know why...say, how about shutting that book and joining me for a visit to the parlour?'

After a while, Anna willingly obliged by shutting the book and she stood up, smiling at Delilah affectionately.

'All right. I am ready.'

Delilah's eyes slid over Anna and once again they rested on Anna's smiling countenance.

'Is something wrong, Delilah?

'You are not dressed to go out,' she said bluntly.

Anna laughed amusedly. 'It's so typical of you to be so straightforward, but I refuse to take offence. Ok, I'll go up to my room and change if just to please you,' she laughed.

Delilah appeared to be slightly mortified.

'I am sorry. I didn't mean to be rude. But I would like to know why you do not show interest in your general appearance. You are beautiful, elegant and undoubtedly attractive, then why must you waste the best years of your life abandoning many pleasures? Why, Anna?' Delilah sounded truly confused and pained, for she had a great affection for Anna, and to see her in this way – treating life as a burden, suffering days and years of her precious life in obscurity was disconcerting; to say the least.

Anna smiled bitterly. 'It would only magnify the bitter memories of the past should I share my grievous thoughts with others. Sometimes it is wisest to keep silent.'

There was a look of deep compassion in Delilah's eyes.

'You have told me all that I wanted to know in these few words,' she said softly, the light of knowledge dawning in her beautiful green eyes. 'You are coming, aren't you?'

'Could you lend me your lipstick?' Anna asked with a twinkle in her eyes, and Delilah sighed inwardly. At that moment she could have hugged Anna. She quickly opened her purse and extracted a lipstick from it and handed it over to Anna along with a compact which contained a mini mirror.

Soon they were seated in a white Mercedes and driving away to the salon, the chauffeur accelerating the speed of the car. The salon's proprietor, Mrs Mai Jung was a well-known hair-stylist-cum-beautician; known for her brand of particular skills.

On their way to the beauty parlour, Delilah slanted an uncertain glance in Anna's direction. Anna seemed not to notice that she was being scrutinised.

'What are you thinking?' Anna asked without turning sideways.

'I was thinking you are too young to be so miserable. You ought to be having fun,' Delilah came outright with it.

The car picked up speed as the traffic thinned out and from there the movement of the vehicle remained unhampered.

'I would wish misery on no one; may they be young or old,' Anna commented serenely. She suddenly happened to gaze out of the window. 'I think we are there. Martin, you may stop the car.' Anna stepped out of the car, and Delilah followed her, standing at her side by the car. 'I think you had better park somewhere. We'll take some time,' Anna said quietly, and a few steps took them to the beauty salon. They had crossed the road to reach the salon.

Once when Delilah had her hair done, they then left the place and walked towards the waiting car. The chauffeur had respectfully opened the car door for both of them. Both had quietly slid inside the car, satisfied with their new hairdo. Anna too had relented after a while, to renew her hairstyle and it had worked. She looked different but lovely. Anna had caught Delilah staring at her and both smiled simultaneously.

'There, you look much more pretty now,' Delilah commented with pure frankness.

Anna laughed.

'I am glad you like my new hairdo.' That was all she said in response to Delilah's flattering comment.

When the car reached home, the two girls rushed through the iron gates quite impatient to reach the mailman, who had just emerged from the right-hand side.

'Any letters for us?' Anna asked with an expectant note in her voice. Delilah wondered curiously, whose letter was she expecting?

Delilah, on the other hand, was expecting a letter from her best friend, Bertha, who was also her cousin from her mother's side. It was a sad thing, she reflected, that Bertha was an illegitimate child, but Delilah had never once reminded the girl of her many misfortunes resulting in her being born out of wedlock.

And contrary to what most people thought of Bertha's misfortunes, Delilah was ready to make compensation for what society should have exhibited; compassion and understanding.

Delilah made certain that no one repeated the irreparable mistake of demoralising her friend in her presence. Her strong and dependable support helped to erase Bertha's feeling of inadequacy.

Bertha's quiet and enduring disposition was often a source of great irritation to Delilah, who regarded her friend's timidity as a weakness on her part when she should have retaliated similarly, and taught all those snobs a lesson in etiquette. For denying her respect and recognition and standing in society, they should have been delivered a jolt, shaking them up a bit. However, she should have made them realise her individuality, irrespective of the fact that she was born under the most unfavourable circumstances. But that hardly being her fault, as presumably, her parents hadn't thought it necessary to endorse their union. And now, the injustice meted out to the innocent offspring was most unfair, to say the least. Bertha's mother was hardly improving matters by behaving recklessly, and as a result signing herself off, as a woman of morally ruined disposition.

But this also was not the whole truth. According to the lady, this was the only resort to escape from the pain and contention not realising that this all merely aggravated the difficulty that lay in the situation.

Delilah came out of her reverie when she sensed the mailman putting the letter in her open palm. She could tell without looking that the letter was from Bertha. She quickly excused herself from Anna's company and went straight up to her room. There she slit open the letter and read its contents; a smile of affection tugging at the corners of her lovely mouth, yet untouched by colour.

It appeared, judging from what Bertha had written; that she was enjoying the attention of some really good-looking men whom she had met at one of the parties that she often attended with her mother. Her mother, with her rare beauty and intellect, was still a much sought-after lady in a male-oriented society. The lady had grit, that Delilah could well appreciate, and the society still accorded her respect. She invariably received flattering attention, especially from the opposite sex even at present.

In her forties... the lady; a tall, stately figure with a face like the proverbial face that launched a thousand ships. She had managed to maintain her perfect figure that never failed to attract admiring, masculine glances, causing envy among the women, and even perhaps generating a definite awe. She was an awesome personality, yet very gentle at heart, as only those close to her knew so very well.

Delilah felt greatly relieved that finally Aunt Marian and Bertha were being accepted in the society, but then, time has a way of moving with great swiftness, and people with the fickleness of their race soon begin to lose interest in the past scandals. They instead start concentrating on the latest in the news, slandering the subject and moulding it conveniently into exaggerated proportions of what would normally be termed as gossip.

After a pause, however, she continued reading Bertha's letter. She had written that she hoped to obtain a job as a junior sales executive, in one of the leading firms dealing in real estate and leasing. Her mother, she wrote, was engaged in throwing grand parties at her luxuriously decorated penthouse at Warren Street left to them by Bertha's mysterious father, who had disappeared soon after leaving Marian with a child in her womb.

Bertha's letter, though warm, was concise and ended abruptly as though she had written in a great hurry. With a reminiscent smile, Delilah slipped the letter inside the drawer of her writing-table set in the corner of a spacious room. The table was installed so that she could engage herself in writing books for children of which few were already published. So far, she had been fortunate and had three of her stories published.

This inspired her to write some more for the children's magazine.

Her stories were in great demand, particularly the one that she had written during the past month.

The cheques that she had received from her publishers for each story were exceptionally generous.

That afternoon, except for Delilah and Anna, no one was present for lunch. Their parents, they knew would return late in the evening and Joan, they were confident would show up as usual, late into the night. It had become a custom with her to arrive home during the night, once she stepped out of the house. As for Dominic, he was the one person in the entire household, who at any rate was difficult to pin down. That man remained a law unto himself. He allowed no one to control his actions. He was out since morning and nobody knew about his whereabouts.

Delilah was beginning to show restlessness.

She wondered where he could have gone, not realising that his life was his own to live; her anxiety had turned her blind to such a fact.

Again, with light perspiration forming on her forehead, she wondered if perhaps he was with his lawyer planning to file a suit against her for the breach of promise.

Fear and trepidation soon killed her appetite.

She got up from the table and retreated from the dining hall, leaving a rather puzzled Anna sitting alone at the table and nibbling at her food without much interest in the delicious spread laid out before her.

Outside in the hall, a sudden click of the exit door also did not hamper Delilah's progress up the staircase leading her to her room. But the sharp command made her turn round, and across the hallway, her eyes met Dominic's icy blue gaze.

'What is it you want?' she demanded with cool hauteur, but a thudding heart.

'Such insolence will someday get you into trouble, so be warned.' He had not raised his voice, but his words carried a distinct warning that Delilah ignored haughtily. With a careless shrug, she reached the top of the landing, and just then Anna emerging from the dining hall observed the scene before her in silent contemplation.

She, however, took a step towards her brother and smiled up at him.

'I'm sorry, Dominic, we did not wait for you for lunch. You must be very hungry. You haven't even had your breakfast, I'm told.' These words were softly spoken and Dominic denoted a note of deep concern in his sister's voice. His smile in response to his sister's concern was slightly lop-sided.

'I am hungry, all right. Say, would you care to join me at the table? You needn't have anything, only your presence there would afford me some pleasure. Honestly, Ann,' he quickly reassured her when she lifted her eyebrows showing disbelief.

'All right,' she smiled at him benignantly. 'If that is what you wish for.'

Suddenly feeling neglected Delilah deliberately spoke harshly with her hands resting indolently on her slim yet curvaceous hips.

'You are not very observant, are you, Dominic?' she remarked caustically, standing poised on top of the stairs.

Slowly he turned to confront Delilah's taunting expression.

'Now I would like to know what you mean by that remark,' he said in a quiet voice.

'Do you not notice any change in Anna's appearance?'

'Yes. She has fashioned her hair in a new style. I am only glad that she had the good sense not to chop off her hair, though.'

'Meaning that I am lacking in good sense?' she asked sharply, her eyes reflecting the anger inside her.

He had this knack for instigating her.

'Have you cut your hair? I hadn't noticed,' he said indifferently.

'So, I understand.' She suddenly felt piqued. He had not observed the change in her hairdo.

'Why... was I supposed to?' He appeared to be quite bored with their turn of conversation.

'Yes,' she remarked with an insulting casualness.

'Your hair looks okay to me.' Then once again turning to Anna, he requested her to order for lunch, and till then, he stated gently, he would retire to his room to bathe and change into fresh clothes.

In order to reach his room, he had to pass Delilah, where she was rooted on the top of the landing and watching him murderously. His every movement was being watched with a look that could have made a lesser man feel nervous for a while, only Dominic seemed unperturbed. Then quite unexpectedly, a strange smile took form on Delilah's lips as she continued to watch him. His eyes too had been fixed on her, and seeing that unexpected smile on her lips he began to wonder what it could mean. And slowly his hand reached out to caress her shoulder-length hair which felt soft to touch and which curled beautifully about her shoulders in the most attractive way.

'Hmm, not bad,' he murmured softly, his eyes never leaving her face, he reiterated, 'not bad at all.' And quietly he turned away from her stare, leaving her side to walk towards his room, and gently shutting the door behind him.

For some reason she had wanted to strike his face; the arrogance had been so pronounced when he had looked at her like he was a monarch of all he surveys. Also, because his tone had been infinitely condescending. With an indrawn breath, she eagerly swept into her room and shut the door fiercely, as though she were indirectly inflicting pain on Dominic.

CHAPTER 3

That night when the whole household was gathered in the dining hall for dinner, Dominic announced briefly that he had to go out of town for some days as he had some family business to transact. And also mentioned, that he would have to put up for a day or two at Warren Street, and if anyone wished to join him, they were welcome to do so.

Upon Warren Street being mentioned, Delilah received a start and she stood up from her chair and nearly turned over the bowl of fruit salad. Her eyes sparkling, she pleaded excitedly, 'Could I come along with you, please?'

'I am afraid not. Some other time, perhaps,' Dominic said quite firmly.

'But you don't understand, I have no wish to be an encumbrance. I'll be staying there with my friend for a while. Please let me come with you.' She turned with pleading eyes that gazed beseechingly at her father, and said, 'Papa, won't you tell him to take me with him? He did make the offer after all,' she added hopefully.

'Sorry, Delilah. Dominic never allows anyone to make his decisions for him.' He stood up and retreated from the hall, and Selena followed her husband out into the darkness, probably drifting out into the garden for a stroll before retiring for the night.

With an exasperated sigh, Delilah once again reverted her gaze upon him, but he wasn't looking at her. His dark head bent; he was silently completing the last course at the table. Joan and Anna were unusually quiet. Frustrated by then, she made a face at Dominic who appeared not to notice, and if he had, he appeared not to be even slightly affected by the childish display of discourteous behaviour. He regarded it as a temporary error he did not wish to tackle at that moment. So, applying tissue to his mouth, he stood up and made as if to retreat from the room. But not easily dissuaded, she ran after him, and standing before him, she stared at him disdainfully.

'Must you always be so mean? When are you going anyway?' her voice sounded surprisingly lost and tearful.

He looked down at her then with a puzzled expression on his face. His low brow faintly wrinkled in deep contemplation. There were times he regretted not being able to understand her better. She was of an amiable disposition, only it baffled him, but what baffled him, even more, was that, frankly, he did not know how to bring out the best in her. It strangely made him feel inadequate as he considered this aspect a failure on his part; failure, as he could only cause her pain and constant disappointment, but never pleasure or even the slightest happiness, or so he believed. He could only afford her unhappiness, and this knowledge produced inside him a feeling of self-loathing, which was the cause of his suddenly grabbing Delilah into his arms and pressing a hard kiss on her lips with a fervour that got him thinking about the unexpectedness of his action long after he had left town for his short business trip.

The warm impression of Dominic's lips on hers had left its mark on Delilah's mind, and its memory would stay imprinted there for a long time to come. Its memory lingered, much after he had abruptly left her to go to his room to pack his suitcase.

Delilah had mounted the stairs that she had confusedly stepped down from. She once again took the first step and rushed to her room rather dazedly, her mouth still quivering from the warm impact of his lips on hers. So tender and heart-warming it had been; a kiss... its memory she would cherish. It had brought tears to her eyes. And she had instantly known the reason for those tears. She had been profoundly moved by his unexpected gentility, as though by that gesture he had wanted to convey a message to her; a message?? At that sudden conjecture, she had undergone a strange feeling of exultation that she had found inexplicable; it being a completely new experience to her. She knew now for certain that Dominic was mainly responsible for the tumult inside her.

She dearly wished that the feeling that she was undergoing was love, yet she did not want to get so deeply involved with any man, especially Dominic, whom she knew if, had he wished, would break down all her resolve and defences. The sudden return of some inspiration enabled Delilah to resume writing. She forgot all else, though not completely and started to concentrate instead on the plots for her latest book. In the middle of her writing, she was disturbed by a sound coming from the corridor outside her room. Ignoring the noise outside, she once more gave her attention to the present involvement. She was furious when the door was flung open and Joan stood there with a broad impish smile on her face.

'Guess who is here to see you?' she said cheerfully. Delilah was too angry upon being disturbed in this manner to be able to share Joan's enthusiasm.

'You should know better than to barge in like that. Now I have forgotten what I was writing.'

'Oh! I'm awfully sorry, I hadn't realised you would be writing so late into the night. You usually sleep by nine,' Joan sounded genuinely apologetic.

'I would like to know who is crazy enough to visit me at this time of the night,' Delilah enquired impatiently.

'Wouldn't you like to know now…' Joan teased, but then, when she saw Delilah's impatience, she became serious. 'Oh, all right! Bertha has come over to spend a fortnight with us. She is downstairs, and I thought since you guys are such good…'

Delilah rushed to her side, and without a word, she pulled Joan after her down the stairs, and straight into the drawing-room where Bertha was seated on the couch, with Selena keeping her company. She appeared to be flicking through the pages of a magazine, rather indifferently. She raised her head to meet Delilah's sparkling eyes and read the message of love there. She stood up and took a few steps forward only to be enfolded in Delilah's waiting arms. Bertha's cheeks were soon covered with kisses delivered by Delilah.

'Bertha, am I glad to have you here with us!' Delilah exclaimed delightfully.

'I was beginning to miss you too, so instead, I made this trip,' was Bertha's quiet rejoinder. Her voice was beautifully warm, low and attractively husky.

'It is just like you to come without Aunt Marian,' Delilah remonstrated gently.

'She is a socialite, and, therefore, she has little time to pay a visit to her family. She is busy in her circle of sophisticated friends. How can she afford to spare time for more earthy creatures like us?' she smiled bitterly.

Selena looked up from the work that she had been engaged in and only Joan; an impersonal observer caught the suspicion of tears in Selena's eyes; tears of compassion for her niece whose life was so incomplete without the love and attention of her parents, who had so recklessly drifted apart for some reason, yet unknown to all. And in doing so, allowing their only child to suffer their separation in the bargain.

For once Joan manifested a sensitivity that no one could have thought her capable of. She gently ushered the girls into another room and offered them drinks. Leaving them sipping at the drinks and talking of their past ventures, Joan soon after returned to the living room. Quietly, she sat down at Selena's feet and looked up at her filled eyes with growing concern.

'You must not allow yourself to get so worked up, Mama. More cause for pain would merely intensify the ache in your head,' she said gently.

Selena lovingly rested her hand on Joan's head.

'I know, dear, but fate has been so unkind to that child. I don't even think she has ever seen her father. As for Marian, she is the last person to exhibit sentimentality even though she truly suffers too. She is too strong a person to allow room in her life for tears and sorrow. But it wouldn't have harmed her to show her daughter some love and understanding. She goes about her life merrily and totally disregarding conventions and scorning the simple things in life – things like love, loyalty and duty towards those who are closest to her. Oh, I admit she is young and vivacious, but that does not mean that she is entitled to flaunt her beauty in the society like a trump card in such...such an uncharacteristic way. The child has to then bear the brunt of society's wagging tongue. They can be so cruel in their judgement,' she spoke vehemently.

'You mustn't be so harsh on Aunt Marian. After all, she was practically deserted by her lover. It is not fair to condemn her in such a manner.' Joan was among the many who genuinely loved and respected the beautiful and kindly person that Marian was underneath that facade which she covered herself with. Joan almost held the lady in awe.

Joan could have cursed the man who had deserted such a wonderful person like Marian, whom she had known for years. In the past, Marian used to visit them too often, but never once had she visited them at their house, though. She always used to book in at a hotel and invite them over to her suite. No one had quite known why Marian had refused to meet Sampson over the years whenever it was subtly suggested that they meet. Although Selena had once been adamant about it, Marian would always win the argument in the end, and the meeting would then be postponed. No one in the family had been able to solve the mystery behind this particular incident.

'My dear, you mustn't try to cover up for Marian. It is not as if you do not know that she has no husband and that it was her lover who had deserted her as you pointed out some minutes ago. And he is nowhere around to make amends for the mistake he committed years ago when he left Marian stranded and carrying his child.' Her voice held marked concern, and it perhaps also carried a slight hint of regret for her sister's present mode of existence, and that the man who had deserted her was entirely responsible for. Only Selena knew just how much she loved her only sister Marian and longed to provide her with the moral support that she had probably needed at the time when she had discovered that her lover had absconded, but Marian's pride had come between them, and Selena could only feel sorry and miserable for her sister's plight. She was offended as she was being denied the right to comfort her in times when Marian had needed her the most. She chose to suffer alone and move about in the society, displaying before the world only the clever facade that she had built around herself, allowing no one to penetrate the strong wall that subtly divorced her from the surrounding mass of human specimens.

It hurt Joan to hear Selena speaking so bitterly of her sister, but she could hardly do anything about the catastrophe, that had befallen, that was by now probably irreparable. Selena had calmed down considerably and Joan had rushed to Sampson's room to give him the medication that the doctor had prescribed for him.

'My dear child, you look decidedly grumpy this evening. What has happened to change your mood, eh?' Sampson enquired jokingly. Joan wrinkled her pert nose.

'Papa, must you be so curious? I have a headache. Will that do?' Joan took the empty glass from his grasp and placed it on the side table sitting next to his bed.

'Aspirin might help, my dear. You must take aspirin if it isn't an imaginary headache... that is,' he jeered with a definite twinkle in his eyes, pronouncing her a liar. 'Are you fooling your own father, girl?' he said reprovingly.

'It...it is Mama.'

He half rose from the bed where he had been reclining.

'What has happened to Selena, girl? Tell me fast.' His breathing had become heavier from the exertion of mental tension. 'Oh, Papa, it is not something you need to worry about. She has simply recalled Aunt Marian's sad story, and it has naturally brought tears to her eyes, upsetting her and resulting in a severe attack of migraine. But I suppose it would pass like she says it would,' she said hopefully.

'It's only natural for one sister to share another's pain and grief.' Joan added and handed over the pills to him. Absently, he placed the tablets on the table and regarded his daughter enigmatically.

'I have never been able to understand why that confounded man ever entered into a relationship with a wonderful woman like Marian only to desert her. From all that I have heard about her, she sounds terrific. Such desertion is virtually a tragedy, almost a crime and a slight that no woman could forgive a man for...' he stated in a firm, decisive tone that surprised Joan, who found it strange that her father should defend the one woman who had refused to meet him so many times in the past.

There was a mystery behind this all, which Joan would have dearly loved to unravel. Sampson then reached out for the tablets on the table and swallowed them followed by a glass full of water. 'The confounded man!' he repeated with an expression of severity entering his face.

When finally, Joan returned to the living room, she found her mother fast asleep on the couch with her knitting lying on her lap, only partly completed. She went to retrieve it and placed it on the glass table while bringing another chair forward, she lifted Selena's feet, and rested them over the cushioned chair.

It was nearly ten o'clock when finally Anna arrived home; looking as cool as ever, but there was a sparkle in her serene, brown eyes that had never been there before. She shook hands warmly with Bertha and politely enquired about Marian after which she hurried up to her room, her steps lighter and her manner, less rigid. She in fact looked full of life and vitality.

After some time when she joined the family in the drawing-room, everybody seemed to notice the change in her and were curious to know what had brought about such a pleasing change in her. Although each one of them kept their own counsel, not wishing to probe lest she might think they were interfering in her private affairs.

Anna was not altogether unaware of the puzzled expressions. She looked at each of them with a quiet smile. Their puzzlement only intensified. She returned to Bertha, who was sitting next to Delilah and asked her pleasantly, 'Do you know anyone by the name of Jarrod Mayfair?'

Bertha blushed a deep crimson at the mere mention of that name.

'Am I to take it then that you know the gentleman, Bertha?' Anna enquired quietly and just as politely. Bertha nodded but didn't say anything.

'You must know his father too?' Anna enquired with a casual shrug, filing her nails nonchalantly.

'I do,' Bertha asserted calmly.

'Then you must also be knowing that his wife was mentally unsettled,' Anna said.

'Why these interrogations, dear?' Sampson asked faintly with some impatience. 'Why this sudden interest in total strangers?'

Bertha had suddenly looked up with a start. 'You just said "was mentally unsettled", didn't you? I don't understand.'

'She passed away last Friday,' Anna interrupted quietly.

'Jared and his father will then surely have to go to Switzerland for the burial,' Bertha said softly, almost as if talking to herself.

'Yes, I am thinking of joining them,' Anna said, still in a quiet voice, opening up finally, and in the only way she could.

'Anna! What is this I am hearing?' Sampson demanded; sounding truly perturbed.

Anna glanced at her father with a serene smile.

'He needs me, Papa, therefore I must go.' She noted Bertha's cool glance aimed in her direction and she smiled even more widely.

'I don't understand, girl. Who is this "he" now?' Sampson sounded quite worried by then.

But taking note of Bertha's evident suffering, Anna immediately put the girl's mind at rest.

'You're probably thinking I'm referring to Jarrod, hmm? Well, as pretty soon Jarrod will be my stepson, I don't see any reason for concealing this fact from you, and more so, I know that this piece of news will bring you some relief.' She smiled warmly at the girl sitting opposite her.

'When are you planning to get married, Anna?' Selena spoke in her customary cool manner. She most certainly did not sound disapproving. Anna caught the look of understanding in her mother's eyes and heaved a sigh of relief. Here at least, there was someone who had not only proved a wonderful mother but a good friend too.

'Next week, Mother,' she stated quietly.

'Papa.' She took her father's hand in hers and looked up at him beseechingly. 'Has this come as a disappointment to you, that I am to marry a... married man and elderly too?'

Sampson refrained from saying anything for the moment.

'Papa, please do say something. Anything!' Anna said, and surprisingly with a note of desperation in her voice.

Sampson in response merely examined his daughter's radiant face and her sparkling eyes. There was a strange kind of liveliness and happiness reflecting on her face, that he had never before seen in all her twenty-eight years that she had grown up to be. There was a new childlike expectancy in her eyes, as though she had wordlessly begged for his comment and approval.

Slowly, he pulled her up from the carpeted floor and to his side. He moved aside to make room for her beside him. His hand caressed her silken tresses lovingly, and his mouth curved into a smile. At that moment, he made up his mind to show her that he was pleased with her decision. Her happiness was what mattered.

If marrying the Mayfair man could make her appear so radiant and happy, then who was he to destroy her newfound happiness by asserting his authority as did most of the parents, and leaving their children stripped of pleasure and happiness only just then granted to them. She was asking for his consent, for he knew, otherwise, her happiness would not be complete. His face did not reveal all that was going on in his mind. Anna resignedly made the move as if to get up, with a suspicion of tears in her eyes.

'Papa, I love Paul, but if it is not your wish that I marry him, then I will respect your wish. Your...your health is so much more important to me.'

'You honestly mean that, you foolish girl? You prefer your papa to your Paul, eh?' he said jovially, his eyes twinkling with mischief.

She stood with her back to him; stiff and unnatural was her posture as tears began streaming down her cheeks unrestrainedly.

'You know I love you, Papa, but Paul also happens to mean a lot to me too. I have known him for some time now, suffering with him, sharing his grief, and accepting the hopelessness of the situation bearing in mind the fact that he could never leave his wife at the time when she most needed him. We were both patient until fate decided to reward our patience. Such endless waiting, when I had almost given up any hope that I might have had of securing happiness for both of us. For the first time in my life, I was really happy, and am really very sorry, Papa, that in my happiness I did not realise that... that your happiness too, counts. Forgive me, Papa, and do try to forget this... this matter. Consider the subject closed.' And holding her tears in check she rushed to go out of the room, but Sampson's quiet voice held her back, almost instantly.

'I shall miss you, Anna, my child.'

At that very instant she turned around to face him, her face positively radiant.

'Papa!' she exclaimed softly, her expression changing miraculously.

'You...you... does this mean that I have your consent? But it does mean that, doesn't it?' she had walked back to her father, for whom she was even prepared to give up the man who she loved so dearly. The privately happy onlookers Joan, Delilah and Bertha tactfully retreated from the room.

'Have you asked your mother how she feels about it?' Sampson enquired, too casually, although his eyes were laughing at his daughter's confused expression.

'Oh, I'm sure Mama does not object. Do you, Mama?' Anna asked, desperately clinging to her newfound happiness, as though it would slip from her tight grasp.

Selena smiled upon Anna, serenely almost reassuringly. 'Here is the question of your personal happiness. What more can I say, but all the best and God bless you, dear?'

'Oh, Mama,' crying and laughing at the same time, she hid her face against Selena's breasts.

'I think you owe me a loving embrace too,' Sampson said from behind.

When Anna put her arms around her father, he chuckled amusedly, patting her head lovingly.

'What a great loss and such a conscientious daughter too,' he quipped with a teasing note in his voice, but his eyes shone with love for his daughter.

***

The lateness of the hour was clearly the sign of the approaching night when Sampson decided to retire to bed, but the girls remained awake till late into the night, excitedly discussing Anna's good fortune. They were happy as Sampson had given his blessings, irrespective of the age difference between Anna and Paul, and giving even less importance to the fact that the man was married with a son as old as Anna herself.

'You are fortunate to have a father as understanding as Sampson if you don't mind me saying so. Some parents would never accept such a... a match,' Bertha said in her beautifully-modulated voice, carrying a tone of warmth.

'Hmm, Papa is indeed very understanding,' Anna conceded quietly, her eyes bright with happiness that even she found it hard to describe in words. Her tone was gently teasing when she said, 'Jarrod is a dear. When is the marriage to be?'

'Jarrod has to complete his studies first. Once he starts practising law, we will then get married immediately. He requires some secured base before he can even think of matrimony. He believes and so do I, that marriage is not all fun and games. There are many responsibilities involved, which we must adhere to conscientiously.'

Anna smiled and said as she stood up, 'You are a very sensible girl.'

Bertha uncomfortably averted her gaze. She did not know how to receive the compliment, as she was obviously not accustomed to it.

Delilah was secretly impressed by Bertha's quiet, firm tone, and her practicality that she hadn't thought her capable of, owing to the extreme timidity of her temperament. Only now she would have to admit that her friend truly possessed a fine character, that perfectly synchronised with the cool determination reflecting in her eyes that were such gentle brown; its charm enhanced by the softness of her expression, something very much characteristic of her. Her face held more character than beauty, but her personality along with the serenity of her facial expression made her altogether quietly attractive. Yes, Delilah had definitely underestimated her friend's unusually beautiful character.

Much later when Joan and Anna had retired to bed, Delilah and Bertha were left on their own. Delilah came and occupied the space on the settee beside Bertha and threw her a friendly lop-sided grin.

'I owe you an apology.'

'What for?' Bertha sounded puzzled.

'For thinking, you were a spineless creature,' she said in her customary blunt manner.

Bertha did not seem to take offence. She merely smiled.

'Have you changed your opinion of me then?'

'All I did was to distinguish the delusion from the fact...being that you are not what you seem,' Delilah shrugged apologetically.

'You wish I were more like Mother?' Bertha asked in a strange voice.

'Never! I merely wish you were less tolerant towards those who treat you so unfairly. I cannot bear to see you patiently endure their constant looks of disdain and scathing comments. No human is perfect and, therefore, no one has the right to stand in judgement of others,' her voice sounded stiff and hard. Her eyes were like flashing green emeralds, glittering jewels, carrying a hard, unyielding quality at that precise moment, and so very unpredictable, sometimes gleaming with laughter, and more often than not, turning like hard bejewelled stones.

'What do you suggest I do? Fight them tooth and nail? Retaliate by hitting them across their mouths? Tell me, should I demand that they keep quiet? Do you think that would silence them? Yes?'

For perhaps the first time Delilah saw her friend's eyes filling up with frustrated tears, and her words, Delilah observed bitterly had indicated her realisation of the sheer hopelessness of her position in society, and all because her father had refused to marry her mother.

Why did such a form of betrayal persist still, thought Delilah, and inviting such condemnation, and from those very people whose standard of existence left much to be desired? To be called a thief by seasoned criminals was the worst form of recrimination subjected to, for petty theft, but to be condemned for being born without a licence and a legal grant by greater sinners was unbearable...unjustifiable!

Delilah quickly went up to Bertha, and said in a small voice, 'Look, I am sorry I brought up the subject. I should have known it would have affected you deeply.' She bent to kiss Bertha on her cheek. 'I am really very sorry, darling.'

'Why should you be sorry? I quite understand why you mentioned it. You are as upset as I am, but the truth is, how can merely two people fight against such a prevalent dogma and injustice? It would not be practical and would hardly serve its purpose.' Gently Bertha carried Delilah's hand to her lips. 'But thanks, dear, for caring...'

Delilah smiled adoringly at her friend.

'I am glad I did not go to Warren Street, after all. What a coincidence! I was planning to stay there with you and Aunt Marian for some days. And here you are...come to spend a few days with me, instead.'

'In a way it's good you did not go, but what made you change your mind anyway?' Bertha asked in her softly-modulated voice.

'Dominic was to stop there for a day or two before continuing his trip further to the north, so I thought to join him. But he refused to take me along,' she shrugged carelessly.

'And who is... Dominic?' Bertha asked casually as Delilah's eyes widened at the question.

'But I always wrote to you about Dagger, didn't I? You can't have forgotten those escapades I had mentioned in my letter so very frequently.'

'No, I haven't, but how could I know that Dominic and the boy Dagger are one and the same person? Is he still just the same?'

'Who... Dagger... I mean Dominic? Hardly. On the contrary.' She made a face. 'The situation has worsened.'

'You have to be exaggerating,' Bertha mused. 'The guy you wrote to me about was the devil himself, judging from the impression I collected from your vivid description of him. But a stunner yet, if I am not wrong, and he could if he wanted to...set a woman's pulses racing. He has to be a "wow" then.'

'He was a devil and "a wow" then, and now he is an enigma plus. A dangerous combination, don't you think? But a stranger yet. And besides...' but Delilah's voice trailed off as though she was not certain of what she had been going to say would be correctly interpreted.

'Continue, love,' Bertha sounded as always; gentle and encouraging.

'Bertha, he has the strangest effect on me.' She had a faraway look in her eyes. 'I feel at times that the... the very thought of him is stealthily stealing its way into my heart, and slowly destroying that feeling of remaining fancy-free. You may laugh at this, but this happens to be the truth. I feel he has a powerful hold over my senses. He...he moves me to such a degree that very soon I may even lose all account of my own identity. He has already managed to break all my reserve which I had taken great pride in once,' she said in a voice not quite hers.

'Then he can't be far from breaking your heart as well. Where would you be then?' And they both knew that Marian was a perfect example of a case of a broken heart. They preferred not to discuss Marian's case just then, as both knew very well what the other meant.

Bertha stood up and walked a few paces, stopping beside the window. 'You must have met some really interesting looking men back in Switzerland,' Bertha's tone was deceptively casual.

'Oh, yes, though not as exciting as Dominic, I must confess. Why?'

'Then you must surely be having some preconceived idea about the kind of man you desire for your life partner...'

'Well... well, yes,' she asserted reluctantly. She still could not understand what actually Bertha had in her mind, to ask such a question.

'Can you honestly tell me that out there you had not met anyone up to your expectations?' she turned round to face Delilah squarely, her gaze steady and probing.

'Well, physically many did... I mean, came up to my expectations.' She blushed at her own choice of words that could very easily be misconstrued.

'I mean, some of their physical attributes had carried a certain appeal for me, but I can't say I was much impressed by any of them. Not really. Surely, there's more to a man than physical attraction, but each time something was lacking, I can't say what, though.'

'Does it not strike you as strange that such handsome men of your acquaintance lacked the potential of possessing the definite overall appeal for you?'

'I did not give the matter a second thought, honestly. And, anyway, I wonder what is this inquisition in aid of,' she sounded thoroughly confused.

Bertha smiled wryly.

'And what's more, the first thing a girl does when she meets a young, good-looking man is talk about it to her closest friend. I do believe I'm your closest friend, then how come you have not yet confided in me all that you may have possibly experienced in Switzerland?'

'Don't be silly, Bertha, nothing really exciting took place out there. Really, this is too much! Why, you are in fact the only person I can talk freely with,' she shrugged carelessly. 'Eventually, I would have discussed everything, however insignificant, but what is really important now is…'

'Dominic, eh?' Bertha quietly filled in for her.

'Very astute, aren't you?' Delilah said sarcastically.

'Yes, dearest, that is why I alone know where your interests lie.'

'Are you implying that it is Dominic I am interested in?' her tone usually assured sounded stilted and a trifle perturbed.

'Well, aren't you?' her smile was knowledgeable but gentle, so much so as to increase Delilah's confusion.

After a moment's contemplation she, however, shrugged resignedly.

'And so, what if I am?' Delilah's tone held a bit of defiance.

'Do not make light of such a matter. I know you are on the defensive, but why must you keep up this act with me? The inquisition, as you called it, was motivated by the urge to prove my point that Dominic is the man who lives in your mind, rests in your subconscious, and has gradually taken permanent residence in your heart. Does that make sense to you?' Bertha smiled gently.

'In other words, you are telling me that I have fallen for him?' Delilah pointed out vaguely, while she wondered if what her friend was saying was indeed the truth.

'Why me? Why not put this question to yourself? Analyse your feelings, and then try probing into the recesses of your mind and see what conclusion you reach. Why then is he so constantly in your thoughts?' her voice was soft and gentle and persuasive.

Delilah got up from the sofa and walked to the furthest corner of the room, now leaning against the open window she stared out in the darkness. Although her eyes were expressionless, her mind was active. After a brief pause, however, she turned to face her friend with a smile. It was apparent that she had come to terms with the fact, and that she no more experienced confusion.

She walked back to the sofa and sat down next to Bertha. And looking at Bertha, she said in a voice that was affable yet audible. 'Bertha, I can't tell if what I feel for Dominic is love, and maybe such a feeling hasn't had a chance to develop. But whatever it is that I am presently undergoing is definitely a powerful emotion which quite often is difficult to control. But I have always maintained that love is a combination of tenderness, gentility and understanding backed by compatibility, so then surely what I feel for Dominic could not be love.'

'Love is known to assume multiple characteristics so like the climatic changes, and, therefore, unpredictable. What you may think of as hatred may well be sure signs of love; complicated... this emotion, yet again it often results in apparent miscalculations.' And it looked like Bertha was speaking from experience.

'But,' Delilah contradicted, 'love is always closely associated with tenderness and understanding and goodwill. Isn't that what love is all about?' Delilah appeared to be confused. 'Is it not an extension of emotional security and peace of mind when being successful in love?'

Bertha smiled faintly.

'True, but tell me where are you when security and peace of mind are denied to you?'

'I don't understand.'

'That's because you haven't realised love yet. Once you do, you will then know what I mean. If love can offer you security and peace of mind, so also it can leave you stripped of it. In love, one moment you touch the skies and the next minute you can fall flat on your face.'

'I still don't understand.' Delilah was obviously puzzled.

She could never imagine herself falling flat on her face. But it wasn't such an impossible dream for her to touch the skies and reach for the remotest star. Delilah had never been denied anything.

'You don't understand, do you? But you soon will. And I wonder if you can try postponing such a tragedy of falling in love. But let us hope for the best.'

'This all sounds so strange to me. I love Papa, I love Mama. Oh, I love you and the girls, but I can't say I have ever regretted loving any of you,' she stated empathetically.

'Yet strangely enough those are the very people who possess the greater power to hurt you,' Bertha pointed out astutely.

'Hmm, I think I know what you mean. Only a few days ago Papa had told Dominic to take charge of me, and I came to know about it much later, and that too accidentally. And it hurt, I... I felt I had been betrayed by him,' she recollected in a soft, pensive voice.

'Exactly what I meant, and well I think it is late enough. Let's go to bed.' Bertha had stood up languidly, stretching her arms above her head and stifling a yawn, while her gentle brown eyes were heavy with sleep.

'No, wait! I just remembered something. Recently... just recently I had felt thoroughly miserable and unwanted. A strange experience I tell you,' Delilah said insistently.

'You?' Bertha showed her surprise and watched her friend with some amusement

'It's difficult to believe. Your whole family dotes over you. Why... they would do anything for you, should you but ask.'

'Oh, they do, but only the other day some incident took place and I can't say I have still got over it.' Her eyes were shaded with pain.

'Would you like to talk about it?' Bertha stifled a yawn with the back of her hand. Noticing that Bertha was truly fatigued and drowsy as well, but was still politely urging her to open up, she decided to keep quiet for the moment.

'Forget it. I'll talk about it some other time.' She then arose from the settee.

'Remember, you can never be indifferent to those whom you love, and you are more often than not affected by whatever they say or do. And I guess that's what love is all about,' Bertha added almost with mock regret.

'Hmm, there is certainly an element of truth in what you just said, however, it's late like you pointed out. Let's reserve some revelations for tomorrow,' Delilah said with a smile and kissed her friend on her cheek.

'But frankly, I'd never envisaged that you would grow up to be a thinker.'

'Experience would turn you too, into a thinker.' Bertha smiled.

'I have a feeling that experience is fast catching up with me,' and they both laughed, the insinuation quite clear to them both.

CHAPTER 4

That very night Dominic was invited to attend a social ball. He was standing with a drink in his hand, discussing political issues with some of his business associates when his eyes fell on a woman of outstanding beauty. She was dressed in complete white with only a pearl necklace adorning her long, slender neck.

He found himself continuously staring at her. She was tall, perfectly proportioned and regally beautiful, and she was now receiving his glance with haughty disdain. Dominic's lips twisted into a faint, amused smile. He excused himself from the circle of his friends and slowly, almost lazily moved to where the woman was standing and surrounded by some of the best-looking gentlemen invited there. He observed cynically that each one of them was endeavouring to hold the woman's attention. He privately admired the way in which she was acknowledging his awareness of her presence, and showing her own interest in him with that peculiar and challenging look, but not without some hauteur. He approached her with quiet assurance, confident that he would not be risking a rebuff. He stood a few inches away from her, his eyes resting on her all the time, but when he spoke in that deep, rich baritone that carried so much authority, he was addressing the gentlemen circling the woman.

'Excuse us, gentlemen. I wish to speak to the lady alone.'

The woman's eyes rested momentarily on the gentlemen, taking note of their reluctance and proving to be terribly wanting in force of personality as they moved away without so much as a protest. She continued to watch them with acute contempt so visible in her lovely cat-green eyes that put them all to shame. With slight murmurs that had excused them from her presence, they had left her side. With some amusement the lady had not failed to recognise the look they had slanted in Dominic's direction; a look of extreme annoyance, but too civil and perhaps too awed, to be able to express themselves boldly.

One thing about Dominic that had arrested her attention was his bold and intent appraisal of her, also his air of confidence with which he carried himself. He was so darkly attractive and self-contained.

He bowed faintly and rather mockingly. She in response dropped a faint curtsy, but her face was set and features beautiful and chiselled like carved out of bronze, only her skin was the lightest shade of golden tan and that in fact served to enhance her appeal.

Dominic thought she possessed an ageless beauty. She could have been anywhere between forty to forty-five.

'You have no right to be so beautiful,' he said with an intent look in his eyes.

'You had better retract that statement,' her voice was firm and abrupt, but only Dominic could have noticed the slightest tremor in her velvety voice.

The intonation with which she talked was breathtakingly attractive, and perhaps if he should have found her under more intimate circumstances, he knew her voice would be capable of carrying an intoxicating quality. She was indeed a dynamic beauty. A rare treat to the eyes and a vision of a woman that he wanted very much to make his.

People were curiously glancing in their direction, but he noticed with some admiration that the lady was totally indifferent to the interest she was evidently arousing in the ballroom by giving her complete attention to him. She possessed an unshaken pride that he found strangely impressive. Her arrogance went perfectly with her stately personality.

Taking her by the elbow he escorted her outside the garden. She surprisingly showed no demur to tally with his wish to have her all to himself. They walked for some few moments silently until they had reached the extreme end of the garden. Very gently but firmly he caught her to him, drinking in her beauty with his eyes and slowly bending to touch her flaming red hair with his lips.

'Why do you want me to retract my statement?' he murmured softly, holding her within his reach, but yet not drawing her any closer.

She shut her eyes and raised her mouth to his. Their lips met in a gentle kiss after which she drew back.

'What is it you want from me?' she asked not quite steadily.

'I want to make love to you,' he stated quietly.

He heard her sharp intake of breath. It was apparent that she was not indifferent to him.

'Where do you stay?' he asked with a quiet yet a faint, urgent note in his deep, rich voice that held such magnetism.

'You wish to escort me home?' she enquired in a quiet voice, her eyes studying him more keenly than ever.

'Did you come here alone?' he knew what the answer was going to be before she could say anything.

He continued perceptibly, 'You perhaps don't need an escort,' but he was certainly not prepared for her calm retort.

'Correct. I do not need an escort. I need a ... man. Now shall we go?' she said with an impatient hauteur.

Dominic realised that she was different in so many ways from the rest of her sex. He would take time to get used to her unusual ways that merely magnified her originality. He draped her fur coat around her bare shoulders and propelled her towards where his Mercedes was standing. But he stopped halfway and turned to her.

'Tell me, which is your car? I will make the necessary arrangements for your safe journey home.'

'A penthouse more aptly described,' she corrected nonchalantly. 'And I did not come by car,' she pointed out quietly.

'Then perhaps you walked all the way here,' he said in a smooth, sarcastic tone.

She appeared to be quite unruffled. 'I came here by carriage.' Her voice was calm and composed.

'Good,' he remarked briefly and helped her inside the front seat of his car.

He walked round his side and got in beside her, shutting his door sharply. He brought the powerful engine to life. She gave him her address. He nodded faintly.

'Wouldn't you like me to know your name?' he asked casually.

'Why not?' she questioned his doubts. 'My name is Marian. What's yours?'

'Dominic,' he grinned wryly. 'Like it or would you prefer me by another name for this particular night?' he suggested satirically.

The flush on her cheeks provided him with a satirical satisfaction.

'The name Dominic suits you,' she said briefly, averting her face and presenting to him her exquisite profile.

He laughed softly, his voice was caressing, when he spoke:

'You are an unusual woman, Marian.'

She said nothing in response to that remark, but casually almost indifferently looked out the window.

A little later she said, 'Take a right turn, please.'

'I know. I wasn't so distracted,' he said offhandedly.

'I am confident of my attractions,' this time she actually smiled, 'but not that confident...'

Very smoothly negotiating a right turn, he pulled the car over by the gates of Marian's house. The sound of the crunch of car wheels brought Marian's housekeeper out of the house. She quickly unlocked the gates and opened them. Dominic drove the car inside the gates and pulled up right in front of the doorstep.

He quickly got out of the car and went to her side, opening her door with a faint, mocking bow that Marian acknowledged with a serene smile covering her beautiful lips. She placed her gloved hand in Dominic's proffered one, her eyes meeting his that were quietly laughing at her with some humour.

'I must give you credit for having your... charming housekeeper fill in the vacancy of a delightful third party. We should make a wonderful threesome,' he remarked sarcastically, as his gaze followed the housekeeper who flitted past them inside the house.

'Sorry to disappoint you, young man. Maggie never spends her nights here as she has her own place and an anxious husband, who I believe cannot do without her,' her voice held a quiet mockery.

'Now, isn't that a pity?' he let out a mock groan, 'and must you flaunt around our age difference like you were showing off your first-class results in the university exam?'

'When most women in my place would have reduced their age to a minimum size of their stunted brains, yes?' she asked smoothly, her eyes brilliant with open mockery directed towards her own sex.

Dominic laughed softly and stopped in the centre of the hall to directly meet Marian's eyes.

'You are original.' There was mild admiration reflecting in his eyes.

'True, women like me never grow stale. With passing years, we have the rare knack of turning almost unique.' Her smile of self-mockery belied the serious almost earnest expression in her eyes.

'You must, therefore, be preserved in the museum,' Dominic said suavely, as he followed her up the stairs.

She turned and looked at him with a tight expression on her face.

'You will soon change your mind about that. The museum is built for the display of inanimate objects. And you'll soon discover that I am a woman with blood running in my veins,' her voice was calm and composed, but her eyes registered the fact that she had indeed been moved to anger by his carelessly spoken words.

And that night he had come to know exactly what she had meant when she had said about being a woman with blood running in her veins, yet there had been something missing... something vital. Dominic was too worldly and far too experienced with women to be unable to recognise a certain restraint in a woman's behaviour. Marian had no doubt responded to his lovemaking in a way that was most assuaging, but some vital part of the woman had been missing. It was as though she was giving without really giving. That she was with him yet miles away from the present itself. He moved her sexually yet he was not able to reach her mind. She was mentally detached. Her body though had responded splendidly to his sexual overtures and yet Dominic found the sparks missing. A complete surrender of a woman ready for love was what Marian was not capable of; a willing, ecstatic surrender of mind, soul and body. Marian's mind and soul remained detached and untouched. No one it seemed could reach her mind and soul, and she remained an enigma for even a man with Dominic's experience.

Dominic respected her reasons for remaining mentally unresponsive. The woman had depths and she was an absolute woman. Without really saying much she gave the impression of knowing too much about life and all that it had to offer her. And unlike most other women, she maintained her reserve.

She scarcely conversed, but Dominic had to admit that whenever she struck up a conversation, she proved she was well-read, unusually intelligent and a student of literature. He discovered that she enjoyed speaking mostly on one subject and that was literature.

So captivated was he by Marian's persona that he postponed his business appointment for a later date and spend some more days with Marian. As days passed giving birth to a new dawn each time, Dominic and Marian became more than lovers. They were friends and companions to each other. Once he had tried to draw her out of her reserve and had failed. She was either a woman of strong beliefs and determination who believed in holding her emotions and reflections in check, or she was too deep to make light of incidents and feelings by taking just about anyone in her confidence.

It could be that she regarded people as extremely fallible. Scepticism could be reason enough for practising reticence so invariably. And even though she regarded Dominic as a friend and a confidant as well, she simply did not seem ready to confide in him. And Dominic was too understanding and patient to demand an explanation from her. After all, what business was it of his to interfere in her private affairs? He was quite satisfied with their arrangement and so was she, until one fine day...

'Marian, mind if I use your towel?' Dominic spoke from behind the doors of the bathroom.

There was no answer. Probably, he thought she was not in the house. She was out for a morning stroll. He knew that she was an early riser, and also that she loved going for her morning stroll. This was not the first time that he had stayed back for the night in her house, and that too was because she had not been particularly well the previous night.

He had remained awake the whole night by her side, nursing her back to health. By morning the temperature had come down to normal again. He had then prepared for her a cup of coffee. Then, on her insistence, he had allowed himself a few hours of sleep.

Much after he went for a quick shower, and minutes later he emerged then from the bathroom with a towel tied securely around his waist. After ruffling his wet hair dry, he bent to retrieve his watch from the side table by the bed and glanced at it. He then realised that it was past seven-thirty.

Those few hours of sleep had made him feel considerably rejuvenated. He quickly changed into his clothes and was just on the verge of buttoning up his shirt, when he heard the front door of the house open and close. That was Marian, he thought vaguely. But something gave him a reason to suspect it was not Marian after all. The sound of the footsteps climbing up the stairs was the kind made by the shoes of not a woman but a man.

Dominic's movements were deceptively casual as he slowly began to button up his shirt. His eyes were fixed on the shut door of the room he was occupying. He waited. The footsteps were getting closer with each passing minute, and suddenly the door was flung open, and there stood a tall, slim man framing the doorway. He was incredibly handsome, his eyes that were as dark as the night were now fixed on Dominic quite emotionlessly.

His features were strong and almost classical. His colouring closely resembled the complexion of a gypsy, yet the classic appearance gave him the distinct air of a polished man. He had an overcoat on and his hands were thrust into his hip pockets. His feet were set apart. The shoes on his feet were black and scrupulously polished, and so was the colour of his thick crop of hair; black and the growth luxurious. Nobody could have guessed that he was not a day younger than fifty-two. There was an aura of strength and power about him.

Dominic continued to button his shirt. After that, he tucked the ends of his shirt inside his slim-fitted trousers. His eyes for one moment remained fixed on the man. Picking up the tie from the bed, he started fixing it around his neck and at the same time straightening the collar of his shirt. The two men continued to watch each other until Dominic chose to break the silence.

'Why, Joseph, what a time and place to meet. Am I to presume we are meeting after a stretch of seven to eight long years?'

Although Dominic's expression which had been cool and indifferent all along had not changed, his voice certainly sounded sardonic.

And the voice was a deep baritone. The man's expression too had not changed. He drove further into the room while firmly shutting the door. And then he spoke…

'With your satanic looks, you are a dangerous man to have around, Dominic. You have undoubtedly grown into a fascinatingly handsome man,' the man, Joseph remarked in a voice that vibrated with emotions.

'Joseph, let us not run about the bush this way. If you have the keys to the front door of this house, then you surely must mean something to Marian. What is it? Why are you here, Joseph?' the deep blue eyes looked steadily into a pair of magnificent black eyes that looked back at him with a quiet message in them that did not quite register.

'Might I ask you the same question?'

'Why? Have I by any chance encroached upon your property or should I turn it plural?' Dominic's words held faint irony and he saw the sudden change coming into the man's face. It was a pained expression. The man turned his back to Dominic, refusing to show his deep suffering. To hear Dominic say those words was like an arrow that had pierced through his heart.

In a few, swift strides Dominic had reached the man's side and remarked very quietly, but this time without any trace of sarcasm.

'The doctor had given Fonda a few grace years. Is she still alive?' Dominic added hesitantly.

'She breathed her last on Wednesday,' came the steady, emotionless reply.

Dominic could not prevent the astonishment from entering his voice which was almost a whisper.

'But that is impossible! I mean she actually survived for so long as these many years. Why, it's almost a miracle!'

'Hardly a miracle,' Joseph's voice was toneless. The man slowly turned, facing Dominic, now.

'Fonda and I had discovered a long time ago that we were not compatible. Matters had reached so far that we were compelled to resort to either separation or divorce. Before she discovered that she was a cancer patient, she fell in love with some Captain Arnolds. A week after she read in the papers about his heart attack. He had died almost instantly. I then decided against giving a divorce. I wanted to wait until she would get over it. But she didn't. Much later I had to come here to attend some important conference. And it was then that I coincidentally met... Marian.

To make a long story short, we discovered we loved each other and we wanted to marry. We lived together even then for quite some time. Then I had to return to Derbyshire, unexpectedly. The telegram I had received that unfortunate day, said very little. What was I supposed to make out of, ''Fonda ... death bed... come immediately'' And because I did not want to frighten Marian, I kept quiet about my marriage, knowing it was a farce anyway, and would not be lasting for long. But when I returned home and learnt that Fonda was suffering from cancer, I quickly dropped the idea of... leaving her for a while.'

After a break, he, however, continued, 'Doctor said it was only a question of a few years. I wrote and told Marian that, at least for the next few years I could not marry her for certain reasons that I could not divulge, and that I hoped she'd understand. She wrote me back assuring me that she trusted me implicitly and that she would wait.' He paused for his breath.

'Fonda was getting from bad to worse. I was all the more determined to remain by her side. I couldn't desert her in that state. Years passed and with passing years Fonda longed for death as her suffering grew unbearable. I... I still cared for her, felt compassion for her, and she was so enduring,' he paused. Dominic waited.

He was deeply moved and was at a loss of words. He suddenly offered Joseph a chair. The bereaved man subsided into the chair, his elbow resting on his knee-cap, and his fingers opening and closing that which indicated his emotional upheaval.

'She never complained. You... you just can't leave anyone when they are down and when they have no one to turn to, but you. Gradually, right before my eyes, Fonda changed beyond recognition. She was the ghost of her former self. In that period, I forgot my happiness... I virtually lost track of time. Almost two decades...I couldn't even bear to think of Marian. I experienced a sense of betrayal. I knew that would be the last straw. I stopped writing to her. It was sheer torture corresponding with her, and yet not being able to see her, to hold her, to love her. After writing a few more letters, she too gave up waiting for my reply, I suppose. It was an impossible situation. This way years passed; eleven, fifteen, and twenty. Fonda continued to suffer and I with her. I cried, man, I cried then several times like a man demented. On one side was a wife, who had endured the torturous pain...the incessant cruel lash of fate...she took it all with a weak, ghostly smile, and on the other side was the woman I loved so completely, so irrevocably, and the mere idea of never having to see her again, losing her completely was one more step leading to hell. From work back to Fonda, and from Fonda back to work... the remaining years passed away, and the day Fonda had been dearly waiting for, had at last arrived. God! You should have seen the smile of gratitude on her face. She had finally been granted a respite. Her reward for years of endurance. And her final words were to me, ''Your life must go on... I love you for what you did for me. I love you for... caring!''

Those dark eyes were filled with tears. He looked up and said: 'And at that moment, Dominic, I swear I couldn't have asked for more.'

Minutes ticked by and silence; a companionable silence prevailed. At last, Dominic spoke, 'Like Fonda, your patience too will not go unrewarded, I think.' There was conviction in his voice. This was his father's brother, and it was up to him to convince him that hope had not abandoned him.

'What can you mean by that?' Joseph's voice was a whisper, and there was a ring of hope that could not have been mistaken for anything else.

'For Marian, only one man exists... and that's you,' he stated calmly.

'But I thought, I rather suspected that you two...er, it's difficult to put it into words, Dominic. Man, say if what I'm thinking is just a figment of my imagination or the...truth,' his voice was insistent, and in his eyes, there was a caged look, and Dominic could find it in his heart to feel sorry for the man.

Very gently, carefully he said, 'Marian is a very desirable woman. You can't blame a beautiful woman such as her for seeking temporary solace in the arms of another man, if she is made to believe that the man she loves, has deserted her. Besides, loneliness can bring about disastrous results, and she too is not exactly happy with the kind of life she is leading. It is the action of a desperate woman... a good woman, but who had been shunned by the society because she brought into this world a child without a father who prefers to remain anonymous.'

'Wait! What are you saying? A child? But she never told me... she never wrote to me... oh, no, it must be... is it a boy or a girl?' the note of desperation in his voice and expression of self-loathing in his eyes made Dominic feel strangely embittered. Even a strong man such as Joseph was not spared the harsh realities of life and could break down.

Dominic himself was a man who was easily moved by the sight of real suffering, and yet he never revealed his feelings. On the surface, he remained cool and composed, but within him, there was a heart that was also quite capable of bleeding for others; a heart which was capable of real feelings.

'Marian has not revealed much except her daughter's name is Bertha, who is in her late teens.' There was a contemplative look in Dominic's eyes when he said it.

Joseph was once more in control of himself. But that pained expression in his eyes remained.

'I can imagine what she must have gone through. My own child, my very own and I could offer her... nothing. Just nothing. Not even my name. Oh, what miseries!' he groaned softly, burying his face in his hands. 'I have a daughter, but how strange... she who has a father cannot tell the world proudly that she has one... who loves her. Dominic, I could forgive Marian anything simply because she did not destroy the beautiful result of our love... our daughter. She raised our child, defying all traditional norms, defying society and I know...I can tell how she must have suffered the brunt of wagging tongues, besides the many hardships that must have followed. But to have a daughter this old and to learn of it now and in this way...' he added in a faint voice.

'Joseph, we have forgotten one other important factor. We are men. We can adjust well in accordance with the circumstances, but for women, it can quite often get very uncomfortable, especially when matters are as grave as they are now.'

It was one full minute till they realised that Marian was standing in the doorway. Seeing Joseph was a shocking revelation at first, but she had quickly gathered composure after the startling shock of seeing him standing there as big as life and talking to Dominic like they were old friends.

It took a while for Joseph to briefly turn and at last feast his eyes on the woman that he loved. Then just as soon he averted his glance, so great was his feeling of pain and pleasure mixed with an almost naive expectancy to see the same light of love in her eyes shining just as vividly for him. But he soon collected composure, and once again turned to meet the eyes of the lovely woman standing at the doorway, and looking so calm and composed.

'With the passage of twenty years, you have grown even more lovelier,' Joseph remarked quietly, as till then, he was not prepared to show the fire inside him for her.

'And neither have you changed much. You look very distinguished as always,' her voice surprisingly carried a faint quiver, but her eyes were in level with his. They did not once waver.

Dominic leaned against the window-side and putting a cigarette between his lips, he lighted it, momentarily looking their way with mixed feelings. He then turned to gaze out of the window, watching the beautiful landscape disinterestedly. But Dominic was wrong in believing that the other two were completely lost in each other. They were, but not quite. Joseph was aware of his presence, and so was Marian.

Watching Joseph very keenly Marian remarked in an almost casual tone, 'It appears you two know each other very well.'

This time Dominic came forward and appeased her curiosity which was only naturally aroused.

'Joseph is my father's younger brother.'

Marian might have been momentarily shocked to hear this news, but maintained her calm. So, she thought resignedly, that explained the undeniable resemblance between Dominic and Joseph.

But she unlike many other women retained her composure and said instead, addressing Joseph, 'You are aware I believe that Dominic and I are... lovers.' She did not know of his sufferings, his grief and the many sacrifices he had to make or she wouldn't have said it so baldly.

Upon hearing those words coming from a woman he truly believed was his, Joseph had inwardly flinched, feeling a stab of fresh pain go through him like shafts of unexpected lightning. Once more Dominic gave him the support he so obviously needed; the strong support that one calls moral support. It looked as though he needed it.

'It would be more correct if you were to say we are friends. To be lovers there has to be absolute spontaneity on both sides. Your responses were automatic, and not spontaneous to say the least. I think Joseph understands what I'm implying.' He turned and saw the clear understanding in Joseph's eyes.

Marian too had noticed and her eyes were now bright with tears. That is all she needed; the look of understanding in Joseph's eyes. It did not matter why he had not come to her in all those years. She loved and trusted him. The explanation for such procrastination could wait. All that mattered was that his return would teach her to live again. And her entire being was already vibrating with feelings. Not unknown to her, she was no longer composed. Her feelings enveloped her in its warmth and which had for so long been dormant within her. Without really touching her, this man aroused the woman in her, and before she even realised it, she was closely wrapped in the warm circle of Joseph's arms.

Dominic stubbed out his cigarette beneath the heel of his shoe and stared at the pair merging into one single frame. He could clearly see that this time Marian's response was not automatic or mechanical. And he knew for certain now that the sparks had been missing because he had held the woman within his grasp and not her soul and mind. He quietly left the room, knowing he was not leaving altogether empty-handed. He still and would always enjoy Marian's warm friendship; its memory he would always cherish. As he lit another cigarette, he smiled to himself. There was still work waiting for him, ample work back in Cambridge. The papers he had come to sign along with a few other shareholders for the commencement of the newly designed project, were subscribed and already dispatched to London. The conference had been a success. Everything in connection with his business had proved more than satisfactory. But his smile remained bitter. It was only after the dinner party given in his honour by a few of his important clients, did he decide to return to Cambridge that very night.

***

It was mid-noon, and except for Dominic, the whole family was gathered in the drawing-room, each engaged in their own activity. It was a Sunday. Selena was knitting Sampson's cardigan. Sampson was absently flicking over the pages of the Sunday papers, his eyes resting occasionally upon his wife, completely unaware of her husband's adoring glances. Bertha and Anna discovered they had one thing in common: the Mayfair men and horse-riding. These were, incidentally, two subjects they realised they would never tire of discussing.

Joan was in a contemplative mood. Her palm cupping her chin, she stared into space, lost in thoughts. Delilah on the other hand was busily writing a letter to one of her school friends. The lights in the room were dim. Upon seeing her father's discomfort, she got up to switch on the main light. Suddenly, everyone appeared to be startled hearing the shrill ringing of the phone breaking the peaceful silence of the room.

Delilah quickly went to answer the phone. She spoke into the mouthpiece and gave her name in an abrupt voice in response to the voice on the other end asking for her name.

'Well, how is my favourite girl?' a pleasant masculine voice queried lightly. Delilah expelled a sigh.

'And, pray, who is this man, who calls me his favourite girl?' she appeared to be slightly amused.

'Have you forgotten Dean Fobster, my dear?' he sounded offended, but she knew he was merely playing a game.

With a smile she decided to carry on from there: a smile of plain mischief tugged at the corner of her mouth. 'Can't say I remember anyone by that name. You must have dialled the wrong number.'

'Sorry, Ma'am, for the trouble,' the voice said apologetically.

'Hey, you were not really disconnecting, were you?' Delilah said with some amusement.

'No, you imp. You should know better than that.' And Delilah could imagine him smiling good-humouredly.

'Well?' she queried indulgently. She was completely at ease talking to him.

'Well, what?' he questioned her query. 'Let's meet somewhere, dear girl, in a day or two. Girl, but you must have changed beyond recognition. As for me, I'm just the same...tall, lanky and blue-eyed,' he said in a mock-serious tone.

'Oh, the colour of my eyes hasn't changed either. And I'm still petite,' she suppressed a chuckle, and just then she heard footsteps drawing closer to the room. She turned and her heart missed a beat. The family greeted Dominic in a casual yet loving tone.

'Hello, imp. Are you still there?' Dean asked in an uncertain tone. Just then Delilah's eyes met Dominic's from across the room. 'Er, look, Dean, do you mind if I call you back later?'

'Girl, you do sound desperate,' he teased ironically. 'Anyway, you do that and don't forget to call me. Bye...' the line went dead.

Delilah replaced the receiver. She continued to look into Dominic's eyes which could only be described as unfathomable.

'How did your trip go, dear?' Selena enquired from across the room.

'Oh, not bad really, not bad at all.' He shifted his gaze that had caught the sight of Bertha sitting near Anna and attentively listening to what Anna was saying. She must have sensed him looking her way, for she returned his cool gaze, her lips smiling enigmatically.

Very slowly Delilah walked to Dominic's side and spoke in an almost formal tone, 'I would like you to meet my very good friend, Bertha. And Bertha, this is Dominic, as you must have guessed.'

Dominic gave a brief nod in greeting and Bertha as cool as ever did likewise, but her eyes were shrewdly passing over the fascinating hunk of a man standing so quietly before her, and subjecting her to deep and thorough scrutiny.

'You remind me of someone, miss...er...'

'That's a stale one, Mr Redford. Try another line if you must. And Bertha will do,' she said with a quizzical smile, absently wondering why he had missed her name during the introduction. His eyebrows lifted questioningly. He noticed that the family were showing open amusement.

Selena was openly chuckling, her hand busily knitting away the cardigan, and her eyes fixed on what she was engaged in doing with such remarkable skill. Dominic once again rested his eyes on Bertha, who was receiving his glance so calmly. His mouth suddenly twitched into an amused smile. He thrust his hands into his trousers' pockets.

'Bertha is far too old-fashioned, er, the name not you.' But his words carried an unmistakable irony. He extended his hand towards her and she instantly put hers into his proffered one.

'Barely do I indulge in unnecessary misinterpretation,' she said in that beautifully composed voice.

Delilah standing beside Dominic was beginning to feel altogether too neglected, but she chose to remain silent. The rest of the family was listening and showing mild interest in their conversation. Dominic was paying only partial attention to what she was saying. Now, who was it that she reminded him of? He still had her small hand in his without really knowing that he was still holding it. But very gently Bertha slipped her hand from his, and she noticed that he had not even realised it. He was still preoccupied.

Selena casually looked up. She was aware of his puzzlement over Bertha's appearance.

'Does Bertha remind you of me, Dominic?' her voice cut through his thoughts.

He mentally shook himself before he stared into a pair of laughing, brown eyes.

'She does, but not totally. She has your facial structure and your admirable composure, though,' but his last two words were edged with sarcasm that was directed toward Bertha.

'This is a rare compliment. Thank you, Mr Redford.' Bertha smiled serenely. He scrutinised her once again and found her composure and steady gaze very familiar. Her tall frame with that beautifully proportionate body contours and those legs: so long and slender. And the girl's complexion too was familiarly golden tan... and, oh Christ! He cursed under his breath; her name was... Bertha.

He soon regained his composure, though still not able to accept the complete irony of the situation, the astounding coincidence was baffling and even a trifle difficult to digest. He could have laughed from sheer amusement, but instead, his expression conveyed nothing. His eyes unconsciously settled on Bertha's lips. But when he saw her flush, he averted his gaze to meet the amused expression on Selena's face.

'She has your lips too, Mother, but not your... figure.'

It was then when Selena looked up and said with a calm smile, 'Bertha is my niece, Dominic.'

For Dominic at that moment, one shocking revelation had followed another. Momentarily, though, he was so confused and non-plussed that even he did not know what to make of Selena's words so quietly uttered. The situation was getting more and more complicated. Bertha was Selena's niece. That was acceptable as far as he was concerned, but the suspicion in his mind that Marian and Selena were actual sisters disturbed him a great deal. And how was anyone to know in the family except for him, that his own father's brother was in fact Marian's prodigal lover, who had deserted the fine lady?

He did not notice the amused smile on his father's lips. And nor did he bother to see Delilah's and Bertha's reaction to his presumptuousness.

Quickly he added, 'Pardon my saying so, but with those legs and figure, Bertha, you distinctly remind me of someone else. Also, your style of looking directly at someone is an added reminder of someone I know quite... intimately,' but he refrained from elaborating on it. He had then moved with quiet ease to where Selena was seated near the hearth and he now had Selena's complete attention.

He could see that everyone in the room was now watching him curiously, however, nobody said anything. With a faint almost careless shrug he moved closer to where Selena was sitting in a cushion-backed, rocking chair.

Selena then asked him a question or so it appeared, and after that what transpired between them was difficult to tell, as they were quite far from the rest of them. But each knew that whatever was being discussed was mediocre and general, nothing in particular as had been the previous subject for discussion.

Bertha who had been standing for quite some time weakly subsided into a chair with an inaudible sigh that appeared to have escaped the notice of everyone present there. Delilah, though remained standing, her eyes fixed stonily on Dominic's back that was now facing her.

Without actually looking up, Bertha said in a faint voice 'Yes, indeed, Delilah, he is what you said; an enigma and maybe in due time I might have the pleasure to encounter the devil in him too.' She was not being provocative but merely expressing her thoughts.

But at that moment, Delilah was undergoing a strange emotion; an emotion synonymous with jealousy which was consolidated by the support of yet another queer feeling; a strong feeling of possessiveness. And perhaps that was the reason why she remained unresponsive to her dearest friend's lightly phrased remark. Although it had been stated without any ulterior motive, and had merely been a verbal repetition of her silent thoughts.

Strangely, though, Bertha was quick to perceive Delilah's present state of mind. Having an idea of what she was undergoing, she most tactfully refrained from pressing the subject into a prolonged discussion that in other circumstances they would have both enjoyed, with a taste for intrigue.

They both heard Dominic laugh over something that Selena had probably said, and then he turned and walked towards them again. But this time, Delilah was not prepared for what followed, and neither was Bertha. Dominic confronted them with a look that was difficult to fathom, although that look struck a definite chord in them, alerting their numbed senses to action. His gaze continued to communicate itself to their active senses, and they could not suppress a feeling of anticipation that followed in its wake. The suspense was heightened and so had their elation. But they were more than disappointed when with a curt nod of his head he abruptly left the room. Together they had turned their eyes to where Selena was sitting, and wordlessly sought some knowledge of the baffling situation from that quarter, but all they could extract from Selena was a vague smile in response to the pronounced question in their eyes. Joan had dozed away, and Anna was now deep in her thoughts. Sampson was engrossed in reading the Sunday Times.

At that moment both Delilah and Bertha experienced an absurd feeling of anti-climax. They were both curious. Their interest that had been aroused was now dampened; the curiosity persisted though. Their eyes met and a question passed between them to which neither had the answer for probably the first time. They were anxious to learn the news that they knew Dominic had been going to impart to them before he had suddenly decided against it.

That same afternoon Delilah met Dominic on the front doorstep of the house. She was alone and so was he. She had still not forgotten the previous incident. She felt feverish, though she was burning not with fever, but with a fury that she had been suppressing all this while, and was now threatening to surface. She tried to pass him, trembling from head to toe, and her face was a beautiful mask of controlled fury. Her eyes were like the sharp pointed edge of a gleaming dagger. She looked bewitchingly beautiful at that moment. She looked a mixture of fire and beauty, and strangely, Dominic was disturbed by such a display.

'Please let me pass,' her voice: a fierce whisper.

He blocked her path and his fingers deliberately encircled her slender throat.

'Where is your interesting friend today?' he enquired in a soft voice, his cool, blue eyes studying her expression with a total lack of interest.

'You leave her alone. She is engaged to be married.' Her voice was surprisingly nonchalant, but underneath she was far from composed. She would have loved to hurl something at him.

'Answer my question first,' he commanded quietly, his grip on her throat tightening.

She was finding it difficult to breathe. His touch on her skin was like adding fuel to the fire burning inside her. She looked into his eyes. His eyes held a hard glint whereas hers were silently blazing at him.

'She is probably taking a walk in the garden,' she answered, though grudgingly. His grip was turning painful.

'Don't!' Her voice was breathless, and it held a note of plea in it with a yielding quality that was disturbingly sensual, and its intensity heightened, which communicated itself to Dominic who after slackening his grip, bent to caress her arched throat with his lips.

'Why are you doing this to me, Dominic?' she asked in a strange voice that had turned husky.

'I'm merely erasing the... hard print of my fingers on your throat with my...lips. Don't you like it? I thought you would like it...a lot.' And his lips continued to travel over her throat and bringing a gasp to her lips. Then slowly, almost lazily he raised his head. His eyes were no longer cold. 'It has rubbed off your anger too, besides clearing your...lovely throat of my fingerprints.'

'Dominic… is it because you like Bertha, that you wish to see her?' her voice continued to remain soft and yielding.

Suddenly he withdrew, releasing her, and his eyes were cold once again.

'And why should that worry you?' then more curtly, 'I have no wish to appease your curiosity.' He moved towards the landing, but she lightly stayed him with her hand to his back that felt like a hard, indomitable wall. She did not know what to do about the tumult in her heart, and the pain that was getting worse every time he showed indifference as he was showing then.

He glanced sideways. The look in his eyes was coldly enquiring. Hers held a soft appeal in them.

'You had something to say earlier, but you never came around to tell us about it.'

'Who do you mean by "us"?' he asked coldly, his hands folded.

'Bertha and me,' she replied softly.

'Whatever it is I want to impart is for Bertha's ears alone. And now if you'll excuse me.' He turned and descended the short flight of stairs after which she saw him crossing the pathway and stopping to the right leading to the garden where Bertha was probably taking a pleasant stroll.

Gradually, when the full impact of the rebuff dawned on Delilah, she changed colour to an angry, almost fiery red and her lips began to quiver. She turned and walked across the hallway, and up the long, curved staircase to her room.

Sampson just then happened to be crossing the hall when he saw Delilah looking upset. But before calling out to her in his usual bantering manner, he moved aside, first mentally assessing her expression, and then trying to reach the correct conclusion about her disturbed expression. Undoubtedly, she was furious, wildly furious, so he thought that a casual greeting would be the best approach under the strained circumstances. To show concern and curiosity would only serve to open the flood of accumulated fury, thereby, compounding the tension in the air and her disturbed mind.

'Hello, dear,' he greeted her, as he crossed the hall to the library which was to the extreme left. He did not wait for her response, though.

He had disappeared inside the library and gently shut the door behind him. Delilah had reached her room. She closed the door ever so gently and in that same state of mind she stepped out into her veranda. She heard the faint voices coming from below, in the garden. She stiffened and found herself listening intently to bits of conversation, its faint sound reaching her above, on the porch. Her knuckles showed white against the varnished railings and the fire inside her accelerated at an enormous pace.

'But... but this is just not feasible that you have... that you are... oh, Mr Redford, please don't play games with me. You don't know what this means to me...all that you have told me.' That was Bertha sounding confused and for once, lacking in confidence. Although the voice sounded intense, it was laden with emotions.

'Every bit of what I have told you is the truth and I don't play games. And yes, don't you think it's time you started calling me by my first name? Bertha, I insist that we dispense with formalities.' There was mild laughter injected into his voice.

'Oh, Dominic, I... I... don't know what to say. Y...you have made me the happiest girl in the world today,' her voice sounded happily tearful and then there was silence.

Delilah slowly turned back to retreat into her room and suddenly she fixed her fingers around a beautiful vase. And again, returning to the veranda she aimed it straight at the garden below, exactly where the voices had floated from. She threw it with tremendous force. It reached the garden with a crash, the glass pieces and the coloured fragments dispersed beneath the feet of Dominic and Bertha, who were too shocked to say anything. They both looked up simultaneously, and something had just then followed the vase on the thick grass with a heavy thud. It was an exquisitely bound book on psychosomatic issues, which Dominic had gifted to Delilah on her previous birthday. It was one of his gifts that she treasured above all others. She adored books; any book that had to do with psychology and psychiatry. She especially adored anything that Dominic had given each time on her birthday, every year.

But now, all those gifts that she had preserved with such care and love were being discarded similarly; out of the veranda and lying in a dismal state at Dominic's feet. Bertha hesitantly stole a glance up at the veranda and then, her eyes rested for a brief moment on Dominic who took a quick glance at all those gifts that he had given to Delilah, now lying at his feet – harshly rejected and disposed of. And before Bertha could prevent him, he dashed inside the house, and up the stairs, dodging steps until he reached the top landing.

Taking a deep breath, he walked down the corridor to Delilah's room, and without knocking he barged into her room, his own temper barely in control. Delilah was standing there in the centre of the room, facing the door with one hand suspended in the air and holding a small box that contained a wristwatch. She remained standing there, meeting the dangerous look in his eyes with a look of her own, no less. Their fury matched, but neither knew about that passion; a burning passion that would eventually follow.

Dominic deliberately shut the door with his foot and advanced into the room, his eyes fixed on the enraged girl, who at that moment closely resembled a strikingly-beautiful cheetah with eyes blazing and body arched for action, ready to take a deadly plunge upon its antagonist. She blindly threw the box at him, but he deftly caught it in his hand and simultaneously ducked just as the next object; a lovely bronzed statue of a woman in a classical pose hit the shut door and with a crash lay on the carpeted floor into fragments.

The next thing she knew was, that her hands were being captured in a fierce grip, and then raised high above her head. In his rage, he twisted them slowly but resolutely. His intention was clear.

She struggled frantically, but with another twist of her hands and she could not suppress the scream that was rising in her dry throat. And then the scream broke the subdued silence of the room. Her body was arched in pain, angry tears filled her eyes. But when her long nails deliberately bit into the hard flesh of Dominic's forearms, he began to show the beginnings of a quiet fury that perhaps Delilah had never before known about. He grabbed a handful of her hair and dragged her to the bed, pushing her down roughly on it. He then bent over her with his hands pressing her further onto the softness of the bed. By doing this, he was also preventing her from rising.

She struggled violently and began using her legs as her hands were put temporarily out of action. He stepped forward and with the aid of one free hand he slapped her hard on her mouth, while the other hand lay across her breasts, holding her captive. His knees were pressing her legs down, also putting them temporarily out of action.

At first, she stared at him wide-eyed. Even she could not believe that he had struck her on the mouth. Her lower lip was bleeding and it looked swollen.

'Get out!' she said in a fierce undertone. She was feeling a strange weakness that was seeping through her body and rendering her physically defenceless. Rage again surfacing, she turned sideways to bite his hand in her desperation, but before she even realised, she felt the stunning impact of his hard length upon her trembling body and then she felt his hands moving...

Even when he unbuttoned her dress and pulled it apart from the middle, all she could utter was a weak groan.

'Dominic, please don't,' she pleaded in a weak voice; her hands now free, she placed them on his chest to push him away quite ineffectively. Her heart was beating at a suffocating rate. She moved beneath him to escape his disturbing proximity, but that action merely served to incite him further.

'You... you have destroyed just about everything I gave you. The watch was spared, though, but now who is to come to your rescue?' he murmured hoarsely, and his eyes gleamed fiercely.

As he said those words, she then sensed that he had virtually ripped open the front of her dress, leaving her body bare and exposed to his scrutiny. And her heart was thudding when she discovered in a quick flash that he had also disengaged her bra and thrown it aside, leaving her breasts too, bare. Her nipples stood taut and erect over the softly-curved mound of her breasts, and upon making such a realisation she shied away from the naked look of desire in his eyes mixed with anger, that no longer seemed curbed.

And before she could protest, his lips came down on hers with a quiet force while his fingers slowly, tantalisingly began to tease the cherry brown tips of her breasts, arousing inside her the wildest, craziest emotion that at that moment she couldn't have recognised for desire; pure desire for more of such an experience. He had set her on fire, and she silently hated him for making her feel this way.

His lips moved from hers to caress her cheek, sliding down towards her arched throat where it lingered deliberately for a while, making her hunger for more before they once more took fierce possession of her lips, and the kiss then started taking her to dizzying heights. She fought, and moaned, but then found herself responding wildly to his kisses and caresses.

'Why did you do it?' he demanded in a fierce whisper, but his hands were gently almost possessively caressing her smooth belly, and bringing a gasp to her lips.

'I... I hated you. That's why,' she said in a breathless voice, all the time strongly aware of him slowly seducing her into submission.

'Why? Simply because I talked to your friend?' he enquired, his eyes now fixed on her quivering mouth.

He bent to kiss her lips and drew back but with some misgiving. He found himself enjoying this experience with her. He wanted her, desired her and knew she felt the same, but refrained from putting it into words.

'You must have done more than...talking,' she said in a voice that held petulant accusation.

'Are you inferring that... that I made love to her?' he treated the question like an irritating fly.

'Well, didn't you?' there was a note of hesitancy in her voice. She caught his lapels and brought his face closer to hers.

He watched her intently before he said with an almost careless tone in his voice, but which had a sharp edge to it, 'No, I didn't. Now are you satisfied?' and with his teeth gritting, he fiercely cupped her naked breast, and at the same time forcing her lips apart with his and taking pleasure in it. The kiss was passionate and searching. It went on for some seconds till she lay beneath him, spent and breathless.

'There was silence down there in the garden for one whole minute when you were with Bertha. Can you explain that?' she challenged his integrity. He merely watched her with a faintly annoying look in his eyes.

'Does silence necessarily have to mean that a demonstration of love is in progress? For Heaven's sake, does it have to mean that something of this sort was amiss? How jealous can a woman get?' he beat his clenched fist against the wall in annoyance.

'Then perhaps you were whispering sweet nothings into each other's ears. How cool...' she put in sarcastically, pulling the blanket up to cover up her nakedness. But he roughly pulled it aside and buried his face between her breasts where the gentle curve of the valley between the white bosom was soft and naturally scented.

'Perhaps,' he said moodily, his lips moving over her breasts in an endless journey and not without some fervour.

'Perhaps? What about?' she asked fiercely and struggled to extricate herself from his grasp, but he pressed her even deeper onto the softness of the bed with his weight that felt like lead, only lead was cold to touch and Dominic's strong, lithe body exuded warmth and rugged appeal.

'Now, what kind of a question is that?' he said impatiently and not without some annoyance. His patience was being tried, she could tell, but she threw caution to the winds.

'And what did you two whisper about?' she persisted, yet she could not tell why she pursued the matter. It shouldn't have bothered her. It wasn't as if they were committed to each other. Then, why? Why was she doubting his conduct with her friend?

He watched her enigmatically from beneath half-closed lids.

'Now, you are beginning to sound like a jealous wife,' his tone was coated with pointed sarcasm. At once he sensed her stiffening. The barb, though unintended, had accidentally struck home.

But Delilah had too much pride for one thing to confess even to herself that she had strong feelings for him. That would in her opinion destroy her pride. Besides, if she had even the slightest vestige of self-respect, she knew she would have to hold in check the desire for his even closer proximity. It was after this that she made a pretence of finding the quality of his humour rather amusing, dismissing it as inconsequential. She found herself smiling upon him, only the smile was forced, but the cynicism was very much evident in that smile. She couldn't have avoided that. Men! How could a woman trust a man with her own friend?

'To be a jealous wife there has to be a much-loved husband to complete the picture. I personally think that bit of humour was in an exceedingly bad taste, as I can't imagine anyone playing such a dominant role of my husband, and that too someone whom I could be devoted to, so much so that everything that he would say or do would rob me of my peace. No chance.' She again smiled amicably.

Deep blue eyes enigmatically smiled into hers and then deliberately he bent to her side and briefly paused before he sought out the soft, full curve of her breast with his mouth and then nibbled titillatingly at the erect nipple. With an inward gasp, she found her treacherous body responding to his overture and melting her very resistance, the touch of his lips light but subtly tantalising, sending through her, arrows of excitement and making her want to fiercely grab at him from behind and draw blood. Her violent reaction matched the sensation he had the power to arouse in her.

Slowly, he raised his head and supported his weight on his elbow, his eyes fixed on Delilah whose breathing had turned uneven. She had averted her face. She refused to meet those knowledgeable eyes. With his other hand, he gently pulled her to him, and the slight smile that he gave her was tentative. His fingers gently tugged at the soft tendrils lying on her forehead.

'Believe me, you'll be far better off should you remain... unmarried. Such a beautiful face and body will be wasted on...one man,' he had added the last words after a deliberate pause.

She abruptly pulled away from him and brought the blanket right up to her chin.

'You are insulting,' she remarked coldly, but her face was again averted, as she began putting her dress on and shakily buttoning it up.

Not changing his position, he observed her every move with careless indolence. An indescribable smile slowly formed on his lips, which she found so firm yet sensually exciting, and that which described him to the hilt and so precisely. She could not help reflecting on his attractiveness and magnetism.

'So, you would like to know what I was talking to your friend about...' he queried through pursed lips, while all the time watching her lazily with a bored expression.

She reluctantly met the enigmatic look on his face, but remained silent, feeling far less embarrassed now that she was dressed up once again.

'Your Aunt Marian has finally married Bertha's father,' he informed with deliberate calm, his eyes smilingly watching her reaction.

She heaved a sigh of relief and made an exaggerated gesture with her hands that confirmed his suspicion of the sincerity of her expressed pleasure.

'That is great news!' she smiled expansively, while Dominic continued to watch her with lazy speculation. Then all of a sudden, her expression changed to one of increasing fury. 'Such a fantastic brainwave! I would like to know just who is this great Casanova who makes my aunt pregnant, deserts her and the child, and coolly returns after all these... these years to put the wedding ring round her finger? What was he doing all these years? If I could just meet him, I would then give him a piece of my mind, oh! The insufferable man! The cheek!' She thrashed the pillow on the bed and temper exhausted, rolled to the other side of the bed to leave its warmth when Dominic's one hand pulled her back on his side of the bed again.

'Where exactly does your sympathy lie, hmm?' his fingers absently stroked her upper arm.

'With Bertha, of course,' she said sharply, her fury had not abated.

'You appear to care for her very much,' he sounded strangely amused.

Her eyes glaring at him, she retorted, 'I do, but that's hardly your business.'

'Yet, a little while ago I believe you were jealous of her,' he said with a deceptive gentility, but after a momentary sharp look in his direction, she changed over to another subject, not willing to admit that what he said was a complete truth.

'You haven't told me yet who this man is.' Her chin thrust out stubbornly, and her eyes took on a cold expression, but which did not fool Dominic at all. He knew she was raging inside. His amusement increased by minutes.

'That man is my uncle: my father's younger brother. Nice family reunion, don't you think?' he mused with some sarcasm.

'How can that be? I don't understand,' she said with a frown and a suggestion of suspicion in her voice.

'You can call it coincidence if you like,' he shrugged carelessly, his boredom turning out to be an obvious trait of his, that he did not bother to conceal.

'Some coincidence,' she smiled scornfully. Then giving him a full treatment of her barely controlled fury, she demanded, 'and how is it that you are the first to come to know of all this?'

Dominic went stiff and with a quick, agile movement he left the bed to stand a little away from it, carelessly buttoning up his shirt, and taking care not to meet her eyes.

'Why won't you answer me?' she demanded impatiently, her palms pressed to the bed and her eyes fixed on Dominic who had his back to her. But he slowly turned at the tone of her voice, his expression one of cool hauteur.

'I resent interference, Delilah. You will be wise not to antagonise me any further. I refuse to tell you what I think is none of your business,' his voice, although quite placid sounded brusque.

'You are hiding something, aren't you?' she persisted, her obstinacy already beginning to rile him, but he admirably maintained his calm.

'You have a vivid imagination,' he stated with faint sarcasm. 'And I permit you to take full advantage of it by exercising it to draw out the conclusion suiting your petty, suspicious mind.' He turned to leave the room when he sensed her jumping from the bed and running to his side with a flush suffusing her cheeks, and her long nails biting into the hardness of his arm.

'You have no reason to call my mind petty and suspicious! Y... you had better retract that statement,' she said through gritted teeth.

He coolly glanced sideways at her nails biting into his arm but did not attempt to extricate himself.

'It is childish to contradict the truth, Delilah, and now take your hands off me. Don't give me an opportunity to fling it aside and do you some injury. You're trying my patience too far.'

On an impulse, she caught at his lapels and murmured endearingly, 'Why, Dominic, why am I filled with such curiosity? Why won't you tell me the whole truth? You...you say it is childish to contradict the truth, and yet you refrain from revealing it. Why? Why Dominic?' her eyes were softly pleading with him, and Dominic's expression at that moment softened.

'You are a strange creature, Delilah. I never anticipated that you would turn so...so very impetuous,' his voice sounded reflective, but his eyes bored into hers, causing her to shiver inwardly from the impact of his hard scrutiny.

'I'm not some abnormal creature to be examined through a microscope,' she retorted with an angry hauteur looking at him with an undaunted rebuke.

He smiled faintly, flicking her cheek with his finger almost indulgently, but she flung it aside impatiently.

'I can't imagine from whom have you inherited such an explosive temper,' his smile was one of lazy amusement.

'Oh, stop it!' she stamped her foot on the carpeted floor furiously, her fists pummelling his chest in a blind rage, and tears of frustration gathering in her eyes. Finally, unable to bear the burden of her inexhaustible fury, she put her arms around his waist and with childlike innocence burst into a flood of hot tears. She was shaking all over from the impact of the emotional entanglement that she was suffering from.

Dominic's fingers gently stroked her hair back from her moistened forehead.

'Please try to understand that it is so much better to hold back the truth rather than having to tell and live a lie all your life.'

She looked up at him with tear-filled eyes and mouth quivering, she murmured incoherently, 'I...I don't, oh, it does not matter, oh, Dominic, what's happening to me? Why...why am I feeling this way?' and a fresh flood of tears flowed down her cheeks as she hid her face in the hard curve of his shoulder, and looking at that moment endearingly childlike and quite defenceless. Suddenly, bringing his hand to her heart, she looked up at him with tear-filled eyes, and cried out softly, 'C... Can you feel the tumult there? I...I feel this way every time you touch me. Why is it so, Dominic?'

Her plea had not gone quite unheard and unnoticed. His hand stiffened beneath hers as he slightly moved away from her.

'Those questions only you can answer.' His eyes bore into hers, but without giving anything away. His thoughts remained a secret. He gently extricated his hand from beneath hers and walked to the doorway.

In acute despondency, Delilah buried her face in the softness of her pillow, her body shaking with silent uncontrollable tears. Dominic paused at the doorway to turn to watch her with faintly arched eyebrows and compressed lips. After a brief spell, he broke the silence that had turned quite discomfiting.

'Look at me, Delilah,' his voice, though soft, carried a tone of authority. She did but with some reluctance. Her eyes were swollen up with wild, incessant weeping. She looked very young and vulnerable; a fact which Dominic found strangely unnerving.

And, although, he endeavoured to bring some order to the disturbed atmosphere, he still did not know what was the best way to handle such a situation.

'You will wipe away those tears and listen to reason.' He paused to watch her wipe the falling tears with a piece of fresh linen. 'That's better. Now, has it ever occurred to you that you are highly temperamental, hence you are more likely to take offence easily, even feel deeply about... matters that really shouldn't be given much importance?' Then more gently he went on, 'Delilah, you are young and lovely. Give yourself time to grow up. Depth of feelings comes with maturity. And this may take months even years, perhaps who knows... much earlier... say, in weeks before you are able to identify your feelings correctly. Do I take it that you have understood all that I have said?' he spoke very gently, almost compassionately. It gave him satisfaction to see her nodding her head in an affirmative, in reply to his query.

'Try to think on positive terms, not necessarily be optimistic, for too much optimism can also prove harmful if certain things don't come up to your expectations.' In a way, even he too did not know what he was indirectly trying to convey to her, but even then, he hoped for her sake that his words would leave their mark on her mind, serving as a form of a lesson to her to be less sentimental, even less emotional and exercise more control over her emotions.

But when he finally left her room, he had experienced an odd sense of trepidation along with an unaccountable feeling of guilt that stemmed from the thought that he had left behind a wounded creature unaided and feeling as insecure as ever before.

Delilah had succumbed to sleep, her tears spent, and her eyes looking all swollen up and red as they grew heavy with slumber.

Bertha, in the meanwhile, had gone up to Delilah's room after some half-hour or so, intending to clear away her doubts about Dominic and her, but upon noticing her fast asleep, she quietly retreated from the room. Verifications would have to be made anyway, but that could wait until morning. She hoped that Delilah would understand and would not be a target for further misinterpretation.

Dominic had returned to the family room and acted as if nothing had occurred to ruffle his nerves. Bertha too acted likewise once she had joined the family, and was surprised at her ability to maintain an admirable calm under the circumstances, which otherwise she would have never believed herself capable of, contrary to what many others thought.

The rest of the members of the family continued to remain in blissful ignorance about the catastrophe that had caused such a stunning impact on the minds of Dominic and Bertha. And apparently, Delilah was the cause of it all. She remained the main culprit behind the controversy that had turned that particular evening into a fiasco; standing out like a torch of configuration in an atmosphere bathed in a cloak of prolonged and seemingly unending silence.

CHAPTER 5

The glass doors flew open from the force of the winds, indicating the approach of inconsistent weather. The morning seemed particularly dull with the sky appearing a shade too grey instead of the customary welcoming blue; a confirmed example of an inception of a truly disagreeable day.

But Delilah's sunny smile presented a startling contrast amid the gloomy weather with which the day had begun. With pleasurable concentration, she absorbed every word that Bertha was uttering. Both were perched on the bed in a comfortable cross-legged fashion, and that morning both looked free from problems. For Delilah, the day couldn't have been more beautiful.

Delilah's expression continually altered from regret to pleasure, from relief to an expression of acute despondency, and back again to the extremity of sheer relief and contentment, as she digested the reasons for her Uncle Joseph's absence from the country for so long as that. She expressed her sorrow for her parted aunt, admiring the lady's courage now that she was no more. And she simultaneously felt gladdened about the happy reunion between Marian and Joseph. Loving hands clasped around Bertha's neck and soft lips touched the cheek moistened with tears of happiness that surpassed all else in its profound triumph and enormity.

'Darling, I can't say how happy I'm for you!' her own eyes were moistened with happy tears.

Bertha laughed and kissed Delilah in turn, before she playfully pulled her from the bed and pushed her into the bathroom.

'A quick shower followed by a nice hot breakfast will revive your spirit even more. Come on, go,' she insisted cheerfully.

Delilah agreed with a slight nod and a radiant smile, and at that moment not even the sultry weather could have dampened her spirits. She ran lightly into the bathroom.

'I'll meet you down in the breakfast room,' she called out to Bertha before shutting the door and quickly peeling off her nightdress, and humming a happy tune as she got under the shower; revelling under the cooling influence of the thick shafts of flowing water. She felt wonderfully invigorated as she emerged from the bath with a towel closely wrapped around her lovely, naked form.

Dressed in complete deep mauve she looked cool and fresh, and with a lace ribbon tied securely round her long, lustrous hair which merely served to enhance her youthful appearance. She raised her hand to sprinkle talcum on her nape and low front; thoughts of the previous night came back to her mind without warning, and she experienced remorse that she could not even begin to explain to herself. Her mouth drooped in a moment of bitter reminiscence. Diffidence was a mild form of describing what she was presently feeling. She was disgusted with herself and felt like she were an object of shame when she began to visualise her behaviour of the previous night. How could she have been so wanting in self-respect that she had gone as far as admitting to Dominic about the way she felt for him? Her naivety and altogether tactless declaration must have surely proved a source of extreme embarrassment to him, she thought with silent scorn and self-loathing as she stepped out of the room. She paused reflectively in the corridor that loomed before her like a dark valley that she was loath to cross; embarrassment and shame checking her desire to join the family in the breakfast room.

But before long the desire was quelled by plain reluctance to join the family downstairs, gathered probably in the breakfast room. She turned to retrace her steps back to the sanctuary of her room, planning a temporary escape from the harsh realities of life, when her progress was abruptly brought to an almost instantaneous halt.

'Delilah,' the footsteps drew nearer till they were barely inches away from where she was then standing; tongue-tied. A coaxing hand clasped her stiff shoulders. 'Come on! We shall go down together. I just happened to realise your fear of the unknown,' Dominic said with an irresistible smile, his fingers intimately curling around her arm.

With a slight hesitance, she stole a dubious look up at him and found assurance in that doubly irresistible smile. She was aware of his touch, his proximity with every fibre of her being, but she continued to retain her outward calm, although she could not prevent herself from saying, 'About yesterday…' she began with a false determination, but Dominic curtailed her weak endeavour to explain her conduct of the previous night.

'Yesterday is past. Anyway, I could have hardly taken you seriously. I know from experience that you do not mean everything you utter when you er…shall we say, throw your tantrums around,' his words lightly spoken were intended to offer her reassurance, and the smile that he threw at her was astonishingly amiable, as he pushed her along with him towards the staircase. Suddenly he scooped her up into his arms and laughed at her weak protests to put her down back on her feet.

Upon reaching the breakfast room he placed her back on her feet as requested and slapping her soft rear in smiling indulgence, he jested, 'You are a lightweight.' Taking her by her resisting hand, he pulled her gently with him into the breakfast room.

'High time, dear,' Sampson remarked lightly, obviously addressing Delilah. His hand was busily buttering the toast. 'You are an early riser. You must have overslept,' he said casually, without expecting any reply. Delilah gave him a quick kiss before taking her seat to his right, at the table.

Selena gracefully poured Delilah and Dominic the scalding tea with cream and a liberal amount of sugar. Delilah stirred the sugar before raising the cup to her lips while Dominic helped himself to a hot scrambled egg and sipped his tea between every mouthful.

Bertha nudged Delilah who directed her an enquiring glance. Bertha smiled with her eyes as she said, 'Dominic is taking us out today. How's the idea, hmm? Why don't you uncurl yourself? You look all coiled up. Relax, will you?' Bertha added with gaiety.

Delilah raised her shoulders slightly in a casual shrug.

'Sounds good enough. Can't say I disapprove of the idea. A change would do us all some good. I mean a long drive somewhere…'

Bertha's high spirits must have communicated itself to Delilah, for she found herself smiling too, her own spirits recovering. She too, in turn, began talking animatedly, and for an indefinite spell forgetting yesterday's incidents for today's forthcoming pleasures.

Dominic observed her keenly but refrained from commenting on it.

Accidentally, Delilah's eyes met his across the table. Quickly touching her mouth with the tissue, she rose from the table. To get rid of the latent hostility inside her, she adopted a cheerful attitude. Turning to Joan she said while adding enthusiasm in her voice, 'Do you often meet Dean, Joan? I'm told his is a field job.'

Joan raised her head to look at Delilah with mischief dancing in her eyes.

'Why, are you afraid he might divert his attention to me?'

Delilah was aware of Dominic's eyes fixed on her. She smiled good-humouredly.

'Oh, not at all. Dean has made it quite clear that he couldn't be interested in other girls while I'm around. I merely asked as I wanted to meet him at his office. I should know when he is available, isn't it?' she shrugged lightly.

'It's a pity you are not jealous,' Joan groaned, but her laughing eyes belied her disappointment. 'I would have enjoyed making you jealous. You are always so self-assured,' she complained and Sampson laughed, joined by Anna who had maintained silence throughout breakfast.

'She has a reason to be self-assured, don't you think?' Pride was written in his eyes.

'The beauty in the family, I should say...' Anna interrupted with a quiet smile.

Gulping down her tea in a hurried movement, Joan said with yet another smile breaking on her face, 'You just have to inform him that you're coming and I promise you he will stay glued to his chair waiting for you.'

Suddenly she swirled around, addressing the family with mock seriousness, 'Word has been getting round in the office that Mr Dean is thinking of settling down at last.' Then directing an innocent glance in Delilah's direction, 'Do you know who he is planning to get married to?'

'We are meeting tomorrow. I'll ask him then,' Delilah said with some amusement.

'Could it be you he would like to settle down with?' Joan piped in, finding it hard to resist such a comment.

'Could be,' Delilah asserted mysteriously, and calmly walked out of the room, leaving behind her a silence that she knew was the grave result of such an unexpected statement that she had made so heedlessly.

It was obvious that none of them were overly pleased with the idea of her settling down so soon after just having returned from finishing school.

Delilah had not stayed back in the room long enough to see Dominic's reaction. She knew that what she had said was superficial and altogether baseless induced by a reckless urge to see Dominic smoulder under that deliberate act of provocation. But the question was that, would he or rather was he in any way affected by what she had said just then? And why should he be for that matter? He was not in love with her, so why would he allow himself to get perturbed or even jealous over such a declaration of her future plans? At this point over preliminary contemplation, Delilah shrugged off the remotest possibility of the exaggerated contents of her premature expectations ever being realised. Dominic would never allow any woman to disturb his smooth existence and least of all evince any symptoms of deep love for any particular woman.

Delilah decided with self-contempt that she had been living in a fool's paradise. But her resolve to penetrate his indomitable reserve did not in any way falter. Certain points were in her favour, though. She was, for instance, aware that he was not immune to her. And she was positive he had a deep-rooted affection for her; consolidated over the passage of time. She would then exploit these facts to her advantage to reach her goal; a triumphant achievement when she would learn of his need for her, from he himself.

Already a plan was beginning to take form in her mind. The smile twitching at the corners of her mouth was youthful but provocative and dauntless, only she did not know then that she was playing with fire.

She was halfway up the stairs when Bertha called out to her.

'Yeah…what is it, Bertha?' She asked absently, her eyes glued to the door and inwardly longing for the sight of Dominic.

Bertha too automatically glanced in that direction, but turned almost immediately; a faint smile of amusement curving her lips.

'Dominic has said he'll be waiting for us outside. He has given us fifteen minutes in which to get dressed.'

'What about you? Are you ready?' Delilah enquired haphazardly, her eyes not moving from the door.

Bertha knew what was in her mind. Almost instantly she said, 'I doubt if Dominic would come out for the next few minutes or so. I gathered he had some business to discuss with Uncle Sampson,' she paused before she said the last two words, still finding it difficult to accept the fact that her father and Sampson were blood brothers.

Delilah threw her friend a sharp look, but with relief noticed that her friend had spoken without a trace of mockery upon mentioning Dominic's name.

Quickening her steps, she reached the top landing and turned back to say in a light tone, 'Give me five minutes.' She had then disappeared down the dimly lit corridor.

She wondered vaguely as she began to change, whether Joan and Anna were coming along too. Much later when she descended the stairs, she encountered all three girls in the hall waiting for her, but without showing signs of impatience.

'Sorry for the delay,' she said in a steady voice.

'You can save that for Dominic.' Joan laughed good-humouredly and the other two had roguish smiles on their usually serene faces.

Delilah raised her eyebrow but did not say anything after that. She followed them out of the house after saying a few words to Selena in her ear and smiling at the conspiratorial wink that Sampson directed her way.

When they reached the car, Dominic was already seated behind the wheel; one elbow resting negligently across the window and the other circling round the wheel, and icy-blue eyes watching them lazily as they drew nearer to the parked car.

Delilah deliberately occupied the seat in the front and not once flinched under the contemplative look of the man sitting next to her. The girls got inside the rear seat. For just one electrifying second, she held Dominic's eyes with hers that were smiling into his in a significant way, and very slowly those kissable lips too soon curved into a smile of great appeal, for his benefit alone.

At once a nerve began to beat in Dominic's jaw, his lips became a hard line as he turned and briskly started the car in the wake of total silence. His silence in itself spoke a lot, and which Delilah understood to be an indication of his disturbed state of mind, and for which she knew she was entirely responsible.

The Cadillac being spacious carried enough room for several passengers. Delilah ruefully glanced at the large space that separated her from Dominic. She dearly wished at that moment that she should have asked Bertha to sit with her in the front. Her candid, frank reflection often contradicting her cool and poised demeanour.

While Joan chattered away ten to dozen, the other two were enjoying some of the anecdotes that Joan was narrating with gay abandon. Delilah stole a quick glance in Dominic's direction. His eyes were staring straight ahead of him, and his profile she noticed with some trepidation looked indomitable and distinctly arrogant.

But her momentary fear was soon dispelled and anger suppressed all feelings of uncertainty, and her determination to carry on with her plan superseded all else. Although, she thought to herself with a definite hint of exasperation that why could he not react positively like any other man to a feminine approach, and particularly to the warm invitation in her tone of speech? Why did he react so differently from others when in feminine company? Why did he have to be different from others? But the questions merely angered her even more, and her hands were tightly clenched over her lap.

A sudden idea occurred to her that she suspected might have some effect on him. She turned sideways and directly addressed Joan in a voice that carried extreme fondness as she said, 'Dean and I are planning to go to the opera next Thursday. They are showing the new release of Hamlet. Tell me, is the play any different from the movie? I presume you have seen the movie?' her smile was friendly and encouraging.

Joan gently exclaimed with a spontaneous smile of her own. 'That man goes for nothing less than the exclusive and the best yet,' she sighed with awe.

'Yes, I have seen the movie, but I doubt if you can make comparisons.' Then after a moment's contemplation, 'Hmm, I should say a drama would appear more realistic. A screen showing would, well perhaps seem unnatural in comparison, if comparisons are at all to be made,' Joan shrugged lightly.

Anna interrupted in her quiet voice, 'I have seen the drama as well as the movie, and in all truth, I can say that the drama won more applause than the latter display of performance. I personally found the drama more preferable.' If the subject could enthuse someone like Anna then obviously her judgement could not have been faulty, Delilah reflected absently.

What had begun as a pretence ended in genuine enthusiasm on Delilah's part as she continued to talk to the girls animatedly on subjects which they all had in common. In her lively mood, she did not realise that her sitting posture revealed every seductive curve of her body and that several times Dominic's eyes had rested on her and deliberately settled on her thin top that stretched tautly over the full curve of her breasts.

A disturbed expression once more entered into his eyes that had been evidently affected by the alluring curves of the girl sitting next to him, and quite unaware that she was unconsciously creating havoc inside him, when in fact she had assumed he was impervious to her attractions.

When the car brakes were sharply applied, Delilah spun around and almost instantly assumed a starch dignity that appeared incongruous in a positively friendly atmosphere.

'Are we going to spend our entire day here?' she directed the question at Dominic, and pointing to the well-preserved park that owed its great charm and attraction to the maintained orderliness from which emanated the strong awareness of uniformity; the park heavily sprayed with a scent of a cluster of flowers of varied species endowed with a radiantly colourful personality. They contrasted prominently with the tall trees that were covered with the lush green leaves bedding against the sturdy brown of the strong, burly trunk of the trees which were in number a minority amidst the beds of wild shrubs and budding flowers of various hues and colours.

Dominic chose to forestall the reply until the girls left the car with the food basket in their possession. The moment they were out of hearing, Dominic turned to face Delilah with a deceptively quiet look about him. 'Now, what was your question?' he asked suavely, his eyes carelessly dismissing the moving public with very little regard for their presence, and finally resting those eyes on Delilah with disturbing clarity. Delilah couldn't even begin to understand why she was feeling so disconcerted upon meeting his eyes.

'Are we going to spend the entire day, here?' she repeated the question, her eyes no longer unwavering.

'That was the general idea,' he replied briskly, 'are you coming?' his hand then settled firmly on the handle of the door.

'Of course, I am,' she said hastily, then sarcasm entered into her voice as she said with a deceptively sweet tone, 'Why, did you think I'd wish to stay behind while the rest of you should enjoy the outing?'

He kept silent for a moment before saying in an abrupt tone, 'Come on, we have wasted enough time.' He glanced out the window. 'I can see your friend coming this way... probably looking for you,' he said in a matter-of-fact tone. And sure enough, Bertha was walking down towards the car.

'Not very tactful, is she? Can't she understand when two people wish to be left alone?' she said critically.

'I should call it an act of consideration,' he said in a severe tone.

She gazed at him sourly. 'What could very well be curiosity, you will naturally interpret as a consideration in defence of her,' she countered in a tight voice.

'What kind of a friend are you?' he added brusquely. 'And why must she be curious when I can clearly see no reason for curiosity?' he returned crushingly and shattering the remnants of her hopes for seeing that special look in his eyes.

'She is almost here...your friend. You will please behave yourself.' It was an order.

She threw him a withering look but remained silent. And when Bertha approached the car, she even managed to offer her unsuspecting friend a comradely smile that sparked a quick response in Bertha, who smiled back relievedly.

'Honestly, you had me believing that you were suddenly feeling unwell or something of that nature. Back there Anna and Joan are complaining that the outing is not quite complete without you.'

For once Delilah had the grace to look abashed. How could she have misjudged her friend? The feud was between Dominic and herself. Then she ought not to have proved unpleasant by being nasty about Bertha who had had nothing whatsoever to do with Dominic's and her differences or was it something else altogether? The question persisted.

Joan looked up to see them approaching and her hand waved out to the three of them as they joined the two sisters.

'Hey, Delilah, what do you know? Our Anna here is getting married next week, but do you like the cheek? She says it's going to be a quiet wedding, meaning civil marriage, and that too being the first marriage in the family!' her expression changed like quicksilver, from gaiety to disappointment to indignation.

Delilah smiled amusedly as she drew closer to them. Her eyes met Anna's and she saw quiet laughter there. Apparently, she too was amused. When Delilah happened to glance around, she found Dominic and Bertha far behind her, and from the distance, they appeared to be talking like old friends. Delilah's expression hardened momentarily before she pulled up straight and turned to the front again. She quickened her steps to where Anna and Joan were sprawled on the thickly laid out grass with a tree languidly looming over their heads.

She dropped down beside them, giving them both a weak smile.

'Not even a party to celebrate such an auspicious occasion?' she said for something to say, while her mind was transmitting waves of jealousy through her entire system. With a stiffening of her body, she sensed their presence without having to look behind.

Dominic occupied the space beside her while Bertha sat down between Anna and Joan, who determinedly brought up the question that had been left unanswered.

Anna answered though with a humorous smile. 'I'm afraid that won't be possible. A party is not possible,' she reiterated. 'The day after the ceremony we will soon be leaving for our honeymoon to Honolulu.'

'Well! That's it, I guess,' Joan said resignedly and the girls began to laugh while Dominic busily lighted his cigarette, his eyes narrowing the moment Delilah shifted a little away from him.

Then very pleasantly he said, 'I assure you I don't bite.'

'Thanks for cautioning me. I had my doubts,' she retorted in a hard voice.

Sensing the interest they had aroused in the rest of the party, he said in a cool, abrupt tone, 'I think a walk will do us both good.'

He got to his feet in a swift movement, and pulled Delilah up with him, his grip on her wrist tightening when she showed resistance, although her face portrayed no reluctance.

'If you will excuse us. We won't be long,' he said suavely.

Delilah ventured a backward glance and her eyes met Bertha's that looked back at her gravely. There was no support to be expected from Anna who was lost in the music floating from the portable gadget that she carried around, while Joan was busily munching some cookies.

'Come along. There is a nice, quiet place further up there where no one would disturb us,' Dominic's words had the effect that shook her already shattered nerves. She looked up wide-eyed. Her eyes were a big question mark.

'We...but why? I don't understand this all...this...this sudden need for privacy.' She looked bewildered.

He dragged her along with him, though not really appearing to do so.

Finally, when they reached an isolated area, he pushed her against a tree trunk, his hands on both sides of her, palms flat against the solid trunk which was supporting Delilah's small back. She could tell she was held captive. She stared at him with a mixture of agitation and with the beginnings of annoyance.

'Now will you tell me why you brought me here?' her lips twitched exasperatedly, and she did not at all approve of the way her heart was reacting to the situation that she knew only too well might prove ungovernable should she behave contrary to his expectations. And she knew the signs of fire and fury only too well, to be foolish enough to try any stunts that she was very well aware of would not be received kindly; irrespective of the fact that they were standing on public grounds.

'What can you have against my conversing with Bertha? I want the truth.'

She did not like the intense look in his eyes, for it made her very uncomfortable. One wrong word and she knew the consequences.

'When you are with her, you completely forget my presence. I feel neglected, naturally,' she blurted out with open frankness. Hands slid from the trunk of the tree to grip her shoulders.

'By George!' he exclaimed in a soft tone, his eyes lighting up with amusement. 'I can't think where you get such ideas from. Bertha just happened to ask me about her parent's intention of meeting with the family and I supplied her with the little that I know. I was merely telling her that they are due to arrive in Cambridge next Thursday. Perhaps there is even a probability that they could be here anytime this week. Like always she keeps asking me all about Joseph which is only understandable, as she would be meeting her father for the first time. Therefore, she is curious to know what he is like in all respects. She is curious and I have the information that interests her. That simple.' His mouth had curved into an incredibly attractive smile that affected her heartbeats a thousandfold.

He scanned the blue of the sky, his forehead wrinkled in mock contemplation.

'Let me see. Now, what else had we discussed?'

A small hand suddenly covered his mouth, and he looked down into gently apologetic eyes, his eyes falling on her lips that were quivering, as they started to form words of apology.

'Dominic,' she murmured in an uneven voice, 'do you think a kiss would clear the atmosphere?' then in a whisper she said, 'kiss me, Dominic.' Her lips were raised and had parted invitingly.

He watched her through half-closed lids before bending towards her and muttering huskily, 'It would merely create fresh trouble.' His lips then moved lingeringly over the smoothness of her arched throat before they took fierce possession of her lips.

When finally, he lifted his head, it was only to plant a light kiss on her forehead.

'Let's go, sweet temptress. It's high time that we returned to the girls.' His half-smile had a teasing quality about it as he ushered her to walk ahead of him. In her present mood, she could not have noticed the strained almost intense look in his eyes that clearly indicated his own agitation mingled with the result of a sensation coursing through his system like a warmly sensuous touch of spreading fire.

For a moment he did not realise that his hand was caught in a softer and more delicate hand. But when he did make the realisation, he chose to feign indifference and causing inside Delilah a sense of inadequacy. Consequently, she extricated her fingers from his and resolutely walked much ahead of him, while silent tears gathered in her eyes. Only this time Dominic did not intervene or try to go after her. He probably did not consider it an act of wisdom to enliven her up. He knew from past experience that too much kindness would prove less amicable and more destructive as the pain or hurt that she was nursing would he knew intensify to an exaggerated degree, if it should be padded with a frequent show of concern. But there was, however, one aspect he was not able to understand completely. It was Delilah's apparent perturbation, and her getting easily offended at trivial matters.

He followed her at a slower pace, caught up in an unwilling entry into a debatable conflict with himself; with Delilah acting as the paramount subject of a controversial nature. The thought as it came to him brought a wry smile to his lips, but without any humour. Never before had he allowed anyone to get under his skin. He had been resolute all along about maintaining a certain detachment and resisting all that had anything to do with emotional involvement.

His smile was one of self-mockery. Where was that well-preserved resolution now? And that strong resistance that had saved his face in the past many times, and rescued him from many tenacious temptations in the guise of plenty of beautiful, desirable women. Sure enough, Marian had worked her way into his system; perhaps the only woman who had managed to sway him in her direction; both physically and mentally, and without any effort. But still, he had to admit that what he had formerly stated to Joseph in the course of their conversation had been a complete truth; that the sparks had been missing, though the memory of the nights spent with Marian, even now could not be completely erased. Their relationship had been considerably satisfactory, more so, because friendship had formed the major part of their relationship. And there had also existed a mutual understanding and affection consolidated by an affinity of the highest degree resulting in the total absence of a guilt complex on both sides.

Even now he could afford to recall those most satisfying nights without a tinge of guilt, and instead, he found it in his heart to envy Joseph for having the complete possession of that golden heart that belonged to Marian; the golden beauty. She was a beauty and a wonderful human being.

There were children everywhere in the park. People were beginning to throng the place that a moment ago had been enjoying a prolonged spell of serenity. Dominic scanned the crowd for the lost sight of Delilah. Resignedly, he thought that perhaps she had already reached the spot where the rest of the girls were lounging on the grass. He realised with a sigh that the public that had thickened had reduced his speed of walking to an almost stilted pace. In a park, he observed not too happily that such a crowd looked out of place. A park was a place of sanctuary.

He had scarcely circled the route to where the girls were anxiously waiting for him when a small plump girl of not more than three came up to him with a nervous smile surfacing the quiver in her voice that he knew was one-stop leading to a burst of a flood of tears. Her finger pointed out regally to a pair of boys who were playfully running about in circles around an old tree; evidently, one trying to catch the other.

'They play alone. They say I am a girl. Mommy say we play all, but look they play all...all alone.' Endearingly and with a childlike trust she took hold of his finger, pointing out imperiously to the boys as if to say, "Let's go and settle the matter once and for all." Dominic complied with the little lady's wish. He thought to himself, he was destined to get side-tracked by damsel's young and old, and all of a sudden laughter rose in his throat and throwing back his head he laughed quite heartily. And at the same time picking the surprised little girl in his arms, and planting a fond kiss on her delightfully plump, rosy cheeks. She chuckled away quite happily, but upon approaching the boys, she sobered up instantly and watched them from her great height with supreme hauteur, as Dominic continued holding her in his arms.

'Tell them. Tell them,' she cried out in her tiny voice, feeling no longer tearful, as she found someone so strong and big to champion her cause.

After settling the disputes between the child and her brothers, Dominic joined the girls. They were getting the food and drinks ready for an early lunch break. He sprawled beside Anna who was busily laying out the drinks before each of them. When he told them of the incident, he had just experienced, the girls laughed outright in sheer amusement except for Delilah who never once looked in his direction. His own eyes, though, lit up with amusement, also carried a certain look of concern when they settled on Delilah. He could see that she was really upset about something.

'It is strange the way the little one trusted you. Children don't normally do that...I mean, make such appeals to practical strangers,' Anna said retrospectively.

'They don't,' said Joan nodding in agreement, 'but Dominic always had a way with children,' her smile cheeky, 'not to mention the fascination he holds for women,' she added for good measure.

Dominic took a large bite from the apple, his eyes once again lit up with lazy amusement as he drawled, 'And you make me out to be quite a Don Juan.'

'The description is a fitting one, I think,' Joan said emphatically, and Bertha smiled with some amusement at their exchange of words.

'You must be joking. I'm a perfectly straight guy,' he contradicted mockingly.

Delilah was fidgeting with the grass beneath her for something to divert her attention while Anna listened to her sibling's exchange with casual interest. Her eyes, though strayed to where the children were playing in the close distance. There was a tender look in her eyes. She was hoping she would be able to give Paul a boy. Perhaps a girl would follow in another few years. Her smile was secretive as she continued to think on those lines; a pleasant reverie that she rarely ever indulged in.

Suddenly Delilah's eyes met hers, and she threw Anna a smile of understanding. The girl had an amazing gift of insight, Anna thought amazedly.

'It would be fun to have a nephew and a niece at the same time, Anna,' Delilah mused with a delightful smile.

'Wish that on somebody else, not me please,' Anna laughed with some humour.

Dominic's eyes suddenly fell on Delilah who unwillingly shifted her gaze from Anna to him. The stare that she gave him was acutely unfriendly. For some reason, he felt like dragging her from her sitting position and delivering a brutal kiss right on her beautiful, scornful lips, but he still carried a certain inhibition which prevented him from being effusive in public. Although, the fierce urge inside him to give her a thorough shaking was getting unbearably overpowering. By sheer will, he managed to suppress it for a brief period.

He abruptly stood up in an agile movement, tossing the cigarette that he was smoking for the last few minutes, and grounding it with the heel of his shoe, then looking up he said with an air of finality, 'Pack up, girls, we are leaving.'

His eyes were like steel; the blue of his eyes glittering in the afternoon light like hard diamonds, as he briefly glanced in Delilah's direction and addressed her in an arctic voice, 'It appears you did not hear me. I said, pack up.' Without another word he turned and strode away.

Joan whistled softly and eyeing Delilah significantly said, 'Looks like you have done it again. What is it this time?'

Delilah had a faraway look in her eyes.

'Joan, please mind your own business,' Anna reprimanded annoyedly.

Joan shrugged, 'All right, but that does not make me any less curious,' then she glanced sympathetically at Delilah whose hands were busily packing up the things along with the other two girls.

'Oh, Delilah, I wish you both would be friendlier with each other.'

'Joan!' Anna reprimanded her yet again, 'Stop it! He'll raise hell if we don't hurry. It was an enjoyable day. Let us not spoil it by aggravating his already black mood. And that's exactly what's going to happen if we keep him waiting for another minute.'

'Disagreeable! That's what he is,' Joan announced judiciously and received a dark look from big sister.

'Enough!' and that had the desired effect on Joan who maintained silence right throughout the return journey homewards.

***

They found Selena in the drawing-room all by herself, engrossed in reading a book by her favourite author.

'Hi, Mom,' Joan dropped down by her chair where she was lounging, her head buried in Selena's lap who immediately left the book aside to caress her daughter's hair.

'Where is Papa, Mom?' she looked around anxiously. 'I don't see him anywhere, here.' She looked around again, her concern growing.

'Have you tried upstairs?' Selena mused with a chuckle. 'You are unnecessarily concerned, dear. Your father is enjoying his precious nap.' She just then saw Anna and Bertha going up to their rooms.

And with careful consideration, she let them, without interrupting their progress up the stairs. But when she saw no sign of either Dominic or Delilah; a perceptive gleam entered her eyes. Yet, she remained outwardly unconcerned as she told herself that they were mature enough to sort out their problem without interference from a third party.

Turning back to Joan she smiled encouragingly, 'Tell me, how you spent your day?'

And Joan had only needed the opening invitation to begin her pleasant chattering, giving a detailed account of their outing, and Selena heard her out without any interruption.

Meanwhile, outside, Dominic was silently parking the car in the garage, but when he stepped out into the lawn; a hand determinedly settled around his forearm. He turned and his glance met Delilah's, who had a wild-eyed look about her. Then his eyes fell on her hand resting on his arm. He looked up again, his eyes like cold steel.

'What's the idea, waiting in the corner like a prowling cat?'

'I... I had to talk to you.' She inwardly flinched at the flash of hard blue eyes, but she stood her ground bravely. Yes, she had grit.

'What about?' he said curtly, shaking her hand off him roughly.

'I would like to know the reason for your... vexation.' Upon seeing the sudden tightening of his jaw muscles and teeth, she hastened to add with a look of entreaty, 'Please, Dominic.'

Taking a deep breath he said in a voice of astonishing calm, 'The questions which I intend to ask you now, would in itself be the answer to yours. Now that you've opened the issue, I would like to ask you, to start with; why must you often wear that sulky expression and give me the cold shoulder the minute anything goes wrong for you?' he asked in a quiet tone.

She hazarded a glance up at him, her eyes a shade too green and clearly reflecting the tumult inside her.

'What can I tell you when I myself do not have the definite answers to those questions? Honestly, Dominic. I'm myself confused,' she said in the softest tone, a soft plea underlining her voice which was barely a whisper.

'All right, then. Let us not ever bring up this issue again,' he said through tight lips and turned to go as if to leave, but once again she stopped him with a light touch of her hand. He glanced at her impatiently; a nerve working in his jaw.

'What's happening to us, Dominic?' there was a note of desperation in her voice that had never been there before, so that for a moment even he was struck by its unexpected entry. Then very slowly and introducing more kindness in his voice he said:

'I don't know, Delilah. And I wish I knew what this is all about, and where it is to lead us both.' Their eyes met. Hers were filled with tears and then what Dominic saw behind the pool of tears made him draw a sharp breath.

'You know something, don't you, Dominic, only you...you like infuriating me. It provides you with some sadistic pleasure, doesn't it?' she ranted on through quivering lips.

In answer he caught her to him in a fierce embrace, taking her face in his hand and gently drawing it closer to his.

'Oh, God! Don't you know anything? Don't you and... don't I know it?' he exclaimed softly before bending to kiss her upturned mouth and in a slow, deliberate way taking a gradual taste of her lips, and causing inside her a strange exultation which sent her into a world of wild ecstasy and near to sexual elation.

'Dominic,' she whispered with closed eyes. 'Oh, Dominic, for God's sake, if you know...I know, then why...why this secrecy? Maybe I know too and maybe I... I'm not convinced.'

His lips moved to her hair, stroking it with surprising gentility.

'Sometimes ignorance can be bliss to... to dangerous knowledge, Delilah.'

'I hate suspense,' she said in a fierce whisper, but her lips were raised to his once again and then their lips met. When she kissed him, it was with a startling ardour which left him shuddering slightly beneath that unexpected impact of such a sensually exciting display of emotion.

After that moment had passed, he then watched her penetratingly but discovered no sign of guile in her make-up. She was completely guileless, he decided with some relief. Very gently he began explaining to her what was in his mind:

'The fact that you're unaware of a certain truth proves that you are still not prepared to accept and acknowledge the solemnity of the situation,' after a pause, however, he continued, 'that we are currently facing. Leave it be, Delilah,' then more gently he added, 'you are still young.'

There came a quick look of indignation in the young lady's eyes.

'Are you inferring that I'm immature?'

A smile flickered briefly at the corner of his mouth, his eyes resting for a brief spell fully on her mouth. Yes, he felt like kissing her again and brutally. She had that effect on him.

'Immature? Why, no. Not at all. I must confess your kiss proved otherwise.' A glint of devilry was evident in his eyes.

She turned to hide the deep blush in her cheeks, but he pulled her to his side. She once again tried to mask her embarrassment by trying to escape his arms, but he held her firmly to his side.

'No, Dominic…' she protested, but his mouth slowly began to journey its way over the long column of her throat in a moment of unrestrained passion that almost instantly aroused inside her a sensation that left her quivering with ecstasy.

'Delilah,' he murmured into her ear, 'you must learn to shed away embarrassment with the approach of maturity. If you must make love, then you must also shed inhibition. You're so innocent, Delilah,' he groaned with some regret. 'I wish you knew how necessary it is to keep an open mind in matters relating to... the intimacy of such a nature,' he said without any hesitation.

'I'm a slow learner, I guess,' she said with an endearing pout.

'Don't get discouraged,' he mocked gently, tilting her chin to take possession of her lips.

But before he could prevent it, she pressed closer to his body, arms circling around his neck and her voice a husky whisper as she murmured: 'Make love to me, Dominic. Now!'

He at once stiffened under the pressure of her soft, supple body; his awareness of her sheer presence bordering on eroticism even as he felt the hardened tips of her breasts pressing tantalisingly against his broad chest.

'Delilah... God, help me!' he swore under his breath, 'Please, don't be rash. Someone might come,' but his voice was harsher than stern; the result of being emotionally disturbed.

He pushed her away with the force of will, his eyes glittering from emotional upheaval, though his lips were set in a firm line.

But she was not to be dissuaded. She put her arms around his waist and rested her head against his chest, and at the same time tightened her arms around him.

'Tell me now, that I'm not slow,' she insisted in a small, uneven voice.

He could not help putting his arms around her, his firm, square chin resting a little above her forehead.

'Is that what you were trying to prove?'

'No. What I did was involuntary.'

'Such involuntary action might turn into an unavoidable rhapsody, moreover, a frenzied impulse that you could very well do without. Quite occasionally, it has a way of leaving behind scars. So, take care,' he warned, his mind and body registering her warm, tantalising proximity.

'Sounds like you're warning me, Dominic. Are you?' she stole a quick glance up at him.

'Merely cautioning you, first hand,' he flicked her cheek with his fingers.

'Mother is probably worried. Let's go inside.'

'So, I will have to learn to crawl before I can walk,' she said jubilantly.

'In face of such logic, how can I contradict,' he asserted with a trace of mockery, 'you can have your way I guess,' he shrugged resignedly.

'Thank you and so nice of you…' she dropped a mock curtsy.

With a suddenness he became serious.

'Delilah, don't grow up too fast. I need some time,' he said enigmatically.

'You need time for what, Dominic?' she asked doubtfully, but he was already walking away from her in his long, brisk strides.

True that Delilah was yet young, for even then she had failed to see the situation in its correct perspective.

And, although, she had her suspicions, they were nowhere near the truth. Besides, doubts would have been shaped into verifications, only Dominic had withdrawn suddenly, making things even more difficult for her in understanding the situation better. Her mind had still not imbibed the fact that Dominic found her altogether too irresistible and in no way settling for his nerves.

CHAPTER 6

Selena looked up from her book. 'Your father was asking for you. He is upstairs in his room. And, Delilah...' she called out to her, as Delilah made to climb the stairs. 'See that you do not upset your father. Remember, you are grown up now. It's about time you train yourself in self-discipline.' She waited patiently for the retaliation which was by then the expected thing, but instead, Delilah hurried up the stairs without so much as a sound.

Selena watched the departing figure of her daughter with a worried expression on her face. She kept the book aside only half-read, her mind restlessly wandering in the darker channels of contemplation. At least for that moment, she was met by a black-out, whereupon obscurity prevailed, and confusion started settling in.

She was undoubtedly a shrewd woman, but her level of understanding was such that it could not accommodate a better understanding of at least her own daughter, therefore, her personal impression of her daughter and her temperament remained clouded. Even after so many years, she had failed to reach out to her mentally. On the other hand, Sampson was endowed with an outstanding perspicacity which made him understand Delilah better, and consequently, it put their relationship on a friendlier plane; sharing the intimacy of thoughts and conceptions with a pleasing and a more satisfying spontaneity.

Both the parents loved Delilah very deeply. There was no denying that, but only one understood her well and completely, and that was Sampson.

There was a slight knock on the door.

Sampson called out absently, 'Come right in. The door is open.'

Delilah entered; a smile covering her face.

'It isn't always open, you know,' she said insinuatingly.

Sampson chuckled. 'That's when I am not alone.'

He was relaxing in his favourite canvas chair by the window with the 'Times' lying open on his lap. She slowly crossed the room to his side and felt considerably better, now that she was in a friend's company.

She silently stared out of the window, her mind preoccupied, for when Sampson called out to her, trying to draw her attention to him, she remained unresponsive. His brows furrowed deeply while his eyes continued to stare at her closely, watching the changing expressions in her eyes that could be so revealing and at the same time mysterious; the message in them quite occasionally difficult to fathom.

She swerved around, her troubled eyes fixed steadily on her father.

'What is love, Papa?' she demanded in an urgent voice.

Sampson was momentarily startled, but he quickly collected his composure.

'Why do you ask, my child?' he questioned her query in a perfectly sober voice that denoted his extreme state of tranquillity.

'Must I confess?' she said in a note of reluctance that came in strong, for she did desire to confide in him, and as well hold back the suspicions and doubts that were crowding her mind. Her expression looked strained.

'Confessions?' he nodded his head in confusion when in all truth, certain things were dawning on him; things that were directly connected with Delilah and the affairs of her heart.

'Confession, yes. Will I have to confess what compelled me to ask you for the meaning of... love? It's all so confusing,' her voice sounded agitated, and Sampson was himself truly disturbed, but he retained his outward calm.

'Certainly, dear or how else do you suppose we can be able to solve your problem?' he said practically.

She turned her back to him as she started in a voice that was shaking with emotion: 'I... I can't properly define my feelings for... Dominic. I mean... oh well, this is it.' She turned and looked straight at him resignedly, her hands spread out in a gesture of frustrated helplessness, her eyes shaded with pain which resulted from the heaviness of her heart.

'I think this feeling inside me is an anonymous killer. Oh, it is agonising at times,' she said, and buried her face in her hands, her body shaking with silent tears.

'Is this a recent discovery, child?' he said, understanding her dilemma that he had suspected all along, but refrained from admitting it openly.

She looked up, her face flushed and moistened with perspiration intermingled with tears.

'No, that's the whole trouble. I have been feeling this way about him right from the very beginning, only now it has intensified.'

'Can't you be more explicit?' he asked gently, bending slightly forward in his chair.

'It's... oh, what's the use?' she cried hopelessly, 'you can't know how complicated it all is. It's difficult to explain.'

After a stretched interval, he said in the quietest tone, 'Take my advice. Concentrate on other matters and try to make light of this subject, until you are able to understand its true implication. I'm aware advice can sometimes act like a bitter medicine you'd rather avoid, but like medicine, it too has its advantages.'

She had quietened down after that, but when she spoke this time, it was with admirable composure:

'Papa, how is it that I see red every time I come across him in the company of other women? I...I just can't stand it,' she sounded emotional and near to tears.

'It is not unusual when you begin to consider someone your...personal property. Crudely phrased I know, dear, but it is only natural to feel possessive about someone you consider your own. You never like to share that person with anybody, if confidence in self should be lacking,' he pointed out gently and watched her steadily, but kindly, almost benevolently.

'Does this then mean that I'm...jealous and perhaps insecure?' she enquired with a startling simplicity.

He relaxed his frame in the chair and smiled up at her, but not unkindly.

'You do realise that Dominic is a free agent, therefore, he is entitled to please himself in any way he wishes. You must never forget this, Delilah. And never show possessiveness towards a man, and never let him be aware of it. Showing possessiveness is the greatest mistake a woman can ever make. Assurance and self-confidence in fact, forms a major part of a woman's charm,' he added quietly, but he threw her an affectionate smile.

She nodded with a weak smile of her own.

'Mother said you'd be upset if I talked to you about anything. Are you?' she lovingly slid her arms around him.

'I never get easily upset,' he smiled reassuringly.

'It's a relief and thanks for giving me your attention. You don't know how much talking to you has helped me.' She planted a kiss on his forehead and walked to the door, throwing him a flying kiss.

'See you at tea-time,' she forced gaiety into her voice.

'Don't forget all that I told you. You are still young. This is the time to enjoy yourself and not get involved in controversies. You must isolate yourself from such a pack of problems. All the best, sweetheart!'

***

The day proved positively bright, inviting yet another outing and heartily promising to sweep aside the lonely feel of desolation. Strongly influenced by Sampson's words as well as nature's warming countenance, Delilah decided to enjoy the rest of the day. She would definitely not allow such a beautiful day to go to waste.

Bertha was in the library, engrossed in looking for a book that might possibly interest her. She was not particularly keen on reading, but she could afford to think of reading for something to do. Idling away her time was not one of her traits, and which she avoided at all cost. Her eyes suddenly fell on a book on the shelf, and she reached for it, pulling it from its corner and dusting it with her hand.

It was a book on knights in shining armours, obviously a book on men possessing great prowess, and which she thought amusedly would make for an interesting reading, helping to while away the long, dragging hours of the day ahead of her. A light tap on her shoulder startled her for a brief spell, but her face lit up the moment she saw who the intruder was.

'Delilah, in future spare me your shock treatment. I'm allergic to it, at least my heart is. Where were you all this time?'

'With Papa. Why? Missed me?'

'Why do you think I'm staying here, if not for you?' Bertha said with a gentle exasperation, 'But, yes,' she agreed with a humorous smile, 'I was beginning to miss you.'

Delilah dropped her glance at the book in her friend's hand. Her eyes began to gleam teasingly as she said with gentle mockery, 'Your choice of books amazes me. Tell me about the thrilling escapades once you finish the book.'

'I will,' Bertha promised with an answering twinkle in her eyes. 'But allow me to start the book first.'

Delilah threw her a cursory glance.

'You are not going to neglect me for that book; a mere pile of bound papers with shallow contents. All childish nonsense!' her tone was slightly accusing.

'Tut-tut, the writer would be highly offended by your uncharitable opinion of his work,' Bertha mused, her eyes alight with amusement.

'Don't be silly. You're being ridiculous! He is not here to listen to my uncomplimentary remarks and good-gracious!' she halted, a wide-eyed look entering her eyes, 'Bertha, you will have to excuse me. Dean is coming here at four-thirty, and I have to get dressed.' And she dashed out of the library.

'A movie?' Bertha asked with an indulgent smile.

'A movie, yes,' she echoed in a cheerful tone, and only when she dashed into something hard, did she realise who was blocking her path. Her eyes collided with a pair of eyes that were hard and brilliant as a diamond.

'You are not going anywhere until I meet this young man of yours.' Dominic had perhaps never before exercised authority of such magnitude, and he himself could not understand the impulsiveness of his words, not to mention the strong, alien feeling that had invaded his being and throbbing heart. For the first time, he discovered he possessed little to no knowledge about how exactly to manipulate such an unexpected invasion. Delilah glared at him for one full second, the expressions fluctuating on her face were extremely unmethodical... discomforting in nature. Finally, an expression of indignation thrust all else into obscurity, and the vexation displayed its substantial proportions with righteous arrogance.

Dominic drew his glance toward his wristwatch and took serious note of the time. He lifted his head, watching her with eased temper and gradual nonchalance that was betrayed by the fire in the shattering deep blue of his eyes. With that expression in his eyes, he looked unbearably handsome.

Bertha had avoided the scene by moving further into the library; diplomacy and tact compelling her to draw a proper distance between them and herself, and by doing so, very successfully obstructing her hearing instinct.

Delilah's eyes met his in a steady glance; the glittering green of her eyes clashing wordlessly with the steely blue of his. The defiance indicating her arrogance compensated largely for her diminutive frame, and as her arrogance towered above the remnants of uncertainty, so did her heightened indignation tower above the faintest tremor in her voice, as she demanded in a strange voice, 'Since when did you decide to enrol as my guardian?' her voice sounded brittle like the quality of her eyes.

'What and when I choose to do things, need not worry you,' he stated curtly.

A crunch of wheels outside drew her attention to it. She stood motionless; a defiant look entering her eyes, although, she did not allow herself to show what she felt then. To retaliate verbally and to exhibit defiance would have proved abortive, for just then, light, brisk footsteps were drawing closer and still closer till they advanced into the room. Dean stood there and then a soft exclamation escaped his lips even as he folded Delilah in a tight, warm embrace, almost sweeping her off the floor and swirling her around within the circle of his arms.

Delilah's eyes shone with delight upon meeting such a dear and a well-remembered friend after a prolonged stretch of five years.

'Dean, but you haven't changed one bit!' she threw him an astonishing look.

'I can't say the same about you. If it hadn't been for those glorious eyes and petite stature, I swear I wouldn't have been able to recognise you.' His eyes lingered on her face with gentle adoration, but politeness bid him to acknowledge the presence of a third party. He could not understand how his mind could have possibly failed to fully register the undeniably magnetic presence of such a forceful and dominating personage; also, a well-known business tycoon, to complete the effect.

Instant recognition had dawned in his merry, light blue eyes. Delilah's face was suffused with bright colour as she suddenly remembered how she had been grabbed into Dean's arms, and in the presence of Dominic. Embarrassment flooded inside her, but at that moment, fortunately, neither of them paid her much attention.

'Mr. Redford, it's a pleasure meeting you this way. A coincidence but hello anyway...' a smile of irresistible charm took form on his lips, giving his face a look of open friendliness. Although, there was not the slightest trace of subservience in his make-up, which won Dominic's favour with a quickness that surprised all three of them. A half-smile took shape on Dominic's lips, as he took the proffered hand in his firm clasp, shaking it warmly almost against his will.

'Mr. Fobster, I suggest we seal our first meeting with a drink.'

'Will Miss Redford be joining us?' his eyes rested cheekily on Delilah, who frowned darkly upon him.

'I think, Miss Redford would prefer to keep her friend company back there in the library. Right, Delilah?' Dominic put in suavely, but the icy look in his eyes brooked no argument.

'Is that correct, Miss Redford?' Dean twinkled at her.

Her fingers were clenched at her sides.

'Miss Redford would like to see more than anything else the movie that you had promised to take her to. Are we going?' Delilah's question was like a pistol shot.

'We still have some time on our hands, Delilah. Take it easy, Delly. Cool it! That temper is again starting to get out of hand. That famous temper,' he whispered, but with some humour.

Excusing himself, Dominic had started walking in the direction of the study. After throwing Delilah a wink, Dean slowly followed Dominic inside the opulently-furnished study which appeared sombrely luxurious.

Delilah watched the door close with some misgiving, but she realised with astonishment that she was no longer angry. Even the fact that Dominic had won his way, in the end, did not give rise to fresh indignation inside her. What puzzled her was the way an instant liking had sprung up between the two men, and that too within a matter of a few minutes. What had endeared Dean to Dominic, and vice-versa? Why had Dominic not evinced any signs of annoyance upon meeting Dean? And lastly, why had Dominic been so determined to speak to Dean in the complete privacy of the study? It was all so baffling. All these questions crowded in her mind like an unsolved puzzle.

Just as she resignedly disappeared into the library, Anna walked down the stairs, crossing the hall in hurried movements hardly characteristic of her, and joining Delilah and Bertha in the library. They turned around together; their lips spread in smiles of welcome.

'I have to break the news,' Anna said in a young, excited voice. All severity was erased from her face and replaced by a look of indescribable happiness. 'Paul is coming. I received his telegram about five minutes ago.' Her eyes strongly resembled stars, and this time Delilah and Bertha broke into smiles of happy contentment, but all of a sudden Bertha grew serious, her eyes a big question mark.

Anna read the silent question in those fine, brown eyes that were slightly shaded with uncertainty.

'Jarrod will shortly be following his father. But it is definite that he will be arriving at Cambridge anytime soon, though it may take him a little longer to arrive.'

Bertha relaxed her frame; suspicion of a smile lighting up her usually serious face that had just for a brief instant turned immobile with a tight wooden expression shielding her vulnerability like a protective cocoon.

'Well,' a masculine voice mused from behind. 'Shall we make a move?'

Delilah swirled round; all doubts of her plans to go out with Dean being jeopardised, fading into nothingness as she met the familiar, mischievous gleam in Dean's eyes. There was no sign of Dominic.

She said her goodbyes to the girls and without bothering to change into another dress, she followed Dean in light steps out of the house and climbed inside his Ford with a quiet, satisfied smile never leaving her face.

The car sped along the stone-paved pathway into smooth, swift progress to further down the valley and descending into the steeper land where tall, brick homes stood on each side of it in systematic order with small, well-preserved gardens fronting the open pathways of each house. And, with a vague brush of scent and floating fragrance emanating from the cluster of flowers that stood out in the gardens; riots of colour amongst looming trees and beds of green sprinkled shrubberies.

Without glancing at him, she asked cautiously, 'You can call me curious, but I'm interested to know what Dominic had to say to you.' She waited for his response to come.

Dean lifted his shoulders casually.

'Oh, nothing that could possibly interest you, love,' he grinned, 'let's talk about you instead. I'd like to say how charming you look.'

Delilah looked bored, but her mouth a stubborn line as she said insistently, 'Please do not evade the subject.

Tell me what he said to you. It's important to me,' she repeated in a firm tone.

'Well, if you really must know,' he shrugged indifferently, 'he asked me about my profession and for how many years have I been working for the establishment, and well, I told him all that he wanted to know,' then in his eyes came a puzzled expression as he said in an uncertain voice, 'but initially, I had the impression that he had altogether something else in his mind, though I don't know. I could be wrong, but otherwise, I must admit that the man, though quiet is basically charming.' He glanced briefly at her.

'Is that all?' she asked doubtfully.

'Hmm, yes.' He nodded emphatically, 'Why this curiosity?'

'You mean, he did not mention me at all?' she slanted him an unbelieving look.

'Now that you come to mention, he did say something about you being too young for any serious involvement but be rest assured... I convinced him in all sincerity that we were nothing but friends,' he gave her a reassuring smile, 'though in all sincerity I would gladly change our friendship into something more intimate er, with due encouragement, of course,' his smile suddenly roguish.

'I'm afraid you're not very explicit,' she said absently, 'nevertheless, we can reserve that discussion for a later date. In the meanwhile, I need your help.'

'If it's in my power to help, you'll get my full cooperation.'

'Then listen…'

***

In the theatre during intermission, Dean left his seat to take a look in the canteen. He returned after a while and handed over to Delilah a popcorn packet. The other half of the movie had already commenced.

'I have never kissed you,' he whispered close to her ear, 'it will be quite an experience.'

'You will be kissing me on the cheek, Dean. No funny tricks please,' Delilah reminded firmly.

He nodded.

'I had quite forgotten that part of the plan. Thanks for the reminder,' he said with dry sarcasm.

She gently touched his shoulder, her eyes in the dark begging for his understanding.

'Please try to understand. You did say you would agree to my plan and…and accept the conditions unquestioningly.'

'The movie was good,' he said evasively, his eyes fixed on the screen.

'Why do you talk in the past tense? It isn't over yet,' she asked, confused.

'Who's watching? It's as good as over for me,' he said dully.

'Dean... please. You did promise to behave at all times,' she said coaxingly.

'And I don't break promises... now, relax. I was only jesting, silly. Though any man with blood in his veins would want to kiss you. I shouldn't think it necessary for a girl as pretty as you to manoeuvre a plan like this to make a man jealous. God!' he sighed, with his cheek resting against his palm. 'The man must be made of stone.'

When the movie got over, the crowd rushed out of the theatre. The younger group chatted nineteen to dozen and raised unnecessary racket as they drifted past the muffled sound of half of the more sophisticated and civilly controlled audience.

Dean grinned as he led Delilah by her elbow out of the theatre, following the rest of the public.

'It's strange,' he murmured almost to himself.

'What is?' Delilah asked casually, feeling an ache in the back of her eyes, as she lifted her gentle fingers to apply slight pressure over her strained eyes that were already beginning to cause her a headache.

'We are of the same age group as these girls and boys, and yet our behaviour sets us apart from them.'

'Maybe if we too were to go round in groups, we would dispense with starched dignity and black sobriety. Our action is occasionally influenced by the kind of people we associate with, however, rare or frequent our meetings.'

'That is of no consequence,' Delilah stated quietly.

'I guess you are right,' he agreed as he helped her inside the car.

Once he started the car, he began by asking her, 'Say, when are we meeting again?'

Delilah's eyes strayed to the hands resting negligently on the wheel.

'I will let you know,' she said hazily, 'Dean,' she began, pausing for confirmation of the doubts lingering in her mind, 'why have you now reduced the speed?' there was no fear in her voice, merely curiosity.

He grinned, looking very much the cheerful, charming man that he was.

'I have a feeling that a slight delay might work miracles.'

'Meaning?' she asked briefly, but not resenting the idea which, though she did not understand perfectly, sounded intriguing to her ears. She was still in so many ways naive.

'This gentleman for whom this plan is intended will then have solid grounds for suspicion. Our anticipation will not go unrewarded. He will suspect that there is more than friendship existing between us.'

She nodded satisfactorily.

'We will have to do this kind of thing more often, Dean. One delayed outing will not do the trick. For the desired effect we will need to take further action.'

'I'm all for it,' he said with quick willingness, but a look from her dampened his spirits, although, he soon recovered it, saying jovially, 'be afraid not, for I'm truly a knight in shining armour.'

'And don't you forget it,' but she was laughing.

He stopped by at a passing restaurant where they had a quiet dinner after which they started on their journey home.

By the time they reached their destination, the house stood before them; a quiet regal observer in the surrounding darkness that covered the atmosphere in a wide-spread sheet of the approaching night. The bright, twinkling stars relievedly compensated for the want of light in the otherwise totally sombre surroundings.

Suddenly the car came to a halt a little away from the imposing house. Dean turned, his hand going around Delilah and gently pulling her towards him, his mouth planting a light kiss behind her ear. With a sigh; a rather heavy one at that, he moved away, his hand still around her shoulders. It was evident that Delilah had been the least affected by that gesture. Regardless of however carefully planned, it had been a purely sexual gesture, and Dean had not at all viewed it in the light of a clever ruse to delude someone the way it was intended to be. He kept his counsel, already regretting his part in the plan, for he was by nature an honest man and disliked any kind of deception.

At the same time, he was earnest about offering Delilah his cooperation, simply because he had observed the desperation in her eyes, and now, he could also feel the anticipation within her as she stiffened, looking alert the moment she sensed that they were no longer alone. And then she turned, her arms going around Dean.

'Dean, say you love me.' She drew closer to him.

'You know I do. I hardly saw the movie. I was too worked up. My hands...I couldn't keep my hands...' his words came out clearly, disturbing the quiet of the atmosphere with their clarity.

His sentence was cut short by a deep, curt voice that held a ring of command:

'Mr. Fobster, you will in future see to it that you bring Delilah home early. In our house, we strictly forbid our women the freedom of spending late nights with young men.' And abruptly turning on his heel, Dominic left them staring at his retreating back.

Dean appeared slightly dazed and Delilah wore a triumphant smile on her face. She nudged Dean with her shoulder.

'I do believe your plan worked.' Her smile though was half-hearted.

'I obviously underestimated the man. Why... he is dynamic. I should have paid heed to the press reports.'

'Sounds like you want to withdraw,' she said with scorn. 'I wouldn't have dreamt that you would turn tail and run.'

He rounded on her exasperatedly.

'Stop being so damned contemptuous, and the description of a coward does not fit me. I'd better tell you that,' his voice, though quiet, carried a hint of annoyance.

Delilah kissed him on the cheek, impulsively.

'Forgive me. I didn't mean to be insulting. I feared that perhaps you might no longer wish to help me, but I was wrong, wasn't I?' she planted yet another kiss on his cheek.

'You most certainly were,' he grinned. 'And stop pampering me with kisses. I will turn into a big-headed oaf. How would you like that then?' his eyes gleamed wickedly, but apparently Delilah did not seem to mind his teasing, for, with the final kiss and this time on the corner of his mouth, she sprung out of the car, and waving him a cheerful goodnight, she disappeared inside the house.

Dean stared fixedly at the shut door before he drove away; a happy sigh escaping his lips.

The moment Delilah stepped inside the entrance hall; her wrist was grabbed from behind. She was forcibly turned around, sinewy fingers biting into the softness of her upper arm.

'What's the idea... coming home late, and then as if that was not enough, allowing the confounded man to make love to you in the car. Are you without shame?' he demanded in a fierce tone. And looking just as fierce.

'You can release me, now,' she said haughtily, slanting him an arrogant glance. 'And quit taking the law into your hands. Father is still around and absolutely fit for giving orders on his premises. He does not need you to exercise authority in place of him.'

'You will not back-answer me, Delilah,' he stated quite firmly, slowly releasing her, but those silently blazing eyes never left her sight.

Slowly he took in the extreme brevity of her dress, and then his gaze slid upwards to move lingeringly on the daringly plunging neckline. His eyes were smouldering, as he said in a grating voice, 'get rid of that dress at once.'

'You can't be serious!' she exclaimed with mock fear.

'Must you misconstrue my meaning?' his voice turned husky, as his eyes once again traced the revealing curves of her partly bared breasts that rose from the beneath the top of her dress like the poetic curve of the half-moon, and subtly gleaming before those scrutinising eyes.

The look in his eyes aroused inside her a tumult, and she could not bring herself to control the unsteady rise and fall of her breasts which were holding an irresistible fascination for the disturbed man standing so close to her and yet not touching her.

She laughed up at him provocatively as she spoke in a tantalising, velvety voice, 'Oh, stop being so ridiculously old fashioned. I wouldn't have guessed it of you. Really, Dominic... does my dress give you no pleasure at all? Take a second look, Dominic, you might start...'

But she was not allowed to go any further, for he pulled her to him so abruptly so as to leave her momentarily bereft of breath. He then started to kiss her... his hands slowly moving over her with a probing intensity, at the same time drawing her supple, young body closer to his hard litheness, and with expertise moulding every seductive curve of hers to his tall, hard frame. The touch of his ignited a fire in her being which sent her nerves quivering and her treacherous heart in turmoil even as it thudded heavily against her ribs.

Suddenly he released her with an abruptness that sent her sprawling on the floor. She raised her hand so that he could help her up, but he merely looked down at her with mixed emotions. His voice as he spoke was deep with a ring of hoarseness which clearly indicated the disturbance inside him.

'Sexy...very sexy, but so utterly shameless. Now get up from there and button up that dress.' He turned to go when she reminded him in a seductive voice:

'Are you forgetting so soon, Dominic, that you ripped open the zip? My dress has no buttons.'

He turned then, his smile bordering on cynicism.

'It must have slipped my memory to tell you that you are very desirable, too. Today I merely ripped down the zip. Someday I might do even worse.'

'Really?' she mocked, unconsciously drawing his attention to the bareness of her creamy flesh by absently toying with her open zip.

'Stop playing with... words. It can be damaging. Correction. It can be very dangerous,' he added softly, his eyes gleaming passionately.

'Help me up, Dominic. Don't be so hard. You did fling me down, you know.' Her eyes were soft with appeal in them that was childlike and endearing.

'You missed your footing. That wasn't my fault,' he pointed out, but he came to her side, nevertheless, and bent to help her up to her feet.

'Carry me to my room, Dominic. Help me lie comfortably on my bed, ah...' she sighed as though in great pain and looking incredibly lovely, 'then, you may leave me.'

He picked her up into his arms in one swift movement, her face pressed close against his.

'Since when have you started throwing orders around, hmm?' but his smile was one of indulgence.

'Oh, wonderful! That feels good.' She closed her eyes in contentment.

'What feels good?' he enquired tersely as he pushed open her door with his right foot.

'Your arms around me,' she sighed with naive pleasure.

'Will you stop this nonsense?' he said in a stern voice, but his eyes mocking its sternness with the desire inside him to reciprocate in like manner.

'I thought I was flirting…' she said indignantly.

He put her down on the bed, pulling the blanket over her. 'That's even worse. As I said, you're quite shameless.' He straightened up, but one small hand unexpectedly pulled him down again.

'I'm going to turn a step more shameless and ask for a kiss.' Her eyes shut rapturously and her mouth parted, inviting a kiss. She waited and after a second or so heard a soft chuckle, and her eyes flew open, her mouth quivering with anger.

'What's so funny, y... you, big ape?' she demanded in a shrill voice.

'Simmer down, lovely shrew. I thought you had a sense of humour,' he smiled attractively, and her heart missed a beat.

She glared up at him.

'Surely you don't expect me to laugh at my own expense?'

'So, you're not dumb.'

'Wherever did you get that idea from… that I'm dumb?' she flung her head up proudly, her eyes blazing and they resembled penetrating, sharp arrows shooting straight at him. The wild cat-like fury could not have been mistaken. And he shrank back in mock horror.

With an unexpected change of mood, she capitulated; her eyes now mildly enquiring, 'Oh, Dominic, did you really find it amusing? You think I ought to laugh, too?'

He watched her in silent amazement for one complete minute, not able to comprehend her, and her quicksilver ways.

'Your unpredictability will know no end. And the answer to your question is most certainly, no. You need not laugh if you see no humour in what I just then said, and laughter without humour is so...baseless.' He bent to kiss her lips. It was a tender, passionless kiss.

'Good -night and don't forget to brush your teeth and er, change into something less seductive. I fear, the night might consume what I believe only a man has a right to.'

'Could that man possibly be you, Dominic?' Her eyes had suddenly grown heavy with drowsiness.

He had become taut, the expression on his face reflecting the fire and heightened tumult within him, but which she could not clearly discern, as her eyes kept closing, however hard she tried to keep them open.

'That only time will tell,' he interjected quietly. Delilah was by then fast asleep.

Dominic quietly closed the door behind him, his heart aching to return to the room and enfold Delilah into the circle of his arms; and to kiss those lips that were meant for wild, passionate kisses. Then with some misgiving, he drew closer to his room. In his mind was fixed a nagging thought produced by a persistent obsession to shirk the dictates of conscience and follow instincts, instead. Upon reaching his room when he grabbed a magazine, forcing his mind to imbibe its contents, he discovered with frustrated hopelessness that constantly thoughts of Delilah were revolving around his mind.

His mind in turn endeavouring to escape from the tenacious hold over his wild imagination as vividly imprinted in his mind as if it were for real; imaginations which directly repudiated all sense of shame and propriety; its highlights directly pointing to Delilah.

It was quite apparently an aspect inherent of a man who is greatly disturbed by a scarred emotion he knows can turn irreparable should it be allowed to mature.

He beat the pillow with his clenched fist, and for once apprehensively anticipating yet repulsing the oncoming of an undeniable urge to rid himself of the resolution to remain emotionally detached. And then for perhaps the first time, he seriously began to think in terms of a steadier relationship.

He jumped out of bed, throwing aside the pillow to one side and striding up and down his room like an untamed beast, ready to succumb to a dangerous yet tempting plunge upon its alluring target. His unsteady fingers started to rake through his thick, black hair. The disquietude grew inside him, and finally, he dashed out of his room like an instigated bull to take a long walk out in the cool, quiet of the night; the only resort, he muttered fiercely to himself and feeling thoroughly miserable.

Damn Delilah and her potent charm, he cursed under his breath, reluctant awareness dawning on him that the potency of that irrefutable charm would never grow dull on him; a fact that merely supplemented his misery. Meanwhile, he decided with finality, that an hour or two of walking would be just the thing to bring him back to his senses again.

***

The following evening found everyone in the house dispersed and engaged in their chosen activities that helped each of them to see through the bleak day with the much hoped for swiftness. Dominic was probably out in the estate, Delilah thought, as he was nowhere to be seen in the house. She distinctly remembered the previous night's episode and began smiling to herself; her audacity exhibited last night suddenly tickled her sense of humour and her smile grew wider. But she instantly sobered up when she felt her mother eyeing her suspiciously.

'Mama, how much longer will you take to finish up this cardigan?' she enquired conversationally.

'I might complete it by Thursday, dear. Yes, and that reminds me,' Selena looked up, her eyes lit up with happy anticipation, 'Marian and Joseph are arriving here on Thursday and we are to receive them at the station.'

'I had almost forgotten about that, and, Mama, did you know that Anna's…'

Selena looked up again with a serene smile covering her gentle features.

'Yes, dear. The news of Mr Mayfair's arrival here on Sunday is known to me. I'm longing to meet the good gentleman.'

Sampson's head which had been buried in his documents and ledgers was now raised to meet his wife's obvious excitement of wanting to establish acquaintance with their eldest daughter's husband-to-be.

'I still cannot digest the inevitable…that Anna's leaving us for good and all so unexpectedly, but you'd think at least she'd stay in England after getting married. I hadn't anticipated that she'd make a permanent home in a foreign country, and thousands of miles away from us,' the benevolent father spoke up for once.

Selena's eyes conveyed compassion, as she tried to put her husband's mind at ease.

'Darling, we must reconcile ourselves to the inevitable, and besides, you're forgetting that she is irrevocably happy, therefore, we must not dampen her spirits by showing our grief. She might then not feel disposed to leave.'

Sampson nodded with some understanding.

'That girl of mine is sensitive,' he said reflectively.

He found soft, young arms going around his neck, and a loving kiss was planted on his cheek.

'Papa, please do not feel so bereaved. I'm still here with you. Joan is not thinking of marrying for a long time yet. So, you see, you still have two daughters... a handful of trouble-makers,' she chuckled as he fondly pulled her over his lap. That had been Delilah.

'Never that, my youngest one. Never trouble-makers, but you both are quite an adorable duo, though.'

'I agree,' Selena put in with mock asperity, her eyes twinkling merrily as she watched on with typical maternal contentment... her daughter getting the full dose of her foster father's affection. She was justified in believing that Delilah deserved it; a belief that hadn't occurred to her earlier until just then.

And then it suddenly struck her with a sharp bite of guilt that all along she had been playing the role of a strict, authoritative parent, never once a warm, loving mother ready to show understanding to her only daughter.

She knew with pleasing positivity that she could not bring herself to see Dominic, Joan and Anna in any other light other than her own children, although she hadn't given them birth. But, with much devotion, she had raised them as her own children. She loved them with the possessiveness of a mother and knew her love was reciprocated. And this link between them proved a never-ending source of contentment for Sampson who adored his wife and all four children with unparalleled zeal.

***

Anna was writing a letter to Paul in the total isolation of the drawing-room when Bertha hesitantly stepped in after a light knock on the door. It had immediately brought Anna's head up in mute enquiry, though typical of her she evinced no indication of even the faintest of impatience on account of being interrupted. Instead, she smiled her welcome; the smile as always reaching her eyes that had an extra sparkle in them.

'I came to ask you a favour since I do not know Jarrod's forwarding address. Would you write and tell Mr Mayfair to inform Jarrod of my present whereabouts? That way he won't be making an unnecessary trip to Warren Street. He wouldn't find me there as expected.'

'You need not worry. Paul will make sure Jarrod gets the message, but what's the matter? Can't you get him on the phone?' Anna asked, throwing her a reassuring smile.

Joan just then happened to enter their midst, standing framed in the doorway.

'Hey, girls, guess what has happened?' she broke into their conversation; her speech not quite coherent.

Looking their way she stepped inside the drawing-room, pulling Bertha along with her, just as Bertha was about to step out of the room, meaning to leave Anna to herself, though, she seemed confused at Joan's strange behaviour

A little confused herself, Anna looked up and stopped them both in their tracks, and spoke in a cool voice:

'Well?' she asked, and resignedly put down her pen, cupping her chin with her fingers.

'I can't wait to hear the exciting news,' she said with gentle mockery.

'Wait till you hear what I have to tell you.' Joan subsided into a chair standing nearby and then she convulsed into laughter that doubled up at the sight of their mildly shocked expression.

'Oh, it's funny! Roger... remember him, Anna? Well... my precious idiot of a former boyfriend has landed himself in the hospital with a disfigured face and a broken leg.'

And it was then when both the girls realised with a shocking discovery that her amusement and elation were superfluous, her laughter goaded by not humour but hysteria. In fact, Joan was hysterical, beads of sweat covering her forehead and over-bright eyes staring widely at them without really looking their way. She seemed a sorry sight, and Anna had never felt more like comforting her unhappy sister who looked distraught; the restlessness inside her exploding and making her quiver with unshed tears that had been unhealthily suppressed by continuous bursts of vacant yet hysterical laughter.

Anna got up from her chair, taking Joan into her arms and was inordinately relieved when by that sisterly contact, Joan quietened down momentarily, only this time to collapse into a flood of tears that shook her whole body like it were a shaken leaf quite unable to keep its balance in the face of the cold thrust of the wind.

'Hush, love... calm down,' Anna whispered into her ear.

'Anna,' she cried. 'Sylvia... the heartless bitch has deserted him. I have to go to the hospital. I... I have to see him.'

'You must leave immediately. If you wish, I will come with you.'

'And to think I... I hated him, oh, how could I have been so blind?' she sniffed, rubbing her tear-filled eyes only to feel the contact of fresh tears that felt hot to touch.

'Who informed you of this?' Anna asked while Bertha remained quiet; a sympathetic observer and her face remained a mask of impassivity.

Bertha too had known great unhappiness made worse by disillusionment and hopelessness, only now replaced miraculously by happiness that knew no bounds. Years of pain and patience were subsequently rewarded by the sudden appearance of her father, whose presence would now rescue her from the scornful tongue of the society as well as their contemptuous look that she had suffered for several years without complaining. And, although, she understood the meaning of suffering, and felt sorry for Joan, quite unable to bear her distress, she preferred not to interfere, though. Anna had efficiently undertaken to calm Joan's shattered nerves and it seemed she had succeeded in her earnest attempt.

'I... I received a call from his sister, giving me the... the news of the accident. A reckless driver he is, but I, oh, Anna, I never thought it would ever come to this. I wouldn't wish it on my worst enemy.'

Bertha found she could not bear just sitting there, quietly taking in that sorrowful sight. And together Bertha and Anna managed to calm Joan down, but with much difficulty, as the girl's shock was more shattering than she had herself anticipated, and which resulted in doubling the degree of her distraught state.

If Bertha and Anna had any suspicions about the intensity of Joan's feelings towards the unfortunate Roger, it was soon cleared after witnessing the subsequent scene in the hospital. They had been escorted by the nurse to Roger's private room, where the sight that met their eyes had been truly awful, only in Joan's eyes they had seen unwavering love and compassion shared by the other two. At that very instant, she had dropped down by his bed; her head buried on the unconscious man's chest, her eyes soon after raised to stare unhesitatingly at the man's ruined face with love and tearful compassion.

For four days Joan visited the hospital regularly, and each time her mind, though slightly numbed, registered the cause for his unconsciousness. A critical condition, though an irreparable concussion that had done serious damage to the brain, and finally realising his failing health which crushed all her hopes of his ever recuperating. And her hopelessness was not unfounded, for on the fifth day she found him covered completely from head to toe with a white sheet. The nurse had stood quietly by the side of the silent figure. She found it quite unnecessary to put it into words that Roger was no more.

As silently as Joan had come, she left just as silently, her eyes absolutely dry of tears and her heart now beating regularly; a calm, silent figure, and no more the Joan; cheerful and packed with mischief and her eyes like ever twinkling stars. It all had changed, though.

The family could offer her no condolence, as she appeared not to need it. Her face continued to wear a mask of resigned impassivity. The rest of the day she kept to her room until daylight when the full realisation of Roger's death came upon her with a stunning impact. Death; a lucky respite for Roger, a total relief for Sylvia, and sadly enough a deprivation for Joan who had discovered much too late her love for Roger; now a broken dream.

But life, if sometimes cruel to mankind, also exhibits shades of kindness blending perfectly with the situation and circumstances created by the skilful hands of fate. Such was proved in the case of the stricken Joan. She found solace in a job in another part of England, transferred to that district by the firm that she was presently working for. A few months away from the home-town, they all knew would help her to forget that particular nightmare, which had literally thrust her from the cheerful, carefree adolescent stage to an almost austere maturity; a premature development in her personality that marked her young-bearing with a prominent touch of melancholy. Her voice too, whenever she spoke, and she barely spoke, sounded distant. She buried her mind in work; yes, her voice too had not been spared, for it too carried a heavy touch of melancholy, though gradually with the passage of time certain memories were being erased from her mind, leaving it quite clear of depression, and prepared to be occupied with thoughts for a brighter future.

She was young and pretty, and men found her attractive. Her mind had blossomed into maturity, and with it, her natural appetite for gaiety was beginning to recover once more. Her love for Roger guided her towards better thinking, a better understanding of herself, and building inside her hope to live free of the bitter memories of the past.

***

Back in Cambridge, Delilah too was gradually blossoming into maturity and here she too was having to face problems of her own. Her treacherous heart constantly suffered, and Dominic remained its tormentor. But would she ever learn that Dominic too was undergoing the problem that was so much similar to hers? Life was undoubtedly full of complexities and every individual was sometime in his or her life compelled to be served as a target for the redoubtable hunter which being fate.

Sampson was taking his second daughter's parting too from the family scene with admirable calm and wise acceptance. Joan had left immediately after Anna's marriage, and it had been a quiet and a quick ceremony. Anna had departed with her husband for their honeymoon. Jarrod and Bertha were engaged and jointly waiting for the arrival of Marian and Joseph whose planned trip to Cambridge had been unexpectedly postponed, but they would be arriving soon, nevertheless.

The past few weeks had been full of events, but now everything had quietened down with an abruptness that was welcoming in a way, and it seemed like almost a blessing in disguise. Every one of them had suffered from a temporary shake of nerves. The occurrence such as it had been and followed by certain developments, each more tragic than the other.

Delilah was standing with her back to her parents, her attention completely taken up by the car outside being driven from the driveway by Dominic. She was thinking that he would probably be returning late in the evening as was his custom. She turned away from the window, and crossed the drawing-room; her mind preoccupied.

'Darling, can't you sit in one place? You appear to be so restless. Really, child... what's the matter, now?' Selena remarked gently, but a warning look from her husband, and she decided against making any further comments.

Delilah excused herself and hastily left the room. In her own room she started to dial Dean's number, installing the pink instrument on her lap, just as Dean's secretary answered the call in a cool, efficient voice:

'Hello...'

'Is Mr Fobster in?' Delilah asked quietly, hoping that her reply wouldn't be in the negative.

'Yes. Who shall I say is calling?' was the polite query.

'This is Miss Redford here,' she said in a brisk tone, and immediately after a minute's break, Dean was put on the line, his pleasant voice profoundly comforting:

'Miss Redford? I'm honoured. To what do I owe this unexpected pleasure?' he responded with a teasing inflection in his voice.

'Could we meet somewhere today?' her voice sounded ever so small and dubious. Dean immediately changed his approach, concern evident in his voice.

'Is anything wrong?'

'Tell me what isn't...' she laughed bitterly.

'Is it all that bad, love?'

'Nothing that you don't know of already, but I must meet you. The plan must continue.'

'You are determined,' he said with an appreciative whistle and then followed by silence.

'Where can we meet?' she asked impatiently.

'Wherever you say, but let's make it this evening. I'm tied up for the whole day tomorrow.'

'That is what I wanted too. Pick me up from here at seven.'

'A little later than that will do?' he hesitated before saying the words.

'All right.' And they simultaneously replaced the receiver.

The day wore on, the hours almost dragging until Delilah felt like screaming. The frustration within her was growing unbearable. Bertha returned to the house during the afternoon. She was alone. Her first thought was for Delilah as she went looking around the house for her. Finally, she found her in her room sagging beneath the weight of whatever it was that was apparently distressing her.

Without turning around, Delilah enquired dully. 'Did you come home alone?'

'Jarrod had to keep an appointment.' She came and stood behind Delilah's chair. 'Let's go for a short spin in the car. The weather is good,' her voice vibrated with life and vivacity that communicated itself to Delilah. It took a good five minutes to see the answering vivacity in Delilah's eyes as she got up to change into a colourful outfit to encourage the cheerful mood that had been indirectly and psychologically instilled in her.

'Delilah, would you like to talk about it?' Bertha asked in an encouraging tone, as they continued walking in the park. It had been some time since they had left the house for a brief outing.

'I think I'm obsessed with Dominic. He is in my mind every time.' She glanced sideways to give her friend a weak smile.

'That I can understand, but why must you make yourself so miserable? It has not gone unnoticed, Delilah. Uncle Sampson and Aunt Selena are worried about you. You hardly even talk, nowadays. You are not the same person. Tell me what's troubling you,' Bertha's tone was softly persuasive.

'Isn't life funny? We had planned to take a spin in the car and we are here in the park taking a walk instead.' Delilah looked around her ostensibly, lifting her shoulders in a resigned shrug. 'Look around us...' She spread her hands in an expressive gesture. 'Everything seems to be at peace and look... the people walking about the street have tranquil expressions on their faces. But I ask you,' she threw Bertha a direct look, 'is all what it seems? Life is comprised of various aspects, and it is difficult to tell one from the other. Likewise, people too have so many facets to their personalities that it is just as difficult to distinguish the real from the facade. Who is really happy? No one is really happy. If they think they are happy, then they are deluding only themselves. People only believe what they want to believe. But here, I'm miserable not because I wish to entertain such distress, but because I really am distressed. Surely that makes me stand out as an exception refusing to hoodwink herself and the world?'

Bertha had heard her silently without contradicting her even once, but she now felt it necessary to put her convictions straight.

'I'm glad, Delilah, that you have yet not sought refuge in lies and deception, and true... that people are actors and this world is a renowned stage, but not necessarily a place where deceit is always practised,' she went on patiently, 'if you will recall that sometime back, even I had been under a lot of strain. I had been the target of public censure, but no matter how hard I had endeavoured to hide the fact, I had only ended by looking even more miserable and under pressure. And, though, I ignored the humiliation meted out to me, I never pretended to be happy when I was feeling far from it. Has it registered, whatever I have told you?' she asked gently almost lovingly, like dealing with an infant.

After a moment's pause, Delilah nodded meekly. 'Well, that makes the two of us. You must be longing to meet Uncle Joseph?'

Bertha smiled serenely.

'Yes. I'm longing to see my father.'

Delilah felt a sudden release of understanding as she warmly clasped her friend's hand.

'I'm happy everything has turned out all right for you. I'm glad... really glad things worked out for you, at least.' Her smile was tender.

'I'm glad too.' Bertha smiled quietly, as hand in hand they both stepped out into the street and headed homewards.

***

The afternoon air was vaguely sultry, lending warmth to the otherwise cool day which was gradually being stripped off its breezy disposition, and just as promptly replaced by the full force of the afternoon heat; the inevitable contribution of the scorching sun overhead.

Sweat trickled down Delilah's back for a moment, teasing her nerves like a tentative finger of an attractive male and just as soon the feeling dissipated. She sighed, quickening her steps. Bertha did not appear to be affected by the heat, though.

They stepped over the pavement, dodging the oncoming traffic, but when they dashed against a particular car, probably being driven by a drunkard, Delilah gritted her teeth. They jumped aside, luckily escaping meeting with an accident, and the fault would have been the wretched driver's heedlessness, without a doubt.

Delilah stepped onto the street once again only to be pulled up on the pavement.

'Delilah, please. Let's not take any chances. Let's stick to the pavement. The traffic is rather heavy.'

'Not all drivers are madmen, but oh, all right,' she capitulated grudgingly, walking in step with her friend, and not finding it difficult to keep pace with Bertha's small, ladylike strides.

'Have you arranged to go out anywhere this evening?' Bertha asked casually, but the expression in her eyes was speculative.

'I have a date with Dean,' Delilah said with a tight look on her face, expecting her friend to probe further into the matter, but she was slightly startled when Bertha said in quite a pleasant voice:

'It would be great if you fall in love with him. Nice guy.'

'Never!' Delilah retorted adamantly, then astonished at her own vehemence she put in falteringly, 'I... I mean he is nice but, well, I don't think I could ever love him.' They had almost reached home when a car zoomed past them at a dangerous speed.

'Of course not... I mean, you cannot help the way you feel.'

Delilah's eyes had followed the racing car distastefully, but she had not missed her friend's words spoken with such deceptive suavity. She glanced sideways to look at her friend suspiciously.

'Do I detect mockery in your voice?'

Bertha had an innocent look on her face, her eyes wide and puzzled.

'What gave you that idea?' but nothing further could be said as they had reached inside the gates of the impressive-looking mansion.

Selena was paused on the staircase, her attention fixed studiously on her versatile daughter. She walked down the remaining stairs, her eyes never leaving Delilah.

'There was a call for you just after you left,' she informed distinctly.

'Don't you want to know who had called?' there was a curious inflection in her calm voice that matched her question perfectly.

'Was it Dean?' Delilah did not notice Bertha slip out of the hall and into the library.

'He will be picking you up from here at five-thirty. He expects you to get ready by then.' Her eyes were fixed on the perplexity that covered her daughter's face.

'But I can't er, I cannot, oh, he must have a reason for coming so early. He... he was supposed to arrive much later.'

Selena shrugged her exquisitely-clad shoulders. It was apparent that she was going out somewhere.

'I can't answer for the change in his plans. You can ask him when he comes home. By the way, your papa and I are on our way to attend a wedding reception. Tell Dominic on his return home that he is to pick us up from Sincombe Mansion. He knows where to find it,' she supplied calmly in reply to the question written in Delilah's eyes.

'But I... I will not be here,' Delilah protested. Dean was ruining all her plans by coming early, she murmured to herself, fiercely. Oh, what a muddle! She sighed half with exasperation and partly with bitter frustration.

'Did you hear me, Delilah?' her mother appeared to be losing her patience, 'I said that Dominic will be returning home today at four. Therefore, it is not likely that you will miss him,' she said and suddenly the sound of footsteps behind her made her turn around, and she missed the look on her daughter's face. It was a look that was rich with anticipation and barely-concealed triumph.

Selena's eyes lit up miraculously at the sight of her husband who looked incredibly handsome; a perfect form of manhood with his fine height that reached a little above six feet, and his lean, handsome features that were almost classical in their perfection, and his lean physique that attractively complemented his overall persona. His still black hair brushed from his low forehead was sleek and luxurious, and the greying at the sides merely added to his air of attractive distinction, and quiet dignity with which he carried himself.

As he smiled at his wife with obvious interest, so also did he notice her looking at him with renewed enthusiasm, and his smile widened. The subtle tinge of copper-like skin taut against his frame appeared smooth and polished, and he could have been mistaken for a statue with a perfect finish. With some amusement, he watched his wife's eyes cover his length with quiet admiration, and taking in the faultless cut of his suit that moulded his admirably fit physique lovingly like a second skin.

At last, she looked up and remarked in a loving tone:

You could have easily passed for Dominic's brother.'

'I will tell you what you could pass for, once we reach the privacy of our room. Coming?' There was a gleam of devilment in his twinkling eyes that reminded one of the beautiful blue of the sky.

In this mood, so like his son's, he too proved to be equally irresistible. He noticed with some amusement and satisfaction the deep tint in his wife's cheeks, as she hastily bowed her eyes before his, quite disturbed by the subtly suggestive look in her husband's eyes.

'You are no better than Dominic...teasing devils,' she accused in a soft tone, but not really displeased.

The deep laugh in his throat again disturbed her, for she turned, intending to give her attention to her daughter, but Delilah had left the room long since.

'Like father, like son, and vice versa. It's in the family. An inherited trait which you must admit brings good results... eventually.' He saw her flush again, and his fingers suddenly cupped her delicate, smooth elbow. 'To the room first, then we shall leave.'

And Selena felt deliriously happy like a young girl once again eager to experience the passionate love-making of her lover.

Delilah had been strolling out in the garden when continuous thoughts of Dominic had driven her to such an extent of turbulence within her that her legs no longer felt strong enough to carry her weight, light though it was. And she subsided into the deep, comfortable canvas chair, closing her eyes to any possibility of invasion of any kind of disturbing thoughts. Particularly, thoughts of Dominic invading her mind usually left her drained of physical and mental strength, and wild, unguarded sensations rushed through her being, making her restless and quite defenceless like she were being invisibly raided.

The sharp ringing of the doorbell was enough to cause her heart to stop, perilously. Involuntarily she rushed into the house from the far end of the main hall and reached the front door first before Bertha could, who had stopped in her tracks with a humorous gleam in her eyes. Delilah was too disturbed to either notice that look or understand the reason for it being there at all. With trembling hands, she flung open the door open, her heart beating erratically against her ribs.

'Hello, Delilah, for a moment I thought you'd faint in my arms.' Jarrod's eyes strayed to where Bertha was standing, and he continued with a smooth charm, 'but I doubt if I would have complained.' When no answering gleam of amusement entered Delilah's eyes, he suddenly grew serious. 'Are you all right, Delilah? You look all flustered, dear.'

'Jarrod... Jarrod, diplomacy is noted to be the crown of charm. Or don't you know that?' a quiet, feminine voice spoke directly to the young man, and he threw Bertha an audacious wink, his hands pulling her to his side, while his fingers moved caressingly over her flat torso.

'What a nice way of reminding me that I'm absolutely charming,' he remarked with gentle sarcasm.

Bertha moved to rest her eyes on Delilah, who it appeared was in no mood to join them in their bantering. She had quickly moved from their side without excusing herself and failing to show even the common courtesy by greeting Jarrod. That gave them both further cause for concern. It was not at all like Delilah to be anything but polite to guests visiting her home, especially those of closer acquaintance whom she was known to always greet warmly; an aspect which was in keeping with her warm and friendly disposition.

Bertha was under the impression that Delilah had expected Dean on the doorstep, but that did not explain the acute disappointment on her face when she had opened the door to Jarrod instead. Only one plausible conclusion could be drawn from it, that Delilah had wanted to see Dean in place of Jarrod. But the question persisted, had her feelings transferred to Dean? Yet it seemed impossible, knowing her obsession for Dominic, and such strong, overpowering feelings they were.

Also, Dean could hardly be the man responsible for diverting her attention to himself after she was drawn to someone such as Dominic. But she was not allowed to reflect further on the matter as Jarrod had put his arms around her, and was kissing her in a way that sent her senses reeling, and all thoughts were swept away from her mind, and quite without difficulty.

Bertha still did not know so many things. For instance, she was not aware of Delilah's plan to attract Dominic's attention by deliberately seeking out the company of another young man. She was not aware that Dominic was to come home much earlier, and that Delilah had imagined that the person at the door would be Dominic, and hardly Dean or Jarrod for that matter. For once Bertha had not been taken into confidence, and so far, as certain other matters were concerned, she still remained in the dark about most other issues.

It was now three minutes to four and Dominic had still not returned home; a matter that caused Delilah a great deal of anxiety, for she was beginning to entertain a lot many unpleasant thoughts with regard to Dominic's well-being. Her mortifications escalated with the speed of lightning. When her parents walked down the stairs ready to go out, she turned eagerly to them. She was relying on them to divert her mind from the nagging torment, and the feeling of acute depression that she knew would drive her up the wall if she wouldn't immediately erase thoughts of Dominic. Unfortunately, her parents appeared to be in a great hurry, and both, in turn, kissed her before retreating from the room and promising to return home early.

Upon their hasty retreat, Delilah hunched her shoulders. Her mouth drooped and her legs which took her upstairs to her room were dragging, and extremely slow in their movement. The moment she reached her room, she started to get dressed. The transparent pink suited her glowing complexion. The dress was long and floating about her small, delicate frame like the graceful sway of clouds. It had short puff sleeves and a high neck but cut from the throat to the valley of her breasts into the shape of a heart. It was a daring dress and narrow from above, accentuating the full curve of her breasts and from the waist, it fell into folds concealing yet revealing every curve of her body each time she moved. The sheerest material clung to her lovely curves, moulding it and pressing lovingly to her shapely thighs and slim, rounded hips, and in doing so, accentuating the alluring contours of her young body by mere means of graceful body language, and the unconscious swing of her hips.

Delilah knew she looked exceptionally lovely. She had coiled her hair in a Greek bun with soft tendrils escaping on each side of her beautiful face of an enchantress and caressing her flushed cheeks. For no reason, she felt exhilarated.

Just as she was about to give a final touch to her make-up, she heard some sound coming from below in the hallway and her heart began to pound crazily. She pressed her hands to the surface of her dressing table with her eyes staring at the door that was not securely closed. She instinctively sensed someone outside in the corridor, and then a peremptory knock sounded on the door that nearly cost her her nerves.

'W... Who is it?' her hands felt cold almost icy, and her voice sounded breathless. Could she dare to think it was Dominic? God! What was happening to her?

The door was pushed open and she looked up to find Dominic standing at her doorstep and looking devastatingly attractive as usual. Her heart missed a beat. He stood there in a cream tuxedo and looked awesome and distinguished. She could do nothing but stare at him, her heart in her mouth. But in his eyes, she sensed a look of censure as his gaze moved all over her in an experienced masculine assessment, and finally rested on the front of her dress with an expression that was anything but complimentary.

'Are you going somewhere?' he asked in a cold, abrupt tone.

'Yes, with Dean,' she said in a whisper, watching him keenly for his reaction, and all the while her heart doing a crazy somersault. But save for tightly compressed lips and a hard, steady stare, he appeared to be quite unaffected by the news.

'That wasn't what I asked, anyway. However, you saved me the trouble.' He stared at her coldly.

With her hands behind her, she frantically tried to pull up the zip of her dress and discovered that her fingers were not steady enough to do their job. She desperately wished that he wouldn't keep staring at her as though she were some kind of an object put up for sale. He stepped forward and her heart missed a beat.

'Here... let me...' And he turned her around, her small bare back now facing him. In one swift movement, he pulled up the zip and stepped back almost instantly. 'So,' his hands were crossed as he continued to watch her sceptically, 'When is this... Dean expected here?'

'He is expected any moment now.'

'And might I ask where you are deciding to spend your evening?' he watched her through hooded lids while he chewed his lips contemplatively.

'Do I have to tell you everything I do and plan? Is it some kind of an unwritten law?' her voice, though soft, sounded defiant.

He shrugged indifferently.

'Not if you don't wish to,' he answered to her former question. She heralded a hesitant step towards the door, but her path was blocked by Dominic, and she was searching for the words to ask him to move aside so that she could step out into the corridor, but he saved her the trouble by moving aside himself upon seeing the indecision in her eyes.

'You appear to be in a hurry and I have no intention of delaying you. Go ahead. Move!' he said harshly.

'Did you have to use that tone?' she threw at him a furious upward glance. He rested his palm against the wall behind her and slanted her a lazy glance that denoted the beginnings of boredom.

'You shouldn't allow my tone to worry you. Now quit acting like the duchess and scram, will you?'

'Oh, you!' her eyes blazing, she delivered him a hard kick on his shin, which took him by surprise, and for just one second, he nearly lost his balance, but he regained it just as speedily. And then one long hand came out and pulled her roughly to his hard length. Their eyes clashed.

And then his mouth met hers in a fierce kiss, while his hands slowly moved to cup her breasts, and even when she gasped at the unexpected contact, he did not release her. Her breath came faster through parted lips, as the hardened tips of her breasts were gripped by practised fingers that began to move over them caressingly and with some deliberation. He had pulled her even more closer to him.

'Here is something that might excite your boyfriend's taste for curiosity,' he said bitingly.

She struggled like a wild cat the moment he brought his lips to the hollow of her throat, moving over its side at first exploringly then teasing its smooth outline with a hunger not new to her. He was aware of its effect on her as she unconsciously arched her throat, her eyes shut in silent rapture. And then without warning his mouth closed over her soft flesh in a scorching kiss once more; the kiss that went on and on... a slow, sensuous motion which made Delilah feel faint with excitement that was seeping through her veins like the scalding touch of fire.

Dominic was the first to draw away, though his arms were still around her waist. Her eyes now opened and lips quivering, she murmured in a husky voice, 'your... your kiss was brutal.'

She then felt his attention go to her throat which he had marked with the passionate impact of his mouth, and a faintly triumphant smile took form on his lips.

'You had better start thinking up an excuse to cover up for that red blotch,' he said, pointing to her throat, 'that is if you have no wish to anger your boyfriend,' he said mockingly.

Her hands went to her throat involuntarily, her fingers nervously stroking the place where he had kissed her, seemed more like he had sucked at her flesh. Her eyes were raised to his that were smiling down at her sardonically.

'I... I had better go.'

'I can't think what's holding you back,' he stated with a cynical smile. 'Unless it is the desire to sample some more of my... kisses.'

'You are conceited!' she threw at him with an angry hauteur.

He shrugged his shoulders, his eyes watching her with shades of mockery soon framing his smile.

'I'm often told my kisses can be very exciting,' he said with that infuriatingly cynical smile.

Dominic was the first to see the young maid approaching them. They were by then standing on the landing of the staircase.

'Madame, there is a gentleman waiting for you out there in the hall,' she informed Delilah politely.

'Tell him I'll be there in a minute,' she told the maid briefly.

Delilah waited for her hurriedly departing figure to disappear from sight before she returned her gaze once more to Dominic.

'Mother asked me to tell you…' she started but was interrupted.

'I know all about that,' he said curtly. 'She had called at the office.'

And because she did not know what to say, she turned to go but found her wrist being captured in a steely grip. She turned sideways enquiringly.

'Do I take it that you're having a sexual relationship with him?' he said in a grating voice, his eyes slits of ice.

With surprising strength, she pulled away from him, her own eyes blazing with an inexplicable fury. Two bright pink spots suffused her cheeks.

'I don't think that's any of your damned business !' her voice was hardly above a whisper.

He grabbed hold of her shoulder, pulling her roughly to his chest.

'Contrary to what you say, I'm making it my business. Now let's have the truth,' he gritted out in a fierce undertone.

A sudden awareness that they had company, pulled them apart. It was the housekeeper and she was looking composed as ever, not the least ruffled by the scene before her. It was as though she hadn't seen or heard anything.

'Miss Redford, the gentleman is waiting out in the hall for you.'

Throwing Dominic, a final killing look, she followed the housekeeper down the stairs.

In the hall, gentle arms circled around her small frame.

'You look enchanting,' he gushed out appreciatively. 'Say, what detained you, love?' Dean was asking her gently.

'Please... not now,' she pleaded in a disturbed voice.

Once she was seated beside him inside the car, she expelled a deep sigh.

'That man is impossible!'

'Because he puts you in such a frenzy?' Dean queried with a teasing quality introduced in his voice.

She sent him a quelling look which made it necessary for him to clear his throat, but his lips were smiling.

'If you have nothing comforting to say to me then kindly maintain a steady silence.' Then after a brief contemplation with a deep frown marring her forehead, she said almost to herself, 'Does he think I'm some kind of a nympho... a... a sex-starved maniac to switch from one man to another at the slightest encouragement? How dare he even imply such a thing?'

'Oh, I'm sure you misheard him,' Dean put in lightly, staring ahead of him as he continued driving.

'Misheard?' she flung him a furious glance, 'he asked if I was having a sexual relationship with you... the insufferable cynic... sexual relationship indeed!' she stared out of the window with a restless look in her eyes, and her teeth biting hard at her lower lip till it drew blood. She felt a sting behind her eyes and she knew she was going to cry. 'To think he doesn't trust me,' there was a bitter edge to her voice that sounded tearful.

Dean continued to drive. He refrained from showing his anxiety by keeping a composed front. To show her that he shared her displeasure would only add to her anguish, and even when he spoke, his voice was calm and composed:

'Look, Delilah, I don't feel like jumping the fences too high, but I think it is time I told you what exactly I feel about this whole affair. For one thing, you are going out with me for his benefit, to observe his reactions, but is it getting us anywhere at all? What are you trying to prove, Delilah? You are easily provoked by anything he says or does. For Pete's sake, why can't you accept the fact that you love him and get this thing over with?' For the first time, he sounded highly infuriated, his fingers tightening around the wheel.

'I love him?' she said simply, but there was a quiet wonder in her voice. She touched his arm lightly, 'Oh, Dean. I need your help, now more than ever,' she stated calmly.

'That's getting to be an old story, now,' he said dryly.

'Does a villain fit anywhere in our plan... rather your plan?' he continued bitterly, as he shifted uncomfortably in his driver's seat.

'It is not a laughing matter.' She admonished gently, yet faintly perturbed by Dean's tone.

'I never said it was.'

'And I thought you were my friend,' she cried petulantly, eyes brimming with tears.

'I was never your enemy.' But when he saw the tears in her eyes, he abruptly put a brake on the car; and stopped to park it in a quiet corner of the street. His arms went around her.

'Oh, you sweet nut, I didn't mean to make you cry. It's just that I happen to care for you and I can't see you make a fool of yourself over that... that arrogant character. We have manoeuvred this plan to make him jealous, but I wonder if it will work,' he said doubtfully.

Her face was buried in the curve of his shoulder and her weeping was muffled, but with sheer will, she controlled her tears and calmed her unsteady nerves.

'Let's hope it'll work', she said in a small voice that sounded curiously like a child's, and Dean's arms tightened around her.

'It just might,' he returned encouragingly. 'If he can ask you questions like that, then he can't be completely indifferent to you.'

She straightened up by his side and regarded him with an air of dignity and pride.

'I never said he was indifferent to me, but the fact that he is attracted to me does not necessarily mean he is in love with me, and that is what I'm longing for,' she informed Dean with a naive dignity and an air of determination that instantly reminded him of a child who could do just about anything to attract attention, and that brought a smile to his lips. Only, his smile made Delilah frown upon him darkly.

'I don't think I said anything funny,' she said in a voice that sounded faintly offended.

'You take offence easily, love. I was thinking to myself how strong-headed you are.'

'And that brought a smile to your lips?' she asked with a disbelieving look in her eyes.

'No,' he assured her with yet another smile which looked more tolerant than amused. 'You reminded me of a child out to attract attention and it brought a smile to my lips,' he explained in all honesty.

'Hardly complimentary,' she said distastefully.

'The truth never is,' he countered patiently. 'Say, are you hungry?'

She nodded, staring out of the window with casual interest.

'I'll take you to a new restaurant that just opened. Hope you like the food there,' he suggested pleasantly, starting the car.

'What is it called?' she asked, matter-of-factly.

'What does it matter what it is called so long as the food is good.'

'Okay. Forget it. I merely asked,' she spoke absent-mindedly, her mind still not able to digest the fact that she actually loved Dominic.

The restaurant ''Palms Hut'' was a small and cool place, and crowded with the younger set of crowds laughing and talking amongst themselves in loud, hearty voices, which carried very little sign of inhibition. Their mood reflected gaiety and youthful banter. The waiter led Dean and Delilah to a corner seat at the far end of the room where there was less chance of their being disturbed.

Dean ordered for their lunch and sat back in his chair, watching Delilah interestedly from across the table.

'Won't you say something? Of course, if you prefer to keep silent it's perfectly all right with me.'

She bent over the table but drew back instantly when she saw the waiter approaching with their order. Soon they were eating and found the food was very much to their taste.

'I'm glad you're enjoying your supper,' Dean said in a pleased tone.

'I'm also glad to be in your company,' Delilah asserted with a quiet smile.

'But you would rather that Dominic were here instead of me,' he said in a hurt and subdued tone; a look of bemusement entering his eyes.

'Your assumption is positively erroneous,' she told him in a quiet voice.

'You don't expect me to believe that!' he said with a bitter laugh, plunging his fork into his tender steak...

She put her hand over his that was lying on the table.

'In your company, I feel so much more at ease, Dean. My appetite doesn't suffer when I'm in your company as it often does when I'm in... Dominic's presence.'

'That's because of your overpowering awareness of him. His presence must have an overwhelming effect on you to be able to actually curb your appetite. As much as I like the idea of putting you at ease all the time, I would have preferred a thousand times if I could have the power to make you feel disconcerted and distinctly aware of me. But this I would not expect a girl to understand.'

'You may be right, but till then, can I expect you to understand that a woman can only feel so strongly about one man?' she enquired patiently.

'You can most certainly expect me to show you that understanding that you so desire,' he said briefly, abruptly paying the bill, 'but the knowledge hurts...what you had just then said about being forever at ease in my company,' he confessed with a wry smile.

The drive back home was a pleasant trip as Dean proved a cheerful company despite their previous discussions, that, had it been avoided could have caused fewer complications and pain. It had ended on a sad note, but Dean had taken it very well, refraining from showing his hurt.

The receding traffic made their journey home a quick one, but hours wore on with rapidity that left them in doubts about the efficiency of their watches.

Upon reaching home, Delilah requested Dean to escort her to the doorstep as she was afraid of the progressing night and darkness. The house was enveloped in darkness except for a dimly-lit hall.

Delilah rang the doorbell and then turned, facing Dean anxiously.

'You know something... you are not playing your role very aptly. It somehow lacks spontaneity.'

With a shaky laugh, Dean immediately put his arms around her waist and brought his lips down to meet hers that were pursed. 'Now, why don't you practice what you preach?' he whispered against her lips. 'Part your lips!'

'Don't be a corkscrew! I... I can't give you any response,' she said in a fierce undertone and was pulled tighter the moment the door opened and Dominic stood there on the threshold, his eyes fixed coldly on the pair wrapped in a lover's embrace.

'Oh, Dean... when are we...'

'You realise you have company?' Dominic's voice sounded like an icicle.

Delilah swirled round and Dean stood there smiling to himself, but he had to admit he did not like the look on Dominic's face that denoted cold fury yet to rise to its full potential. Delilah's smile was superfluous, something in the nature of sarcasm.

'Yes. Now, I do realise that we have company,' she said with a defiant look in her eyes.

'That's a comfort,' he said sardonically, standing before them both in a completely black suit, like a magnificent jungle beast with an uncertain temper.

His hands crossed, he surveyed them coldly.

'And, pray, why did you take the trouble to open the door when the house has no scarcity of servants?' she flung him a suspicious look.

'They have been dismissed till tomorrow morning, and as I was on my way out... it was no trouble at all,' he answered suavely, his tone smooth.

'And what occasion prompted the urge to give them the evening off?'

'I just happened to feel like it,' he said curtly. Then moving his glance to Dean, he said, 'Dean, it is a request... henceforth, please don't bring her home late,' he said briskly, and with a brief nod he left them staring at each other with some puzzlement.

'What do you make out of that?' Dean enquired lightly.

'That he is arrogant and self-opinionated,' she said with a tight expression on her face.

The sound of a powerful engine coming to life attracted their attention. Dean turned back again.

'Yeah, arrogant and self-opinionated, and also that you love him,' he reminded her with a charming smile.

'Fine time to remind me of that,' she said annoyedly, her mouth drooping in utter dejection. She looked up then. 'Are you coming in?'

'And risk that man's temper. No thanks. I will call you, tomorrow. Bye...'

'Goodnight, Dean, and thanks for all that you are doing for me.'

'The pleasure is all mine,' his smile was ironic as he got inside his car, and drove away.

As she entered the hall, her hands instantly went to the switch and the cut-glass chandeliers came to life, illuminating the room with its dazzling brilliance.

She breathed a sigh of relief. Brightness always had that effect on her. With light steps she mounted the stairs to her room, switching on the lights of the corridor as she went up to her private quarters. Once in her room, she undressed and leisurely changed into her nightdress; a delightful pink negligee of pure chiffon that reached just above her knees. In the tall mirror, she could see the seductive figure that she cut. She looked softly alluring and beautiful, and every man's dream with that glowing complexion; attractive features and a seductive body that unconsciously boasted of a display of soft, titillating contours.

She started brushing her shoulder-length hair that fell in soft cascades against her shoulder blades. The bony structure of her shoulders no longer looked prominent as she had put on some weight, and which merely served to add to her attraction instead of minimizing the effect as it would have done for most other women.

She strolled across the room to her bed and began thumping her pillow, her mind absorbed in thoughts of Dominic. As she climbed to bed, she realised with dismay that Dominic would be coming home very late; an unwelcome possibility that left her virtually empty of anticipation. It was obvious that he would not be coming home alone, as he would be going to pick up Selena and Sampson from the party that would probably be getting over by midnight. And the opportunity of being alone with him, she knew would not arise, at least not tonight when she would have loved to meet him in the dark corner of the corridor and have him make violent love to her. And so immersed was she in her private thoughts that she did not realise that she walked to the dressing table and stared at her reflection quite without knowing why.

And when she did realise, she was sitting before the mirror, her hand picked up the brush, and once again reaching for her lovely tresses. Now, was she staring at her reflection with the idea of looking more beautiful for Dominic? But such a discovery that had so far been only the subject for her subconscious now immerged with full force into the open. Must she, however, condemn herself for such an indulgence though, so brazen in nature? Such a reaction of body and mind was not to be entertained by a morally straight person. But was her assumption veritable or was it merely a pretence, what one only wanted to believe or cling to as a compensation for the clearance of conscience, rudely interrupted by uninhibited ideas; highly magnified?

If only people wouldn't have to pretend to be anything but themselves and live with a clear conscience without continually deluding themselves and the rest of the world. Delilah preferred to be honest with herself. So, she was quite shameless, but was being hypocritical as the rest of the world any better? Her revelation carried a sure touch of cynicism. So what, if she was hungry for his kisses and she wasn't going to pretend otherwise, she told herself resolutely. The world could very well do without one more hypocrite to pollute it with the artifice of thoughts and twisted manipulation of one's own life.

Yes, Dominic had seen her in Dean's arms, but, thought Delilah, what had he concluded from that scene was hard to tell, as he hadn't behaved as though the scene had disturbed him in any way. She wished she knew what had been circling in his mind behind the surface composure that generally proved a source of great annoyance to her. His inscrutable expression quite occasionally made her feel thoroughly inadequate. It put her quickly on the defensive. And, which eventually resulted in a verbal conflict when she would have preferred to be in the circle of his arms instead, and experience the thrilling touch of his hands and lips.

She languidly stretched her hands above her head, her mind open to such a possibility, however remote, of seeing Dominic tonight while her body felt warm and moist from the mere thought of his virile proximity that exuded so much of his latent sensuality. Hours ticked by and she could no longer fight sleep. Minutes later when Dominic pulled up the car at the gates of the house; the sound of the car apparently produced no response from Delilah, as she was asleep. It did not penetrate her subconscious, thereby providing her with some relief and joy. She slept on.

CHAPTER 7

Delilah and Bertha were relaxing out on the open veranda and helping themselves to a cup of evening tea. Bertha seemed in a state of preoccupation and Delilah, though curious, kept her counsel, quietly sipping her tea.

'Jarrod wants us to get married before the end of this year,' at last Bertha opened up, putting her empty cup on the saucer and waited for her friend's reaction to her statement.

Delilah looked directly at her.

'Are you against the idea?'

Bertha pulled back the chair and stood up for a minute, not able to answer the question precisely.

'I'm not sure if I want to get married so soon. I care for him, but I still believe it is too early for such an important step as matrimony. I don't want to risk a broken marriage,' she said in a steady voice that carried a tone of conviction.

Delilah's eyebrows shot up.

'I thought you said you cared for him enough to be serious about this issue. Then why these doubts?'

Bertha gave her a faint smile.

'Are you of the opinion that marriage is founded on mere affection? Darling, there is more to a marriage than affection and love, however deep.'

'I'm afraid I don't understand. Are you trying to tell me then that you're not sure if he is the man you want to marry?' She felt strangely disappointed in Bertha.

Bertha smiled again. But it was a wise smile.

'Maybe it's because I care for him so deeply that I don't want to plunge into marriage so soon. We need more time to get to know each other better, to discover our likes and dislikes, our plus and minus points, so that when we eventually marry, we should be prepared and more inclined to exercise patience and understanding. This being perhaps the only resort that has helped to save many a marriage. But at least our eyes will be open to all the difficulties ahead of us and neither will accuse the other of deception, as both of us will be perfectly aware of each other's shortcomings,' Bertha explained gently. 'What is love if not a combination of attraction and spiritual bonding, and the urge to forever remain one and united?' she carried on contemplatively, 'If I had to, I would even go through trial marriage simply because to me it is not the case of hasty marriage and just as hurried a divorce,' she concluded in a voice that trailed off.

'Whew! You are a deep one.' It was apparent that Delilah had understood her friend at last, but it had taken some explaining. It provided her with relief to discover that Bertha did in fact love Jarrod, only she believed in exercising circumspection.

'Hardly that, dearest, merely cautious and practical. It never pays to be sentimental. It's a question of a whole lifetime, and the decision taken should be the correct one, I suppose, or it doesn't take long for love to shape into hatred and condemnation,' Bertha added and sounding matter-of-fact.

'Still, one can never be too sure whether he is taking the right decision,' Delilah observed with simplicity so typical of her.

'At least, one can have the satisfaction of having tried in straightening out their priorities, and if still, things should not work out as per expectations; the regret then is never so profound,' Bertha put in thoughtfully.

'I wonder if I have my priorities straight, but I know now, what exactly I want the most,' Delilah stated with a dreamy look in her eyes.

In Bertha's eyes flashed a sound knowledge of what Delilah had in mind. It's as though two minds were interwoven into one, as Bertha had immediately read what was in her friend's mind.

'Is loving and wanting Dominic the way you do such a fiasco, Delilah?'

Delilah's bitter smile had not gone unnoticed.

'My... My... such sharp perception, but I thought you suspected me of having a relationship with Dean,' Delilah remarked with yet another bitter smile, and poured herself a second cup of tea.

'True, but the suspicion if any had been very vague, though deep down I always knew that there could be no one but Dominic, who possessed such extraordinary powers of attraction for you. Pour me a cup too.' Bertha once again subsided into a chair that she had formerly occupied.

'Then you must have wondered that loving Dominic the way I do, what was I doing dating Dean, and so often?'

Bertha's smile was one of knowledge.

'At first maybe, but those doubts were soon cleared. Correct me if I'm wrong but I have an absurd feeling that you're dating Dean to spite Dominic, even perhaps to make him jealous.'

'You do understand me then, and so perfectly, but tell me... is it so very obvious... the motive behind such an arrangement?' Delilah for once sounded worried.

'Only to those who know of your love for Dominic, while others will continue to believe what you have set out to make them believe.' She gave a light shrug of delicate shoulders.

Delilah expelled an inaudible sigh in the course of their conversation, and the restless look in her eyes could not be misinterpreted.

'God! Confusion and more confusion keep building inside me, and steady progression in the matters of the heart continues to remain a fool's dream,' she sighed, her eyes lowered in silent anguish. Her heart felt heavy.

'However, such revelations are enough for today. Let us move on to another subject. Let us discuss the arrival of Aunt Marian and Uncle Joseph. Their love is again such a surprising discovery, don't you think? Their relationship so unexpected, but they must indeed be making such a beautiful pair,' she reminisced.

'Is Father really so handsome?' Bertha asked absently. 'Mother is a stunner. She still continues to fascinate men; young and old.'

'A fascinating woman... Aunt Marian,' Delilah reminisced yet again with a smile that brought an answering smile to Bertha's lips.

'But have you seen Papa personally? He had been away from home for so long. How do you know that he is so handsome like you just said?' Bertha asked confusedly.

'No. I haven't seen him personally but I guess he has to be a stunner, judging by Papa's looks and Dominic's, more so. Inherent, I should say.' Delilah's smile was like sunshine. 'I too am equally anxious to meet Uncle Joseph if he can attract someone like Aunt Marian. Must be quite a man.'

'Yes. Take for example Uncle Sampson... he has the look of a distinguished aristocrat and with a brain that could only be described as brilliant.'

Delilah denoted admiration in Bertha's voice.

'Who should know that better than you, that Aunt Marian is very choosy about who she associates with. A man devoid of intelligence and looks below average would be the height of deficiency so far as Aunt Marian is concerned, and what she would reluctantly tolerate with some misgiving.'

At that Bertha laughed.

'God! You must still be carrying a torch for Mother to become so totally blind to one of her most reputed shortcomings. She is so perfect herself that she would never... mind you, never accept anything, anyone less than perfect. As for tolerance...I doubt if she understands the word,' Bertha remarked caustically.

'Have you forgotten that you were not the only one that had suffered in the past? The only difference was that she had suffered behind an impenetrable veneer of sophistication and icy composure, and what people falsely interpreted as egotism, but how wrong they all were. She had been exhibiting dignity and not arrogance, and you're being unfair by showing such resentment towards her,' Delilah reminded her friend promptly.

Bertha had her back to Delilah.

'You don't expect me to forget the kind of life she was leading?' Bertha queried dully.

'Bertha...' Delilah said in a soft intonation, her hand reaching out for her friend's shoulders. 'Don't blame her for all that happened. Many people do a lot of things which they shouldn't be doing because they feel insecure and lonely. A drop out in society and which ought not to be existing anyway, as it's one big farce,' she had stated contemptuously. 'She brought you up, didn't she? She sent you to a good school. She provided you with luxuries that every young girl dreams about. Oh, she gave you virtually everything.' Delilah spread her hands expressively.

'You're forgetting love, Delilah,' interrupted Bertha in a quiet voice.

'She tried to offer you that too, but you did not give her the chance to prove herself a mother to you. And her efforts have always been far too obvious. Even you can't deny that,' she cried out vehemently.

'You care for her, don't you?'

'You care for her too, and I don't understand what's this all about. For Pete's sake, doing injustice unto someone is detestable to me and you're not justified thinking so low of her.'

'You may be right. I'm being much too harsh in my judgement. But her previous capriciousness just cannot be ruled out. However, it is undoubtedly her life, and the privilege to live it the way she pleases is, I guess it's entirely for her to decide. Who am I to judge?' Bertha uttered in a low voice.

'You are her daughter, yet nobody has the right to pass judgement on others. No one is perfect,' Delilah said firmly. 'Now, are you willing to take back all that you said about Aunt Marian?'

'For that, I'll have to get to know her all over again. My opinion, when I make it, is steadfast, and it is not going to be easy for me to revise my opinion of Mother so fast. And, Delilah, you need not look at me so accusingly, for despite everything I still happen to love her just as much.' Her smile, though tired, was reassuring.

Delilah kept silent for some seconds before she suggested mildly, 'I have some shopping to do. How about joining me?'

'I have a little shopping to do myself.' Bertha's grin was cheeky, as she said, 'it will prove a fine distraction.'

Delilah nodded.

***

It was some hours after when Bertha and Delilah were crossing the hall with their purchases wrapped in their arms when suddenly they got distracted by a voice that stopped them short. They turned simultaneously.

'You may go, Bertha. I want to talk to Delilah alone,' Selena spoke in a quiet voice, though it carried gentility and so did her eyes.

Nodding silently Bertha left the mother and daughter alone, while she went up to the room allotted to her.

'What is it, Mama? Delilah asked in an equally quiet voice, but there was in her eyes a look of cold enquiry.

'Come sit beside me, child. You need not look so speculative. What I have to say to you will not displease you.' Selena's mouth was curved into a warm, encouraging smile, and that which dispelled all Delilah's initial fears about her mother likely to rebuke her as she did so very frequently.

Stiffly she came and occupied the chair across from where her mother was seated. The parcels were still tucked in her arms.

'Why don't you relieve yourself of those parcels?' Selena suggested softly, her hands reaching out for the parcels and gently putting them on the side table. Then turning once again to Delilah who was by then looking pretty impatient, 'Delilah, just lately I've discovered you are not very communicative. You don't even smile very often as you used to. Won't you tell me what's troubling you?'

'Why this sudden interest in me, Mama?' she said with mild sarcasm, 'I don't remember you ever showing me such concern. You were too busy being critical to notice that I've been under strain for quite some time.'

Selena did not flinch from the sharp impact of her daughter's remorseful words, but her eyes had turned a shade deeper brown, and her cheeks were flushed while her mouth had the slightest quiver which gave away her feelings of repentance. Momentarily, her lids had closed over her eyes before she looked up and met her daughter's bitter smile with her own that was lacking in spontaneity.

'That was a mistake I don't think I will ever repeat again. I haven't been very affectionate towards you, dear, but it does not alter the fact that I love you very dearly,' she uttered in a low voice, her eyes streaming with unshed tears.

'You have a strange way of showing your love, Mama. Is neglecting a child your idea of affection?' she queried in a dry, sardonic tone.

'You were always so far beyond my reach,' Selena said in an unsteady voice, 'You were always more attached to Sampson than to me.' Her eyes were shaded with pain and bright with tears.

'But that's because Papa was more a friend than a parent, so much less hard and stringent than you. I'm not such a virago as you make me out to be, Mama, or I would not have been so popular among my friends. Oh, I admit that I'm short-tempered, but no one is completely perfect. I always hoped you'd make allowance for my shortcomings, but I was soon disillusioned.' She stood up, thrusting her hands inside the pockets of her denim, and ordering the maid who had just then entered to deliver her parcels to her room.

Selena gently pulled her down again, shifting the chair closer to her side, her fingers curved round Delilah's wrist.

'Don't be so harsh in your judgement, child. Can you blame me for overlooking what I haven't been able to understand? I'm referring to the problem that is evidently driving you up the wall.'

'Did you ever try to understand what I was undergoing?' Delilah watched her mother with accusation staring out of her eyes.

'Honestly, I have tried and I'm still trying. I don't like to see you this way. Those dark circles under your eyes and that slight droop to your lips… it's apparent that you are very upset,' she said softly, her words sounding almost like an appeal.

Delilah pulled up from her chair, her face wooden as she retorted coldly, 'you could have tried harder, but maybe you don't love me enough…' she walked away, her back stiff and her feet quickly mounting the stairs.

'Delilah… wait!' Selena had stood up too; a look of sheer anguish entering into her eyes.

Delilah did not turn round but continued to walk up the staircase.

'Delilah, your purse. You have left it behind.' Selena attempted to call her for the last time.

'Ask Mary to bring it up to my room.' She then disappeared down the corridor.

With a heavy heart, Selena once again subsided into her chair, her hands holding her head that felt like lead. The pain in her head was returning and it started spinning. She was feeling dizzy and the pain persisted and worsened with every passing minute. When Sampson entered the hall, he found that his wife had fainted and sprawled on the floor while one hand still covering her head; a protective gesture. He quickly knelt down beside her unconscious form. There was a worried frown on his unlined forehead, and his lips were pursed tightly, revealing his inner turmoil. He pressed the bell near the settee and no sooner had he done that when the housekeeper stepped into the room. She took in her mistress's still form in one glance and silently helped Sampson carry Selena up the stairs into the master bedroom.

***

It was over an hour when Selena finally regained consciousness, her pain dispelled, but the memory of what had caused that pain still remained vivid, and she shut her eyes as though trying to erase that picture from her mind. Sampson was right by her side and his fingers were lovingly caressing her hair that was now lying about her shoulders in a luxurious spread. At fifty-plus she still managed to look beautiful; a sight worth beholding with her soft, delicate beauty.

'How are you feeling, my love?'

Selena looked up, her eyes looking for something in her husband's eyes.

'I. Oh, I...' and then her head was buried in her husband's chest and she burst into a flood of tears, her body quivering from the force of it.

'Sampson, please hold me tight... I mean, really close. Oh please...' Her voice sounded broken and her tears had doubled up, but as Sampson's arms tightened around her, her crying soon abated and a companionable silence followed soon after that.

Quietly, Sampson began to stroke his wife's small back while his lips gently touched her tearful cheek and wiped away her tears with his soothing touch.

'Would you like to talk about it now, darling?'

Selena knew what her husband was referring to, but out of concern for his health, she pretended ignorance and waved away the question with a show of indifference which she was far from feeling.

Instead, the smile that she gave him was unusually radiant as she put her lips to his in a long, passionless kiss, and once more Selena was taken in her husband's close embrace. The lights went off. The embrace became passionate and Selena responded to it by exploring her husband's lips in a sweet, exciting kiss. And all else was forgotten. Selena felt safe in the warm circle of her husband's arms.

***

Back in Delilah's room, Bertha looked upon her friend with some annoyance.

'Are you planning to sit here and sulk all day?'

'Don't be silly,' Delilah frowned.

'I can't think what's got into you suddenly. You seemed in perfectly good spirits when we were out shopping. Did Aunt Selena say something to make you this way?' Bertha asked perceptively.

'Ask me what I told her,' Delilah said in a guilt-ridden tone and her eyes looking straight ahead of her.

Bertha came and sat beside her on the bed.

'All right. What did you say to her?' Bertha asked patiently.

'I guess I spoke to her very unpleasantly and I'm sure I've done the wrong thing. I... I can't understand what came over me,' she added with a note of regret in her voice that sounded small and unsure.

'But of course, you've done the wrong thing,' Bertha asserted abruptly, sounding understandably disapproving.

'God! She must have surely taken it to heart. Oh, I know I was wrong, but I swear it wasn't a deliberate attempt to offend or hurt.' She looked up at Bertha with an appeal in her eyes.

'Of course not,' Bertha agreed. 'But why did you have to be so unpleasant to her? I mean, I don't recall her ever doing any harm to you. How could you be this way, Delilah, and that too after handing out long sermons to me about being fair and just with my own mother? You won't even tell me what induced you to give vent to such... such a... a verbal onslaught?'

'A one-sided onslaught of which I'm not extremely proud. Oh, you know what I mean,' Delilah ranted on hopelessly.

'I always had the impression that you both shared a fine compatibility and now, all of a sudden everything goes wrong,' Bertha reminisced.

'Mother and I were never compatible, so whatever happened was nothing sudden. It was long overdue and quite inevitable,' she sounded dull and resigned.

'Is it something to do with Dominic?' Bertha queried in an uncertain voice.

'Well,' she spread her hands out in a gesture of helplessness. 'She wanted to know what was troubling me and instead of confiding in her I... oh, well...instead of confiding in her...' her voice trailed off, her head bowed in shame.

'Which you should have, but anyway continue...'

'Well, instead of confiding in her I tried a little sarcasm and...and as if that wasn't sufficient, I ended by accusing her of being an... unworthy parent... not capable of understanding,' she said lamely.

'My belief is that you were never an ideal daughter, then what right had you to judge your mother so harshly?' she said, and there was an angry flush on her cheeks as she said those words in a stiff voice, her eyes watching her friend disapprovingly.

'For Christ's sake, will you give me the chance to explain before blowing your top?' Delilah demanded in a loud, excited voice; her every word coming out clear and crisp.

'Go ahead. I'm listening.' Bertha crossed her hands and did the same with her legs, making herself more comfortable on the bed where they were both lounging.

'Okay, so I was wild and impetuous, but that was no reason for Mother to neglect me the way she did. She never tried to understand me, never had a kind word to say to me, and even when others treated me unkindly, she kept her reserve, never once rushing to my defence.' She paused, shaking her head in an attitude of defeat, 'when I cried, I don't remember her ever wiping away my tears. When I wanted to be loved by my mother, all she had to offer was scorn, and never has she taken me into her arms, and kissed my fears away every time I used to experience a sense of desertion and dread of alienation. True, for the first few years of my life I must confess she gave me all the affection that she was capable of giving, but it's now some years since her feelings have undergone a change; a radical change and there's no denying that,' Delilah concluded bitterly, her head lowered in silent dismay, and tears were silently trickling down her cheeks.

'Perhaps what she failed to understand was that you were always different from all, far too rebellious and that temper rather tricky, though not exactly disreputable.' She wiped Delilah's tears away with a fresh piece of linen.

'My only crime was I could never be a conformist. Maybe that is what she finds so irksome. She never could understand that every individual stands apart from the other in the context of thought and deed. Why can't she face the fact; the indisputable fact, that every human is a puzzle in himself, and therefore at certain junctures difficult to pin down? And that a non-conformist like me is even more difficult to pin down as I think and act as I please and refuse to conform to the norms chartered out by the society as the only acceptable necessity,' she went on with some vehemence.

'Has it ever occurred to you that she is far too conservative and therefore mentally unprepared for your nature very opposite to hers?' Bertha chided her. 'By clinging to the past and strict upbringing, her sense of security remains unshaken and undisturbed, you understand? Her mental pause is static and for her, it represents security and a guiltless, comfortable existence. She clearly cannot adjust to change which for you and me indicates progress. She cannot help being what she is just as we cannot help being what we are. Our minds are more open to reason, but hers remains shut, though unintentionally, to the racing times; the jet-set age I think is how it is generally termed.' Bertha had in her quiet fashion made her point clear.

'Is it the fear of the unknown and the unexpected that urges Mother to cling to the past and monotony, or is it something to do with the generation gap?' Delilah asked a bit more gently, obviously making a conscious effort to understand, for however intelligent, she was by far too much of an egoist to possess the capabilities to understand the intricacies of human nature.

'Generation gap, did you say?' Bertha laughed softly, amusement lurking in her eyes. 'Take Mother for instance and Uncle Sampson... they are so much like us...free of prejudice and forward thinkers. They possess such flexibility of mind that nothing would shock them and nothing that they would not accept and without any regret. So, the answer is not the generation gap but Aunt Selena's own private grievances with the present trend of behaviour,' she added gently, thoughtfully.

'After all that you just said, I feel like she suffers more from insecurity than me, for it is obvious, that Mother behaves like she hates parting with old toys and fears the complicated mechanism and operation of new toys. Sounds like I was cribbing for nothing when it's actually, Mother, who needs to be shown understanding,' she sighed but her tone was lighter.

After a moment's contemplation, however, Bertha continued, 'Maybe Mother could try explaining to Aunt Selena and she would begin to understand that the fault does not lie with you or even her, only that you are two individuals poles apart from each other and alterations in personalities cannot be forced. If at all alterations can be made, then it should come naturally or distortion in character and personality would soon take control; a very risky venture I should call it. Well, something should work out, for, despite their many differences, they have always been great friends.'

'In a layman's language,' Delilah sighed, 'someone needs to knock some sense into Mother's head, isn't it?' but she was laughing, though not unpleasantly. 'But I must confess, it is nevertheless a good idea, only you have to approach Aunt Marian now for her support,' Delilah said with an amused smile almost in the nature of gentle provocation.

Bertha laughed.

'You're making it sound like I'll have to approach some dangerous opponent. Christ! When are you going to understand? Just because I adopt a cynical attitude where she is concerned, it does not mean I find her unapproachable and unkind. You'd be surprised after all that I have said, how well she responds to all those who go to her for advice or understanding.' And there was actual admiration in Bertha's voice.

'She can't be all bad, then,' Delilah remarked deliberately.

Bertha had a strange smile on her face.

'On the contrary, she is all goodness itself. She is wonderful, but like you, I now suspect that I have misjudged Mother. Perhaps in the past, she had merely reacted to the circumstances that were apparently not in her favour, and what I had wrongly interpreted as a manifestation of her actual character,' she said with a note of regret.

'Who can claim to possess a flawless character?' Delilah's smile was bitter once again.

'How wrong I was,' Bertha sighed heavily; her head lowered in retrospect.

'You can see how one story or rather confession leads to another and which proves how hasty we were in our assessment.' Bertha smiled quietly.

'Hardly flattering to us, for it also proves to us that we are not old and mature enough to sit in judgement of others,' Delilah commented reflectively.

'Ah, Delilah... now you are quite forgetting what you had once said to me that no one... simply no one has the right to sit in judgement of others, and I believe you were right, and I must strongly dispute over your recent statement, for however old and matured a man may be, he is not without flaws, therefore he is not entitled to point out the flaws in others,' Bertha added patiently.

In deep retrospect, Delilah looked strangely lovely; her brow furrowed in contemplation.

'Yes, indeed you are right,' Delilah said at last. 'For maturity does not necessarily come with old age, and an elderly person need not necessarily have to be an emblem of wisdom. As a matter-of-fact, maturity, wisdom and experience can also be acquired at a tender age, and this all reasoning has brought one major factor to my attention.'

'And what may it be?' Bertha asked casually.

'No man however matured and experienced should have the right to sit in judgement of others, as no man can boast of perfection. I abhor people who judiciously stand in judgement of others,' Delilah said with some asperity.

'We have certain convictions, but do we always follow them by way of practice?' Bertha looked up and her gaze was just as steady.

'Yeah, convictions without practice would soon lose their significance and meaning,' Delilah agreed quietly. 'True, mostly things said at random are rarely given consideration and serious thought, and then they remain just words; empty words in place of which silence would have been so much more preferable,' she again continued, but her voice sounded like it were coming from a distance.

'Hmm, but it still wasn't a confession I was seeking from you, love,' Bertha inserted gently; her expression serious. 'Let me explain. Like we have admitted; the seat of judgement ought not to be occupied by man, and yet I can assure you that we will do the very thing we are up against, whether intentionally or unintentionally. Only man has been granted the privilege to think, reason and decide. And consequently, it is a man's birth right to judge and assess or how else would law and order be maintained, discipline and civility be practised? Get the picture?'

'I cannot but agree with you,' Delilah inserted thoughtfully.

'However, I wonder whether we have not deviated from the main subject. To start with, our subject was Mother, so an apology is in the offing and I might feel the better for it,' Delilah said in the quietest intonation so unlike her.

'Do you promise never to be rude to her again? As I said, she can't help being what she is, just as you can't help being what you are.'

'Alas, my dear Bertha... it would be so simple to turn words into an oath and yet again, how many keep their promises?' her smile was cynical.

'Dear Delilah, just then when you said, an apology was in the offing, you made it sound like a conviction. Are you beginning to have doubts now?' Bertha sounded faintly contemptuous.

'I guess to maintain a conviction or a belief one has to learn to respect it first, and for that one has to have a sense of values. There are but a few who possess it, but quite occasionally they show it little regard. Never having cherished it, they begin to ignore it instead by quite forgetting its existence, but don't you know yet that I'm a different kettle of fish altogether?' Delilah smiled cheekily.

'Who knows that better than I do how original you can be, only keep your promises in the future.'

'I will try. I'm not a very patient person. However, when did I ever tell you that I'm without flaws?' Delilah teased.

'You're full of it. How's that for a first-hand compliment?' Bertha returned suavely.

'Never did a compliment sound so great,' Delilah laughed merrily, humour lurking somewhere in her eyes. 'Some more of such compliments and it would be difficult to bring me down to earth. I'm already experiencing elevation,' she said, but she was smiling; that typical slight smile so much part of her and her irresistible charm.

'Have you tried inviting Dominic to your level of elevation? I'm told he's not exactly averse to heights. He enjoys them instead. Revels in it,' Bertha said with mild sarcasm.

'Where did you get that idea from?' Delilah asked confusedly.

'Come on, don't you know it is you that I'm talking about? Aren't you the height? Presumably, he is drawn to heights, only the man is opting for dizzying heights,' Bertha laughed with rich humour.

'What next?' Delilah queried absently. 'A pity, though, I can't imagine him losing his balance and falling on his face,' she trailed away thoughtfully.

'Why? Is it perhaps your secret hope to lovingly break his fall and gather him into ready arms?' Bertha smiled; her eyes gleaming with amusement.

'Now really, Bertha…. you are letting your imagination run riot,' she said, but she was blushing, her eyes lowered in some embarrassment.

'Relax… I was only kidding.'

'Oh, I'm relaxed.' Delilah stretched herself on the bed, her hands going behind her head, acting as a pillow.

Bertha got out of bed, entering the adjacent room where there stood a small refrigerator that she opened to let out the jug of water. She poured the water into the glass and returned to the bedroom.

There she found Delilah with her eyes closed and lying prostrate in bed.

Delilah just then sensed her presence. She opened her eyes and the smile that she threw at her friend was quietly pleasant as she extended her hand to take the glass of water, and put it to her lips.

'Now, what was I saying?' Bertha urged with yet another smile.

'Not again, Bertha. I've had enough for today. There are plenty of other subjects that could be touched, and would instead prove a pleasant diversion,' Delilah said evasively. She had turned round to her front with the glass in her hand.

'Perhaps,' Bertha decided with a secretive smile that... enough was enough.

'Where are you off to?' Delilah asked her, as she again made to dash out of the room.

'To get some ice cubes. I just love them,' Bertha responded gaily, throwing her a half-grin.

'You love ice cubes? Are you out of your mind?' Delilah asked, surprised at her friend's unexpectedness.

'Who knows... maybe I am.'

'Get some for me too, please.'

'Really? What are you trying to prove?' Bertha looked at Delilah with mild astonishment.

'That I'm just as mad as you are. Now hurry, will you?'

Bertha soon returned with a box full of small ice cubes.

'Aunt Selena would have fits if she would know of this. Eating ice in this climate!' and both broke into a laugh. The merry mood was back and the girls took full advantage of it.

***

The day slowly began to drift into a listless evening that only had a cool breeze to its credit, and otherwise totally lacking in buoyancy. When Delilah much later ventured into the drawing-room she found it was occupied by her mother who was smiling at her warmly from across the room. It was as if that scene between them had never happened. For a moment she stood by the doorway, her eyes thoughtfully fixed on her mother. And then before she even realised it, she was in her mother's arms.

'My child... my very own child. Oh, how I adore you!'

'Mama, you know I love you too. It's... it's just that I had felt so.... neglected, and you must know how that feels... to be ignored and misunderstood.' She bent to kiss Selena on both her cheeks that were moistened with tears.

'Let's start all over again. How about it, my sweetheart?' Selena murmured affectionately amid tears sliding down her cheeks.

Just then a tall figure strode into the room but stopped midway, and a smile took shape on Dominic's lips as he took in the scene before him.

Seeing him standing there and watching them impudently, Delilah; feeling a little embarrassed, had moved away from her mother's side, as her eyes continued to survey Dominic suspiciously with angry hauteur.

'Now, if you are about to make some nasty remark, then you had better change your mind. I warn you I will not take kindly to it,' she informed him coolly and watched him with icy distaste. Why did he have to be so damned attractive... so fascinating with that peculiar smile of his, mocking her make-believe nonchalance? This being her personal view on this particular issue.

Dominic slowly began to move towards her, and that smile never leaving his devilishly handsome face. Delilah remained standing where she was, fixing the full battery of her eyes on him. But before he could say anything in response to Delilah's verbal onslaught, Selena gracefully intervened even as she covered the space between them.

'Dominic, my dear, I can't think where you had disappeared lately. You had me worried, son.' She looked up into Dominic's eyes which had softened considerably. He bent to kiss Selena on her cheek.

'Mother, you worry unnecessarily. I had some estate business to settle in the neighbouring town and well, I got home a few days late. That's all.' He indulgently flicked her cheek with his finger as he stared down at her with genuine affection.

'So, lovely Delilah, any progress that you may have made in the path of true love with young Dean?'

She threw him a disparaging look that was received with a satanic smile that carried a charm of its very own.

'Hmm, but maybe your mind is interested in varieties, and you have mercifully packed off the Dean chap.' He was obviously enjoying her increasing indignation.

Apparently, Selena's attempt at keeping them at bay had not worked, for both looked already involved in a wrestling of minds.

'Er, Dominic, I'm going up to your father. Come along with me, dear. He'll be glad to know you're back home. He has been asking for you,' she made a final attempt, but already knew through instincts that it wouldn't bear fruits.

'I'll be joining you later, Mother. You go ahead.'

Selena looked at Delilah and Dominic with obvious displeasure before she left the room with a shrug of her shoulders. Slowly almost leisurely, Dominic turned to Delilah.

'Well now... where were we?' his smile was far from pleasant.

With a faint shake of her head, she turned to go when quick fingers curled around her arms, pulling her to a hard frame.

'Not so fast, Delly,' he said caressingly.

She flashed him an angry look.

'Stop calling me by that ridiculous name!'

'Delilah then...' his tone was soft and tolerant but the smile on his lips was decidedly one of wry amusement.

'I wasn't jesting when I said, provoking me won't be wise, Dominic. Now let me go.' There was a tight expression on her face which Dominic observed with careless disdain.

'Tell me what would you do if I should continue to incite you,' he teased, then suddenly his eyes were smiling down at her.

With an unexpected abruptness, she broke away from his slackened grasp and stood with her back to him.

'Please, Dominic, I'm not in the mood for playing games,' she swirled around, her voice tearful. 'I don't know what's come over you. Why do you always have to pick on me for your sardonic game of sordid cynicism?'

'You're so susceptible and such vulnerability... such fragility weakens my resistance to succumb to the temptation of provoking you. And besides, you look so... irresistible when provoked,' he drawled, his eyes straying to her lips with some deliberation.

And, although, her heart was thudding crazily, she subjected him to a steady look, and inhaling a deep breath, she said in a discouraging voice, 'If the temptation is so hard to resist, then I suggest you continue to play the game. I won't be surprised if, within the briefest span of time, the novelty should wear off,' she smiled morosely with a deep tinge of bitter cynicism.

'The novelty will wear off only when you become immune to provocation,' he said with lazy deliberation which was in itself a mild form of provocation that turned Delilah's colour to a deep pink, and her eyes flashed daggers at him.

Her fingers were clenched at her sides and it was obvious she was trying very hard not to give way to her pent-up emotions.

There was a light knock on the door soon after which Mary the housemaid entered the room, announcing the arrival of Dean Fobster. The timing was just perfect for that announcement, for Delilah's anger melted into a welcoming smile as she saw Dean entering the room. His face which was covered with a smile that was oddly attractive as he crossed the room to where Dominic and Delilah were standing.

'Dean, what a nice surprise,' Delilah crooned in an affectionate tone. She put her arms around him and enthusiastically kissed him.

'Er, how do you do, Sir?' Dean greeted politely, and though, Dean's arms were around Delilah's waist, his eyes were on Dominic, and even he had to admit that the man's scrutiny was extremely disturbing.

Dominic gave a curt nod, his eyes as hard as clear-cut diamonds.

'Are you a frequent visitor here, Mr Fobster?' his voice matched the quality of his eyes.

Dean was a bit taken aback by the pointed question and asked in such an uncompromising tone, but he soon regained his composure.

'My visits to this place are rare,' Dean answered surreptitiously.

'However, I hope you will stay back for lunch, Mr Fobster,' he said politely.

But this time Delilah answered, as she stepped away from Dean; her mouth a firm line.

'Sorry, this is not possible,' she intervened hastily. 'Dean and I are going out for lunch.' Her hand clasped Dean's who was beginning to feel quite bewildered by then.

'Was this arrangement pre-planned or you got this brainwave a moment after I suggested you stay back for lunch?' he queried smoothly; a half-smile appearing on his face, and which was for once devoid of humour.

She threw him a murderous glance, but her voice was perfectly composed when she spoke, 'We are meeting some friends at the restaurant and from there we are invited over to Dean's granny's house. We will be having our evening tea there.'

Watching Dean quizzically, Dominic enquired politely, 'Mr. Fobster, you did say your grandparents were away on a small tour to the Continent. It was discussed during the conversation we had on our previous meeting if you remember,' he reminded in a fathomless voice which carried a sure detection of measured suavity that was not completely without sarcasm.

Dean at first looked confused, then stealing a vague look at Delilah who also appeared to be quite disconcerted, he said with admirable ease, changing his expression to one of pretended calm, 'True, but they returned to Cambridge, just yesterday,' he added hurriedly, his smile convincing, but he was experiencing butterflies in his stomach. Lying didn't come easily to him.

'But weren't they scheduled to arrive much later if I'm not mistaken?' Dominic stated composedly, his hands thrust in the side pockets of his coat.

'Correct, Mr Redford, but while the tour continues, my grandparents owing to grandma's sudden illness, took another flight and are now back home. They couldn't have possibly continued on their tour under such grave circumstances.'

And, though, there was a faint look of suspicion in those diamond blue eyes, the uncompromising owner of those eyes accepted the explanation with careless boredom, as the subject was no more of any interest to him.

'All right, Mr Fobster, you've proved your point. I will not offend you by doubting your... sincerity,' he said, although he put heavy emphasis on the last word, his interest in pursuing the subject had evidently ebbed out.

With another faint nod, he abruptly left the room to swiftly mount the staircase two at a time, and quite apparently anxious to meet his father who had been kept waiting for long enough.

'Christ, help me! Delilah, each time I meet the man, my conviction grows that he is certainly not the man to play games with. I'm surprised if he has actually believed my fabricated explanation to be the truth.' With a resigned shrug, he moved a little further into the room, with his back to Delilah.

Delilah had a hopeless look in her eyes as she said quite tonelessly, 'You may not know this but I could see he was plainly not interested.'

'Then let's quit acting the eternal lovers.' He had turned, and for once he had spoken with unrestrained irritation, but when upon seeing the offended look in Delilah's eyes, he apologised immediately.

'Please let us continue for a little while more. I have a weird feeling it might work out even though it appears he is far from affected by all this,' she appealed softly almost half-heartedly.

Dean subsided into a nearby chair, hunching his shoulders.

'Am I so bad, Delilah? Won't I do?' He had a mock, forlorn look on his face.

'You are a fine person, Dean, or you wouldn't be devoting yourself to someone like me the way you do.' She stroked his hand fondly.

'We are friends, remember?' he said with an air of a defeatist, but he had uttered those words good-humouredly.

'I don't think I will ever stop thanking you enough for everything you are doing for me and so sincerely. You believe that, don't you?' she asked in a gentle tone, her eyes reflecting what she felt from deep within.

'I'm a fool!' he said in an undertone. 'Pretending to be your lover. I won't wonder if I end up falling in love with you.'

Her laughter was like a soft tinkle of bells.

'I like you best in your teasing mood,' so saying she just then spotted Bertha outside the room. She confronted her with a dazzling smile and hurriedly approached her friend in light footsteps. Unintentionally, she left Dean behind, and for a moment forgetting him. In her excitement, she had failed to recognise the seriousness of all that Dean had just then said to her, though playfully uttered.

'Bertha, I insist you come along with us today. Wouldn't it be fun, Dean?' she called out to him enthusiastically.

Dean was standing, supported by the long couch with his hands folded, and keenly observing the girls with a vague smile, his mind far away.

'Not a bad idea,' he said sincerely. He liked the look of Delilah's friend and decided it would be fun to get to know her.

The young man thought that no friend of Delilah's could be boring and the girl was also unusually attractive, dressed in a simple blue dress that reached demurely to her delicate knees.

He had noticed with growing interest that the fine material was subtly moulded to the perfect body; a streamlined figure with long, slender legs.

'What are we waiting for then?' Bertha said amusedly, her eyes twinkling brightly, but her voice was quiet as always. It carried no trace of what she really felt.

Dean had shifted from his standing position. He then started moving towards the exit door and feeling absurdly light-hearted as he casually beckoned the girls to follow him outside the house to his car.

The drive to the city was a pleasant experience as they each had something interesting to talk about. The discussion, though varied, proved amusing. They were nearing their destination, and throughout their journey, a new subject was touched and each more amusing than the other. Their discussion continued with a total lack of inhibition. Bertha appeared to be visibly enjoying Dean's company which brought laughter to her lips and tears to her eyes. She was enjoying a man's company the way she had never before enjoyed, and all her reserve was shed away in moments of spontaneous laughter and light-hearted humour.

They had lunch at "Abba's Café", a new restaurant which was mostly frequented by the younger crowd. Very few elders were to be found there, and the partially loud sound of Rock 'n Roll music reduced everybody's voice to a bare whisper. With some luck, the music was hardly deafening. On the contrary, the music floating in the room was pleasantly stimulating, despite the volume. And the number being played was a seductive rendition; the lyrics and music playing havoc in the minds of many listening to it so intently. Thus, with gradual ease, a romantic atmosphere was created.

It was a little wonder the restaurant was crowded since it was newly opened, and besides the food was exceptionally good and the service was prompt. Everything was served hot and fresh by the smiling and graciously obliging waitresses.

In the middle of the second course, Dean asked Bertha which field she had chosen as a career. Bertha had replied that she had previously been in the employ of a large textile company, but for some reason, she had to resign from that job. Also, that she was presently on the lookout for another job. She hoped to get the job here in Cambridge, as Jarrod her fiancé was planning to settle down in Cambridge. Dean appeared at first taken aback at the mere mention of a fiancé, but he got over it within moments and was in fact listening to Bertha talk about

Jarrod with keen interest. He even discovered that he liked the sound of the fellow Jarrod.

On their drive back home, they stopped by a small cafeteria for a cup of tea. There again they spent another half an hour until Dean suggested they leave, as he had an appointment to keep. Four-thirty was closing in, and it was an important client that he had to meet.

When they finally arrived home, Delilah asked casually, 'Well, how did you find Dean?'

Bertha grinned and said with a teasing inflection in her voice, 'Your choice can hardly be criticised. He's really good and fun to be with.'

'Did you ever have any doubts about my taste in male company?' Delilah enquired with a responding smile.

'That was before I met Dominic,' was her brief rejoinder.

All of a sudden Delilah's expression altered. It became cloudy and even perhaps a little sad. But she did not rise to her friend's bait; unconsciously rendered, and instead, she quipped lightly, 'Coming upstairs?' she shrugged her shoulders. 'I thought perhaps you'd like to meet the family. Mother is probably up in their room with Father.'

'Delilah, I have a feeling Uncle Sampson is not keeping well. He has paled considerably. I wonder if you noticed it at all,' Bertha remarked with quiet concern. And then silently she followed Delilah up the stairs where halfway they encountered Selena who greeted them vaguely. It looked like her mind was diverted to other important matters. Delilah, although, with some hesitation, stayed her mother with a hand on her arm.

'What's the matter, Mama?'

Bertha looked on quietly, observing the worried expression revealed on Delilah's face and the forced smile on her aunt's lips.

'Darling, would you mind keeping your father company?' and so saying she hurried down the remaining stairs, her strained voice calling out for Dominic who was nowhere to be seen. Wordlessly, Delilah proceeded up the stairs and Bertha followed behind her quietly.

When Delilah opened the door to her parent's bedroom after a momentary hesitation, she couldn't suppress a gasp when her eyes fell on her father's motionless form. She ran towards him, but a sigh of intense relief escaped her lips, as her fingers came in contact with the regular beat of the pulse under his wrist. On impulse, she held the bony wrist passionately with unsteady fingers.

Then a soft, soothing voice said from behind her; 'It is not what you fear. He is merely in a state of slumber.'

'Yes, I can feel his pulse,' Delilah commented in a small, tearful voice.

'That's exactly what I meant. Let him rest soundly, sweetheart. He needs an uninterrupted sleep,' said Bertha in a gentle tone. When she turned around, she found Dominic standing in the doorway with an elderly man following behind him.

He had walked in quietly, introducing the doctor to the two girls. Just then Selena too walked into the room. She went up to where her husband was lying in bed and gave him a light shake, soon after which Sampson awoke.

His heavy lids opened slowly and with some difficulty. His face was slightly contorted with pain as he strove to sit up on the bed. The doctor made him lie back on the pillow again. Sampson showed no resistance. Dominic silently gestured to the girls to leave the room which they did without question, but not before Delilah enquired in a soft, quivering voice:

'It is nothing serious, is it, Dominic?' she said, while her tear-filled eyes pleaded for reassurance.

His arms automatically went around her shoulders. His smile was quiet and reassuring. 'It's nothing serious.'

***

Once Delilah and Bertha were seated in the drawing-room, Delilah's eyes were invaded by the flood of tears that she had no control over. Bertha let her, and after a few minutes she poured her a glass of water that Delilah found hard to drink, as her throat was blocked with tears, but she gulped down the water, nevertheless.

'Do not upset yourself like that. Uncle will be all right soon, I'm sure,' Bertha said comfortingly.

'I... I hope you're right, you... you don't know what he means to me.'

'I know, darling,' she said in a quiet, loving tone.

As the door of the room was opened, Delilah noted the doctor descending the staircase with Selena and Dominic walking behind him. Delilah got up from her chair and rushed out of the room to where the doctor was standing on the landing. Her face raised to his was full of fearful anticipation as she whispered, 'Is... Is he all right, Doctor?'

The doctor's smile was answer enough, but seeing the girl's obvious suffering, he took a step forward and said in a hearty voice, 'My girl, Sampson will be right as rain by tomorrow. That much I can promise you.'

Her face was transferred miraculously, and it radiated pure happiness as she repeated the doctor's words to herself.

'Right as rain by tomorrow. Oh, Doctor, I could love you for putting my mind at ease. It's such a profound relief.'

Selena lovingly put her arms around her daughter, her face completely devoid of worried lines. She was once again the cool, composed lady of the house except for her eyes that were warm with love for her tender-hearted daughter. Dominic followed the doctor out and politely helped him inside the waiting car.

'Just remember this, Dominic, those pills are a necessity without which I'm afraid his health is very likely to deteriorate. Goodbye, my son.' He patted Dominic's shoulder.

'Thanks for coming, Doctor.' He stood there for a minute, watching the car moving through a cloud of dust, his expression contemplative. His eyes though were staring at nothing in particular.

When he returned to the house, his eyes fell on Delilah standing on the landing by the baroque staircase. Her expression remained quizzical as she moved her gaze all over Dominic, standing in the doorway with his eyebrows slightly elevated. He otherwise seemed altogether unperturbed. His stance almost lazy and casually unconcerned.

'Tell me, suddenly what do you find so interesting about me?' his voice was not without dry amusement. She found his current mood difficult to pin down.

And because she felt strangely disconcerted by his deep-set eyes watching her steadily, she moved from her position and began walking towards the library, her back stiff and straight.

'Where is everybody?' he followed her inside the library, in his slow, lazy strides.

She turned, her heart thumping madly. Yet again she managed to shrug carelessly.

'Oh, they must be somewhere. Probably, Mama and Bertha are with Papa.'

He was soon in level with her despite his slow strides which brought him to her side, and he was now standing merely a breath away from her with her small, stiff back facing him. But he didn't attempt to turn her around, and nor did he touch her, though his proximity was enough to set her pulse racing. She was standing without really moving, and he too did the same.

'Turn around, Delilah,' he insisted. His voice; low yet persistent.

Slowly she turned on his bidding, and then he was kissing her on her parted lips with mounting passion. For a startling moment, she became still, then responded fervently to his kisses and urgent caresses on her body.

'It has been so long, Delilah.' His face was buried against her throat, and his lips lightly, titillatingly moving over its smooth texture and arousing inside her all those familiar disturbing emotions which had the uncanny power to render her breathless and turn her weak in the knees. She had to grab the front of his shirt for fear of losing her balance.

In doing this for support, their bodies were moulded into one; an impression that was created so perfectly in the late evening light, 'Dominic,' she cried breathlessly, her eyes raised to his, 'don't you care anyone might see us this way?'

'Why? Should I be caring?' he raised his eyebrows mockingly.

'But, Dominic, they are likely to speculate on our… behaviour.'

He gave a soft laugh that made her feel oddly excited, and her heart again missed a beat.

'No, I don't care if they should speculate on it,' he whispered, laying special stress on the last word, 'but the question is, does it matter all that much to you?' he started kissing her again, his kisses more fervent and insistent this time.

'Don't...' she mumbled as she began to struggle, and finally managed to pull herself away from him, though his arms were still around her, 'What... what will they think?' her breath coming faster through her lips.

'It is quite obvious that I'm making love to you,' he whispered, and before she could prevent it, he had slid the dress from her shoulder and his lips began to explore the bare flesh which tingled under the fiery touch of those firm, sensuous lips.

'Dominic, oh, how can you be so heartless so as to move me in this... this way! Oh, please...' she breathed the words, her eyes shut in a moment of silent frenzy.

'Please what?' he said with a disturbing drawl, his lips doing their own thing.

'Let go of me. It's... it's unbearable!' she uttered in a whisper.

A deep sigh escaped his lips as he lifted his head to watch her with a smouldering look in his eyes.

'I could move you a hell lot more if only the opportunity should present itself,' he whispered hoarsely into her ear, and so saying creating havoc inside her.

'Opportunity? What can that mean, Dominic?' she asked in some confusion. She looked as though in a quandary.

He cupped her chin so that she would not have the chance to avoid the smouldering fire in the deep blue of his eyes.

'Look at me,' he commanded. 'Does it matter... the answer to your question when my eyes tell you that I'm on fire for you?'

She gasped.

'Dominic,' she cried, fighting for strength, 'please, don't make it worse for me by... by saying such things.'

'You think it's any easier for me?' he shook her fiercely by her shoulders.

'I try hard to avoid you, but every time I see you, I learn to my dismay that resistance as far as you are concerned is a... damn it, make-believe thing for me!' he exclaimed in a fierce whisper, 'and it has to be you; you who are... oh, I really did a fine job of messing up my life,' his smile was infinitely acrid.

'Am... am I all that bad, Dominic?' her voice was laden with torment, mortified by what he had just said. It had hardly sounded like a compliment.

'Oh, you're bad all right. You drive me insane,' he said through clenched teeth, 'you make me want to kiss you... make wild love to you; the works, you know,' and watching her passionately, 'and what's more; you are totally, utterly damaging for my nervous system. And if you doing these things to a person is bad, then you are no angel, damn it!' he shook her with a fierce desire to do something crazy to her, anything but keep away from her voluntarily.

'You needn't throw accusations at me!' tears spilt down her cheeks. 'I don't do that intentionally. I... I didn't even know you felt this way.'

'Well, now you know,' he said with a hard expression on his face.

'I... I'll try to keep away from you. That should stop you from complaining,' she murmured as though taking a vow through quivering lips.

'That won't improve matters,' he stated curtly, his hands crossed, and he looked decidedly uncompromising.

'Then why don't you try finding a better alternative for your peace of mind?' she threw at him in a husky voice, and tears were not far.

'Hmm, the only way perhaps I can get you out of my system is by going to bed with you. How's that for an alternative?' he said sardonically, and then pulled her to his side and pressed his lips to her throat that burned from his fierce touch.

'You can't mean that!' she looked taken aback, and almost scandalised, her eyes widened in surprise.

'I never realised you were such a prude,' he jeered softly, his tone taunting, 'and I don't joke about such er, delicate matters.'

'No!' she exclaimed softly, her eyes again widening unbelievingly.

'Yes, Delilah, did you think I'd be content with a couple of kisses and light caresses? You must be naive then. You're dealing with a man and not some yellow-faced callow youth,' he remarked scornfully. He then pulled her even more closer to him and once again his mouth sought hers, parting it with an urge to drink in some more of her sweetness and that which left her quivering from head to foot.

'You did say an alternative could be sought out to end the battle inside me? Well, I found the only alternative I could think of, but it appears that you've been living in a cocoon for far too long to realise that there is an outside world there, that if viewed without pink spectacles, is cruel and selfish and hell for prudes and a wretched innocent like you.'

She looked up then, still reeling from the shock of what he just said, and there was fury staring out of her eyes, where a moment ago love had been shining brilliantly.

'Have I ever told you that you are abominable?'

He appeared to be quite unmoved by such a display of righteous anger. His lips curved into a disparaging smile as he said mockingly:

'That's about the only adjective describing me that had never occurred to you before,' he mocked again, 'an apt description, though, I must admit.'

Furiously she tried to move past him, but a hand shot out and long, sinewy fingers curled round her upper arms and pulling her to a hard, masculine frame; the contact already giving trouble to her breathing.

'Trying to overpower me with your strength?' she accused him with barely suppressed anger. His grip on her arms became a degree fiercer.

'You're not struggling, Delilah,' he reminded her in a soft, mocking tone, his hands suddenly gripping her even more fiercely.

'Oh, leave me alone!' she gasped, as his mouth closed over hers, and subjecting her to a raid of lips that she found sensuously exciting despite the fact that she was angry with him for behaving in such an abominable fashion.

After much struggling, however, her arms involuntarily slid round his neck and she experienced an odd thrill when she sensed the tip of her breasts hardening upon making contact with his bared chest. His kisses had become sensuous in quality and turned her head a little tipsy. Her eyes closed of their own accord. She then started giving him the kind of response that his lips and hands were commanding of her by way of subtle seduction. With smooth expertise, he was arousing her entire being; her nerves of late becoming extremely sensitive to his proximity and the touch of him.

Suddenly she did not know what came over her, for she literally pushed him away from her with angry distaste, her eyes brimming with tears. He did not attempt to take her back again in his arms, and instead, he narrowed his eyes speculatively, his lips tightly compressed as his eyes moved over her with icy contempt. Only, she in her rage was blind to everything.

'How low can you stoop?' she flung at him in a low, furious voice, 'You know very well that you are messing around with my vulnerability. What... what do you hope to achieve from all this?' she whispered fiercely.

His hands were crossed. The blue of his eyes had turned deeper blue with hidden depths shooting misty emotions to the surface which even then seemed unfathomable and vaguely disconcerting.

'There,' she accused him pointedly, 'you can't even answer for want of a rational reply, though your every action is motivated by an urge to torment.'

'Your baseless comments hardly merit an answer, and I'm not going to enter into explanations of any sort. You can damn well think what you please. By the way, you certainly know how to dampen my spirits. Looking for ulterior motives, are you?' he mocked gently, his smile infuriating.

His mind seconds after that seemed preoccupied, but the words delivered had been curt and almost cutting, and the volcanic expression that came to Delilah's face did not quite register. Consequently, he was unprepared for the hard kick that was delivered on his shin with true force, rendering him momentarily unprepared, and it was only with natural agility and a quick reflex did he prevent himself from falling headlong on the floor.

There was a queer expression on his dark, handsome face as his eyes moved over her only to linger deliberately on her heaving breasts; its rise and fall being acutely measured, and he could tell why this was so. The young woman was obviously disturbed, judging by the apprehensive tumult of her uneven heartbeats. Then when she was not looking, he caught her around the waist and roughly pulled her to his chest, his eyes narrowing to slits as she attempted to pull away from him. His grip became unbearably cruel and she couldn't suppress the gasp of pain and the tears coursing down her cheeks, unchecked.

His breath was warm on her neck as he put his lips to her ear that burnt from the light touch of his. He murmured in a fierce undertone:

'You kicked me, but I will do better. Instead, I have in mind something more effective that will do perfectly for a penalty device.' Then he was dragging her struggling figure to a large, polished wooden table upon which he nonchalantly rested his leg. With a forceful swiftness, he put her over his lap and his hand came down sharply over her soft rear.

But, before he could subject her to further humiliation amid angry protests and outrageous shouts coming from her quivering mouth, Selena had entered the room. She stopped short in her tracks when her eyes caught sight of Delilah receiving a sound beating on her rear. At last, she found her voice that held mild censure, but her eyes carried more than that. There was now arrogant indignation reflected in her eyes.

'Dominic, you will stop that at once!' she said with an air of command and cool authority.

At the sight of Selena, Dominic had released Delilah who forgetting the offence inflicted on her was now watching her mother with a shocked expression on her face, which gradually turned to a mixture of love and gratitude towards her. Selena had perhaps for the first time come to her rescue when she was being so heartlessly subjected to humiliation, and that too at her age. It was unthinkable!

Dominic had in that moment, extracted the cigarette packet from his pocket, and coolly choosing one, he calmly put it between his lips. Thereafter, he lit it with his lighter with some deliberation. Selena watched him with a puzzled air of a parent who is not able to comprehend the strange behaviour of her beloved son, although her voice still sounded cool and composed when she said:

'Apparently, you had forgotten that Delilah is now no longer a child to be spanked so. She is now a young lady and should be treated like one. I hope that is clear.'

Dominic met Selena's eyes through a haze of blue smoke. Slowly he turned his gaze to Delilah, his smile dry and mocking.

'If that's true that she is indeed a lady, then I will most certainly apologise, but how was I supposed to know that it is merely an act of grace and utter femininity for young ladies to go round kicking people, or else I wouldn't have retaliated the way I did,' he said smoothly, his smile sardonic.

Delilah gave him a murderous look and stalked out of the room. After she had left, Selena found herself smiling amusedly to herself.

'It appears that Delilah hasn't changed completely as I had feared. She seemed so lost and has been looking it for the past few days. I'm glad, though, that she has reverted to her old self again. A relief I'd say, so much more preferable to looking like a tombstone,' she reflected almost to herself.

Dominic grinned wryly; his eyes were shaded with mild disbelief.

'Such a baffling statement coming from you, Mother, has shocked me.' He looked anything but shocked.

Selena smiled faintly, and taking a chair opposite the fireplace she subsided into it. She then stared at the fire thoughtfully.

'I thought you were shock-proof, Dominic.'

'That's a possibility,' he shrugged carelessly, 'but I wish to God that young lady wouldn't constantly be on the defensive with me. It is then a sure way of instigating me.' He then went out, leaving behind Selena with sufficient food for thought. Much after, her contemplation persisted over what Dominic had just then said. Gradually she was beginning to see light, and a smile began to form on her lips.

CHAPTER 8

Bertha lifted her eyes and looked straight into a pair of handsome jet-black eyes that were staring back at her with a warmth that was rich in intensity. Then she was in her father's arms where she knew she rightly belonged.

'My daughter, my little Bertha...'

She looked up from his chest where her head had been resting a while ago. He bent to kiss her tear-stained cheeks and shining eyes that were looking up at him with mute admiration. She knew she was home, at last.

Delilah shook hands with her uncle and then Selena followed, shaking hands with her brother-in-law who so happened to be her husband's brother. What a coincidence! She was also privately shocked at the sight of a man who strongly resembled her husband, and was in fact of the same height and build, only the smile was different. It was open and friendly. Sampson had a kind of smile that was capable of sending jitters down a woman's spine, so like his son's.

The two sisters: Selena and Marian soon embraced each other warmly, and then Marian was gently pulling Delilah close to her side and planting a tender kiss on her cheek.

'Sweetheart, you have grown into an attractive adult. One would never tire of watching you,' Marian complimented genuinely; her smile warm and captivating. Then very slowly her enchanting mouth formed into question, 'How is it Dominic hasn't come along with you all?' she said, and her husband was the only one who did not manifest any kind of astonishment, at least it wasn't obvious.

Instead, he appeared to be quite unconcerned with what was being said by his beautiful wife. His smile was confident and the look in his eyes slightly indulgent and even perhaps a trifle amused, but he kept silent.

'He had to attend to some work at the estate, so he couldn't come, but I wasn't aware that you know him,' Selena put in softly, but she looked as always; calm and poised, although, she lacked the perception to understand that something could have been amiss between Dominic and Marian.

'Hmm, I understand that he works himself too hard,' Marian responded in the same calm voice.

Selena nodded.

'It's an understatement. It appears you know Dominic very intimately,' Selena finally spoke, but unsuspectingly.

Marian's mouth curved into a tantalising smile.

'You can say that again.'

And it was apparent from Selena's blank expression that she did not quite comprehend the subtle implication behind those words.

Finally, they all got inside the car and drove homewards. But on their journey home, Delilah invariably watched her aunt with a mixture of curiosity and perturbation. She thought about Marian's insinuating smile, and those words uttered that had carried far deeper meaning. What could it all be meaning? She pursed her lips, her frown deepening even as her mind came to a conclusion which was so perilously close to the truth.

The atmosphere, when they finally reached home was loaded with electric tension, and its awareness was felt very strongly by each and everybody present there.

All seemed affected by it. The tension in the air intensified once Sampson stepped into the entrance hall upon hearing the sound of the crunch of car wheels. In an ordinary but immaculate suit he looked charming and extremely debonair. He was prepared for the sudden return of the prodigal brother who was now married to his wife's sister; the golden beauty as he had imagined her to be. His incredibly blue eyes moved slowly, indolently over his brother's handsome form. Yes, he had to admit it, his brother excelled in extraordinary good looks. His smile fond, but those eyes giving nothing of his latent feelings away. Then for just a second more, Sampson's eyes rested on his brother's wife who was looking him over with cool appraisal, as though summing him up. Finally, she broke the uneasy silence.

'So, at last we meet, Sampson,' she stepped forward, and so did he, meet her half-way. Their proffered hands came into contact; the gesture was instantaneously warm and friendly.

'It was a long wait, but worthwhile, I must confess,' he said with a faintly teasing gleam entering his eyes, and his mouth slowly shaping into an incredibly attractive smile.

Selena came forward; a lazy smile tugging at the corner of her softly beautiful mouth.

'A family get-together I think calls for a celebration. What do you say, Sampson?' Selena's gentle fingers curled affectionately around Sampson's elbow. The smile that he threw at his lovely wife was answer enough.

The girls drifted further into the room and watched their parents with silent adoration.

'Sampson,' a hesitant pause and then Joseph continued, 'I heard you are not keeping well,' the remark carried deep concern.

'Nothing to worry about really,' Sampson stated evasively, his smile slow and genuinely warm. 'I suggest we move into the family room. A nice cool drink is what we all need. Come.'

Meanwhile, Delilah was finding it difficult to move her gaze away from her aunt. Apparently, Marian appeared unaware of the speculative rather complimentary appraisal of her presence. On the other hand, Delilah thought, why had Marian sounded so anxious to meet Dominic at the station? And upon finding him absent from their midst she had evidently looked disappointed. Delilah decided, that perhaps she was being too hasty in her judgement of the odd situation, she had reminded herself firmly, yet the thought persisted. Could it be... no, it couldn't be possible!

'Delilah, please see if Nelly is hovering around somewhere in the kitchen. Tell her she is required here immediately,' said Selena.

Delilah cut short her train of thoughts; wild thoughts they were, though not totally unfounded, but how was she to know that in such a short time?

She quickly left the room, her mind still probing even deeper into the thoughts that stubbornly persisted, and her peace of mind soon deserting her. Upon being told to serve the guests, Nelly had left the kitchen to enter the family-room.

Bertha still occupied the family-room with the rest of the members of the family. She wondered vaguely where Delilah had disappeared to, but not wishing to keep tabs on her friend's reasons for leaving the room, she kept her counsel. Although anxiety was strongly felt by her, she knew if she were to go looking for Delilah, then her action might be wrongly interpreted.

Upon returning in their midst, Delilah stood gazing out of the window facing the garden. She appeared to be deep in thoughts, yet going unnoticed by all. She had then moved restlessly away from their midst, to the room adjacent to the family-room. The evening was unbearably warm. Languidly, she stretched her hands above her head and letting them remain there for a while, only this time her languorous movements did not go unnoticed.

The sound of brisk, steady footsteps was deadened by the thickly carpeted floor as they drew further into the room where Delilah was paused by the window-side, quite preoccupied. Her back was now facing Dominic even as he drew nearer. She was not aware of his presence, though.

'Just what is so interesting about the view outside?' the deep, sardonic voice broke into her thoughts, startling her out of her reverie. But she did not immediately turn around; her mind numbed for a moment.

'When did you return?' she asked in a soft undertone. Her fingers clenched to her sides she continued to speak with forced calm. 'Aunt Marian was asking for you. She is in the family room with the rest of the family,' she stated coolly, and waiting with bated breath; anxiety spreading in her system like wild flames scorching her. It was further enhanced by a queer kind of anticipation she couldn't for the life of her understand.

'So?' he countered after a second's silence.

'Well,' she finally turned to face him, 'wouldn't you like to meet her? She seems anxious enough to... meet you.' A naked fury reflected in her eyes, but that which had still not been expressed verbally.

'And so?' he asked in a brief rejoinder, the tone sounding vaguely discomfiting. He was watching her very closely; a steady gaze and disturbingly direct.

'I had the impression you'd rush to her side the moment she'd step inside the house.' Her breathing had turned uneven, and her fingers clenched and unclenched in a bid to control the rising temper.

Dominic's eyes rested momentarily on the movements of her fingers and once again settled on her face that now revealed raw emotions and wordless fury. Then he smiled; a smile of lazy indulgence.

'I did not exactly rush to her side as you described it, but I did meet the lady. Now, I would like to know what you are doing here all alone while the others have collected in the family room,' he added, and folding his hands across his chest, he observed her from beneath hooded eyes. At that moment he looked disturbingly attractive, and Delilah could have hated him for looking the way he did.

Delilah lowered her eyes before that intense scrutiny.

'Why did you come looking for me?' she asked evasively.

His brows were knitted and his lips were pursed, as he continued watching her.

'I think you had better come right out with what is in your mind. It's apparent that whatever it is, is eating you up from inside,' he said with some irritation.

She shot him an upward glance, her eyes coldly enquiring.

'What... what exactly is your relationship with... Aunt Marian?'

'Should there be something between us?' he shot back in a tight voice.

'What is she to you?' she demanded fiercely, her eyes filling up with tears of anger and helpless frustration. 'She has grown even more beautiful with advancing age,' she added deliberately, and looking for an answering response in his eyes.

'Stop hurling questions at me! I don't take such crap from anybody, you understand?' he snapped furiously, but there was also an undercurrent in his voice that she failed to sense.

'I'm not anybody, I'll have you know that, and... and I have a right to know,' she whispered fiercely.

'Just because I happened to have made love to you once or twice, you think you have the right to know about my personal life? Grow up, Delilah. And stop annoying me,' he uttered with careless disdain.

'It may be your custom to kiss and make love to women and dismissing it as insignificant, but to me, it carries a far deeper meaning, and therefore, it maddens me if you should even look at another woman. I happen to possess a strong sense of identity, and I would hate to share you with any other woman... however beautiful, inclusive of Aunt Marian. Do you get the picture? I refuse to be toyed with, Dominic,' she said in a firm undertone and looked at him with a disturbing directness.

'Toyed with? What nonsense are you talking?' he demanded quietly.

'You know very well what I mean and now let's have the truth,' she flared up suddenly and looked primitively beautiful in the moment of unrestrained fury that she did not attempt to suppress. It was obvious that she was extremely worked up, but so was he, though not too obvious. 'You... you think you can treat me any way you like and the ugly truth stands before me without any warning; the fact that you are involved with... my own aunt. Now that is hardly a pleasant discovery,' she jeered softly, 'Why are you so quiet? Why aren't you saying something?' she said in a fierce tone, her eyes never leaving his sight.

'I rather not dispute over it. It would be pointless. And it certainly wouldn't serve its purpose, so forget it,' he stated briefly, almost curtly, and turned sideways to light his cigarette with a nonchalance of an antagonist.

'That still does not answer all my questions,' she said in a voice that carried violence and which did not go unnoticed by Dominic.

'The reasons are insufficient and the allegations uncalled for. Now, simmer down, will you? I had better go now. Are you coming? They will all be anxious if we don't join them soon,' he said absently, and carelessly flicked the ashes of his cigarette unheedingly over the richly-carpeted floor.

She did not move. The stare that she accorded to him was cold and direct.

'Is she just as fascinating in bed as she is to look at?' she hurled at him tonelessly. She continued to look at him unflinchingly. And she stood there before him and looking bewitchingly beautiful with sparks shooting from such luminous eyes.

He moved then slowly almost casually, his eyes narrow slits of ice. There was a sadist in him that Delilah had not yet encountered.

'I'm not easily riled, Delilah, for which you can thank your lucky stars,' his voice, though soft, carried a latent hardness that went unnoticed.

'A man of iron control,' she commented scathingly.

He glanced in her direction with some suspicion. At that instant, he looked uncompromising.

'What exactly is it that you are angling for? You're playing a dangerous game with me, Delilah, I'll have you know that. So be warned,' his voice too soft for any comfort.

'I have already put forth the question, and I never repeat myself, Dominic. I would like you to shed some light on the matter under discussion. Clear my confusion if you can... please, Dominic.' Her expression softened momentarily.

He flexed the muscles of his shoulders, and expelled an inaudible sigh, his own expression giving nothing of his feelings away.

'All right... if it's of any consolation to you. Marian and I are more than friends. We have in the past shared certain intimacies that had brought us very close to each other. It has been a fine and a most satisfying relationship, but far too delicate and intricate a subject which if discussed elaborately would be doing it a dishonour. And a lady's reputation too would be severely damaged, especially if it is someone of Marian's calibre; an outstanding woman, yet. So please don't press me any further to utter things I might later regret, not that I cannot restrain myself,' he added quietly. 'You may call it purely accidental with regard to our... relationship, but believe me when I say it wasn't planned or deliberate. And I have no regrets. She is a wonderful being and her independent nature extremely exemplary, to say the least. And now, any more questions?' his voice for once sounded coldly distant.

'Perhaps my pattern of thinking is different, and that is reason enough why I find it difficult to accept the fact that two friends can also share out of mutual consent a relationship which I understand involves the union of mind and body,' she said in a voice unlike hers, like she were speaking from a completely different perspective, unknown even to her, but just as soon she descended to reality. Her tone when she spoke; mildly cutting, 'But you could have come out straight with it and said that you were lovers. Practising circumspection? Hmm, perhaps you thought I was too naive to understand what you were indirectly implying...'

'That will be enough,' his voice arctic, but the blue of his eyes was glinting dangerously as he continued in the same tone, 'The family is waiting for you. Don't be too long.' And he turned on his heel and strode out of the room, leaving the door ajar...

'Your impatience to return to that room is far too obvious. A little bit of subtlety wouldn't harm you, you know,' she called out after him, but he was gone.

She sought the support of the chair standing nearby, and dazedly subsided into it. She felt her body shaking tremulously and consumed by a fierce emotion that she now knew to be jealousy: a surging feeling sweeping through her nervous system like the accelerated flames of the fire. And it was then she discovered with a startling impact that she was lost to Dominic completely, and irrevocably.

Her treacherous heart was pounding crazily, and she couldn't repress the raid of every part of her being by the persistent assault of deep regret and a sense of utter mortification. The seeds of love had been sown ages ago. Love had reached its peak. And she knew with some misgiving that there was no turning back now.

Slowly she rose from the chair. Her mind was made up about something. She then experienced a spread of serenity. She smiled as she walked out of the room; a secretive smile.

When she entered the family room, she assumed a cheerful approach that fooled all but Dominic who was keenly watching her with an enigmatic look in his eyes. He didn't trust her current mood, not after being exposed to the liberal display of her capricious temperament. It was then when their eyes met, and what he saw in her eyes made him take a sharp, indrawn breath.

For perhaps the first time he received a mental and physical jolt. He shook himself mentally. It was not conceivable and yet it was very clear. Delilah loved him; loved him with an intensity that was vividly disconcerting, and almost intimidating. Amidst the pleasant chatter, both their silence seemed incongruous, though no one appeared to have noticed the oddity perhaps more so the graveness of the situation that only Dominic and Delilah were unexpectedly caught up in.

Delilah was the first one to come down to reality. She moved but found her path being blocked by Dominic. His fingers curled around her elbow as he whispered in a hoarse voice, 'let's get out of here!'

Once they were out of everyone's hearing, he pulled her to him, his expression disturbed and strained.

'It is crazy! I mean the whole idea is absolutely crazy!' he exclaimed and watched her wonderingly, his fingers unconsciously biting into the tender flesh of her upper arms.

'Inevitable is the word,' she stated calmly. 'You venture so close and expect a woman to feel indifferent, perhaps? She has to be practised then and strictly professional to dismiss such intimate moments with a man as purely incidental. And I'm hardly that, I think,' she said suavely.

'I... for God's sake...I don't understand...I mean, how could you have allowed such a thing to happen?' he muttered fiercely, and without realising, his fingers had circled around her throat, his grasp tightened as alien feelings inside him grew erotic until he could not bear its fierce pressure on his mind and being. And before long, he had buried his face against the long, slender column of her throat; an inexplicable shudder going through him.

Delilah gasped at that contact in a moment of unrestrained emotion that they were both experiencing, but found it hard to verbalise. It was all too much for the both of them, and unconsciously they took shelter in mouthing unnecessary words to mask their initial discomfort.

'These things just happen. You can't prevent it from...'

'Quiet! Now just kiss me and hard!' he commanded in a not quite composed voice.

'Where? Where do you want me to kiss you?' she whispered into his ear huskily, while her arms went around his neck, drawing herself closer to his hard length. 'Tell me, Dominic, where should I start from?'

His body went taut as he pulled away from her proximity. Tilting her chin, he gazed intently into her eyes that were partly closed in a moment of unbridled ecstasy, her body as always on fire for him.

'You are one devil of a woman. Feel me with your body, and, my love, you'll know exactly where and how to start...' he bent to touch her arched throat with his lips.

'Oh, Dominic, I want to feel you, love you... not wanting to spare an inch of you. May I? Say if I may!' She cried as if in pain, tears gathering in her eyes as her hands struggled to make contact with the private channels of his anatomy. 'Oh, Dominic...' she again cried in pain and part ecstasy, her voice breaking suddenly, 'You...you can't... know how much I want you... how much I adore you!' and convulsively she broke into a flood of tears, burying her head in the curve of his shoulder.

'Are you a woman or dynamite!' he fiercely caught her to him and a bit more fiercely, his eyes growing a shade darker now. 'For heaven's sake... this... this is utter madness! I'm beginning to lose all control, Delilah. Let go before... God! Tell me, you little fool! Tell me! Can't you feel my crazy urge for you?'

'Take me, Dominic... make me feel wanted and ... loved. Now... please...' her tears, though silent were incessant, and her quivering mouth slowly covered the width and length of his bared chest in a tenderly passionate kiss while she allowed her hand to feel the hardness of him, her fingers not quite steady yet with gradual precision, arousing his latent passions to screaming heights. 'This... this is not enough...' she moaned, 'Oh, Dominic, can't you understand? I have reached you, oh, how can you hold back?' she cried frustratedly and pummelled his chest, but he pulled those hands away and brought them back to where they had a moment ago settled, his eyes now shutting in a frenzy never before experienced with another woman.

'My control, darling, is already ebbing away,' he managed after letting out a groan indicative of restrained anguish combined with an exalted ecstasy that he was soon losing grip on.

His fingers still steady, languorously pushed aside the dress off her fair, slender shoulders and feeling its silken texture; the gesture caressing and disturbingly explorative while they slowly began to journey over her front and finally settled over the fullness of her breasts that were palpitating beneath his probing touch. The impact had proved undeniably heady as periodical gasps escaped her lovely, soft lips.

'You respond so beautifully, my sweet... every part of you,' he drawled, himself disturbed. 'I don't think I could withdraw now, even if I tried,' he said huskily, his thighs and then the hardness of his knees coming into contact with the extreme tumult pulsating erratically at the base of her moistened body; the part he knew was extremely sensitive to his touch, and he couldn't resist feeling her tantalising sensitivity with gentle, probing fingers that continued its journey in a never-ending probe, to ecstatic heights.

He felt her arch her body in silent ecstasy, just as her mouth parted a little to expel a soundless gasp. As the movements of his fingers became a degree faster... more probing, she murmured between a soft intake of uneven breathing, 'let go, Dominic. I... I feel weak and faint... I... I think. I'm... oh, Dominic!' She moaned, finding such exhilaration unbearable yet irresistible.

But not to be dissuaded he continued, his mouth gentler and more soothing and succeeding in exciting yet calming her erratic nerves. She was beginning to feel a strange languor, not having experienced anything like this before and her untried senses gradually entered into oblivion. She lay across him only partly appeased, but for those few blessed moments, she was lost to passions unrivalled.

He gazed down tenderly at her sweet countenance and bent to feel her now soft, swollen lips with his own. With calmness, he accepted the fact that this had just not been a pure desire for flesh, but something more tangible, more meaningful. Yes, and he could now call it love, for plain desire, would have been bearable, but this drive for fulfilment had been so perfectly matched and synchronised. And besides, all that he had just then experienced had even for him been so much more overpowering. The effects of their love act still persisted, although the urge had cooled down a little, though not altogether.

It had been a dynamic experience, although exhausting. He for once experienced emotional fatigue and a trifle drained out, but grateful for this moment of respite.

He was certain he would have lost all sense of time and propriety, forgetting the place and uncompromising situation they had both been in, were it not for their family gathered in the adjacent room. He sighed, his eyes growing heavy with sleep; sweet drowsiness. The control he had exercised over his emotions had helped, for he could imagine the consequence they would have been subjected to, had anybody witnessed the erotic scene.

Fighting drowsiness dulling his senses, he stretched her form with some effort on the settee, and making her posture as comfortable as he could, then moving to a chair opposite, he subsided into it, shutting his eyes relievedly. Before he drifted into a temporary sleep mode, sudden thoughts of Dean crept into his mind, but thankfully sleep and mental exhaustion defeated his resolution to give that particular issue a bit more careful thought.

Yes, Dean would have to be dealt with. He wasn't going to be let off so easily. Delilah, the sweet enchantress was his and he would allow no one and nothing to alter the fact. She was his... his... his, but heavy sleep attacked his revelations and brought them to a standstill.

Much after, Delilah stirred and the first thing she saw was Dominic's sleeping posture reclined in the chair, his dark head resting against one broad shoulder, his own. She quickly moved to his side and lifted his head in her hands, cradling it with loving care while her mouth planted a gentle kiss on his wide, intelligent forehead.

'That you, Delilah?' he said drowsily, his hands reaching out for her.

She chuckled softly, moving out of his reach, her smile provocative.

'A cup of tea might revive you. Would you like me to prepare it for you?'

Extending one hand he pulled her over his lap, now fully awake.

'To hell with tea!' he brought her closer to him and his mouth once again captured hers in a passionate kiss, more possessively this time.

'Surprising,' he remarked absently, 'I still don't see anyone around. The discussion must be pretty enthralling to keep them all glued up in that confounded room. Now, why are you so fidgety?' his hand absently caressing her tiny feet and rather fondly.

'Fifteen minutes or so, is not a very long time, surely?' she watched him tenderly while her fingers began to fondly ruffle his crown of luxurious hair.

'Ah, do that some more, my sweetest. I like it.'

'Hmm, I'd like to do a great deal more,' her eyes were twinkling merrily.

'So would I. Want me to prove it?'

She hastily withdrew from his side, her eyes no longer laughing.

'What's the matter?' he frowned; his expression sombre.

She avoided his sharp scrutiny, her back facing him.

'Dominic, tell me something truthfully,' she paused for a second before continuing, 'do you feel the same way as I do or is it the case of mere flirtation, as a sound substitute for someone who is quite out of your reach now that she legally belongs to someone else?' she enquired sharply, her eyes narrowing suspiciously.

'No legal arrangement would stop me from taking what I believe only I have a right to, but let's just say that the beautiful lady has returned to where she actually belongs, and, therefore, my intrusion would hardly be a wise move, and besides, it is not my custom to take into my possession what I know was never mine.'

'Sounds fair enough, but I still don't know why I have these... these nagging thoughts,' she said in a soft whisper, her face averted and looking small and lost.

He appeared to be studying her stiff back very intently. Suddenly his eyes lit up with dry amusement.

'Nagging thoughts, did you say? Nagging suspicions more likely, sweetest, but quite baseless really,' he smiled caustically, 'and what was that again, flirting with you, substituting you for another woman's charms is what you meant, hmm? That is some opinion you have formed of me, charging me with the exploitation of your... tender feelings, only more explicitly put, I think,' his tone now hard and bitterness had crept in his voice; his smile humourless.

She turned then, nodding her head in vehement denial.

'For Christ's sakes, it is not my opinion that you could be this way. I... I merely asked you a question to which I'd like a straight answer. I'd... well, I'd in fact like you to clear my doubts if any.'

'If any? My God! You're full of doubts. What next?' he laughed harshly.

'What kind of an answer is that, pray?' she returned haughtily, her anger slowly surfacing.

He then slanted a cynical glance in her direction.

'Asking me to clear your doubts for you?' his smile contemptuous. 'You're blind and ignorant if you claim to have any doubts about my sincerity,' he spoke briefly almost in an impersonal tone that carried a close to steely dismissal.

Sensing his cool withdrawal, she felt her heart sinking. Weighing down with regret, she rushed to his side in a few, quick steps and looked up at him beseechingly, her beautiful eyes brimming with tears.

'Oh, sweet darling. Pray... forgive me for doubting you like that. Words uttered prematurely can, I know, leave their impact on a troubled mind. Forgive me...' she put her arms around his waist, resting her head against his chest and crying between irrepressible gulps, her throat contracted and her body shaking convulsively as she reiterated the apology with self-abasement.

When all of a sudden Dominic folded her into his arms, she found it all the more difficult to check the flow of tears. His apparent tenderness and gentility it appeared had all the more power to upset her extremely vulnerable disposition.

'Emotional... altogether too emotional, I must say. Where do you find the space to store up all that inside the delicate, small you, hmm?' then shaking his head slightly, he continued with a fondly amused smile, 'I find it difficult to coax you into a better temper. Here,' he offered her a fresh piece of linen, 'Now dry up those tears and let's have a smile.'

'But I don't feel like it at the moment,' she muttered, her voice small and tearful.

'Then perhaps you'd like me to kiss you or better still... you kiss me.'

His smile was irresistible and Delilah thought that he had never before looked more attractive, and suddenly she too broke into an engaging smile.

'Oh, Dominic!' she laughed, almost against her will as she tip-toed to reach his lips with hers; his lips inviting shy kisses with a tantalising grace.

'Now then, before they should come looking for us, I think we ought to return to them. What do you say, my love?'

She nodded in agreement, but disturbing thoughts of Marian still persisted, completely disorganising her mental parity once again. Although, somehow with great difficulty she managed to retain her surface composure so as to not destroy the promise of such a cleaner understanding of each other.

The idea of Dominic and Marian being lovers somehow did not seem feasible to Delilah, not that the acceptance of facts did not come easily to her. She was basically a realist and accepting of facts, however painful, came naturally to her. Then why did this particular fact seem like some unimaginable nightmare she wanted to escape from?

She would have dearly loved to obliterate the thoughts of yesterday and concentrate instead on the promising future, but did the future really hold for her bright prospects or would it prove just as tenaciously oblique as yesterday? It was difficult to tell, while she knew destiny was quietly deciding her future. Her smile was disappointingly perfunctory as she unconsciously shifted away from Dominic's side, not realising that he was not unaware of what was troubling her mind. He, on the other hand, preferred to keep his counsel for that moment at least, and for similar reasons as hers.

Upon reaching the family room they were met in the doorway by the butler.

'Miss Redford, a gentleman by the name of Fobster was here. He has left behind a note for you and a message.' He handed over a sealed envelope which Delilah accepted with unsteady fingers. She could feel Dominic's eyes burning through her back like laser beams.

'Thank you, Dennis.'

'And what was the message to be conveyed, dear fellow?' Dominic intervened in a voice that was far too quiet for comfort.

Delilah directed him a wide, troubled look, but Dominic was looking straight at the butler who appeared not to be aware of the tension permeating the atmosphere.

'Mr. Fobster said he would be calling up Miss Redford tomorrow evening with regard to the letter to be delivered to Ma'am here.'

Silence ensued after which Dominic spoke in a brisk, abrupt tone. 'That will be all, Dennis.'

The moment seemed charged with electricity. Delilah began to feel apprehensive of the consequences that might follow. At that moment she wanted to be miles away from Dominic. The silence was beginning to be interminable. His back seemed so stiff and uncompromising, and suddenly when she sensed him moving, she realised with dismay that her legs were threatening to give way under her weight, and the envelope was slipping from her fingers to the floor.

A strange sort of weakness was engulfing all else along with the power of resistance, entirely superseding her conscious state. When arms went around her, she endeavoured against her failing will to assess the reason for that sudden gesture. The foreboding look was slowly being replaced by an expression that denoted concern and perhaps even something akin to disappointment written in the deep blue of his eyes which she found unfathomable. A second after, she lost consciousness.

***

It was only much later did Dominic discover that Delilah was suffering from a temporary break of nerves. Everything was happening at a stretch and getting harder yet to place in their correct perspective. With a sigh, Dominic had returned to the family room and had found everybody in the middle of some discussion that he had no inkling of. Sampson looked his way and Dominic knew what was coming.

'Where is Delilah?'

'She is in her room,' he stated briefly, lighting his cigarette.

'And what is she doing there all alone, might I ask?' he enquired without any preamble.

'You must surely be knowing what's the matter with her,' Selena spoke for the first time, her voice composed, but the expression in her eyes belied her composure. There had been the faintest of concern entering her voice, yet managing to retain her cool.

He shrugged carelessly, pretending indifference while the rest watched on with open concern staring out of their eyes.

'Mother, you had better go up to her,' he suggested after a slight pause.

Instantaneously she excused herself from their midst to hasten to her daughter's room. Sampson stood up to follow his wife when Dominic requested him to stay behind, as he had much to discuss with him; matters pertaining to some business settlement. Moreover, a contract which he was to sign subsequently after having met with his approval. And, though, for some more time, Sampson's mind was diverted to business matters, it was troubled about Delilah's unexpected disappearance from their midst. Only at that moment, whatever Dominic was painstakingly imparting to him seemed a great deal more important.

Marian and Joseph appeared to be involved in an argument, and presumably, it was Joseph who appeared to have won the argument, for his smile that he exchanged with Bertha sitting at his feet was one of amusement and faint triumph.

Marian seemed not to mind their exchange of conspiratorial smiles. She, on the contrary, appeared to be thoroughly relaxed and content.

'Papa, I would like you to meet Jarrod,' Bertha suggested gently and watched him adoringly.

'The man you have decided to marry?' he asked with an indulgent smile.

'Yes,' she nodded, her eyes all the time resting adoringly on her father who in turn was watching her with a similar expression in his eyes, though the smile of humour still persisted.

'You must tell me more about him before I finally meet him in person, but I must confess the little that your mother has told me is sufficient to double up my approval.'

'Hmm, there isn't much to tell, but I'd like to tell you the little that there is,' Bertha put in contemplatively.

'Well, go ahead then, dear,' he smiled serenely at her, his hand lovingly stroking her head.

Marian allowed herself to gaze at Dominic, and a smile of tender reminiscence took slow form on her lips. Minutes after, her eyes once again were reverted to her husband and daughter and settled there upon them with unspoken love and tenderness.

Upstairs in Delilah's room, Selena was seated by the side of Delilah's sleeping form, her hands moving affectionately over Delilah's forehead and flushed cheeks, as tears of remorse and regret poured unheedingly down her cheeks. She did not bother to wipe them away.

'Delilah,' she called out softly, bending towards her lying posture, her eyes shaded with pain as she noticed her pallor for the first time.

She had observed that Delilah's face now looked pale and cheeks sunken. There were dark circles around her eyes, and the mouth seemed to be drooping even in repose like an unattended flower only meant to blossom. Delilah was ill, she could see, and her heart wept for her daughter. Impulsively, and with her heart brimming with love, she lifted her daughter's head to her breast and cried as she had never cried before.

Later when the doctor was summoned, he had promptly diagnosed a slight bout of nerves and added that it could also be a case of hypertension yet not fully matured. The condition was not serious he proclaimed, but lots of attention and care would have to be looked into, as matters could very easily take a critical turn.

The next morning when Delilah awoke, she found the sealed envelope lying next to her pillow, unopened. Almost instantly she could tell that it was not tampered with, and she also knew who could have put it there. It had to be no one but Dominic. She was feeling considerably better. The headache had subsided. Gingerly, she reached for Dean's letter, slit it open and started reading its contents.

The contents of the letter addressed to her were not too pleasing to Delilah, judging by her tight expression.

***

That evening when Dean had arrived there, he was ushered straight to Delilah's room by a very gracious Selena, but who did not in any way evince surprise, courtesy demanding that she pretend ignorance. When

Selena left them alone, Dean couldn't hold back the exclamation:

'My goodness!' he went to her bedside and tilted her chin, his expression worried.

'You look thin and awfully weak. I wonder if something is being done about those pale cheeks,' he flicked her cheek gently.

She did not look up at him immediately, her fingers absently turning the pages of a magazine.

'Say, what's happened? You don't look too pleased to see me,' he frowned.

She looked up then, her eyes looking directly at him.

'What do you mean, you can't go on with the plan? You can't ditch me at the last moment!' she threw aside the magazine, her angry eyes fixed stonily on Dean.

Dean had a sheepish expression on his face.

'I met a girl, Delilah. I… we decided to get…' he said falteringly.

'Oh, so that's it!' Delilah smiled broadly, her expression changing to one of delight. 'I quite begin to understand your reasons, Dean, for withdrawal.'

'You do?' Dean appeared to be doubtful, and he averted his face awkwardly.

'I do. I think I will have to learn to fight my own battles. Maybe, I now realise I did the wrong thing using you as a crutch to gain my own ends,' she sighed heavily, shrugging her delicate shoulders resignedly.

'Look, Delilah, for how long can a woman fight such... such a never-ending battle? I mean... well, nothing seems to affect the man. He can't be sufficiently interested, as I have sensed in him no pangs of jealousy. Give up, Delilah,' he said gently.

'Never!' she blazed, a determined look entering into those eyes that shone like polished steel. 'I'll have you know that I'm no weakling and for me to strike a defeatist attitude would be unthinkable. I'll fight for his love even if it should take me a lifetime,' she said determinedly, then with more gentility, 'you can't imagine what this means to me, Dean. If I don't put up a good fight now, then I would feel that I had never tried hard enough. It's that way with me. But...' she threw him a quick smile, 'you need not worry about me. I am well able to take care of myself. By the way,' she added as an afterthought. 'Who is this young woman who has apparently caught your interest? Anyone I know?'

'Her name is Shelly Dantich. No, you do not know her.'

'I'm glad for you, Dean... really glad.'

After he had left, she started to think in earnest about the future that was looking so bleak somehow. But she also knew that her fighting spirit would never die. It was so much an integral part of her. When someone knocked on the door, she called out absently for that person to enter, her thoughts faraway.

A tall figure framed the doorway, watchful eyes resting indolently on the open letter lying on the rug below and crumpled up into an untidy ball. Delilah strongly aware of Dominic's presence noticed it too, and hurriedly made to avert his attention.

'I feel considerably better now, Dominic. I... I thought you were already gone. Fancy you still being at home,' she laughed, but it sounded nervous, and all the time aware of his glance fixed much too casually on the discarded letter. And then he was steadily, purposefully walking towards it, and bending to retrieve it.

She held back the gasp of fright when he bent to pick up the ball of paper. Her mind tensed she waited with bated breath for him to read its contents. Slowly he looked up, fixing his gaze on her, and silently watching her expression rather speculatively.

Not able to bear the suspense, she blurted out in an uneven voice, her look one of open defiance so typical of her: 'Are you meaning to read it?' her heart was palpitating at an increasing speed.

After a stretched silence, however, he asked nonchalantly, 'Should I be reading it?'

'I have heard it is unmanneredly to read someone else's letter.' There was a cautiousness about her that he noticed almost immediately.

'Hmm, so have I.' He then hurled the ball of paper into the fireplace located in the furthest corner of the room.

And it was only then, did she begin to breathe more freely. Dominic turned sideways to stare at her, his eyes narrowed to slits.

'It is not surprising that you should feel better now. Dean's visit here must have done the trick,' he said in a clipped tone.

'A friend's visit can help a lot,' she asserted defensively.

He turned to face her fully with a fierce look, now controlling his composure.

'Don't give me that crap!' his voice had a steely quality and putting sudden fear inside her, though she was not the one to show it.

'But he is in fact my friend, Dominic,' she protested in a small voice.

'That wasn't what I was given to understand,' he stated curtly, his face set, and his expression tight and foreboding.

'I can't be blamed if you take it upon yourself to draw hasty conclusions,' she said impatiently. Her own temper was beginning to show, though she knew it was through no fault of his.

'How then would you account for his getting married the following month, if as you seem to believe we are more than friends?' she charged at him while her impulsive declaration defeating the very purpose for the farce she had planned entirely for his benefit.

Privately, her heart reached out to him. She knew she was being unfair to him, but why she was doing this, she could not even begin to understand.

His smile was unpleasant as he said by way of reply, 'That is not inconceivable.'

'Meaning?' she flung at him, her face changing colour.

'Just what you are thinking, spitfire,' he quipped back sardonically.

Her expression was contemptuous as she imperiously pointed a finger at him.

'You have a dirty mind. It is not as if you are a saint. Considering all that you and Aunt Marian have…'

'You had better stop right there.' A dangerous glint entered his eyes.

'Why?' she retaliated, 'Does it rankle?'

'I'm not prepared to listen to nonsense. Don't stain that name by messing it up with… uncultured thoughts. It is Marian that I speak of, so take care,' he bit out with some exasperation.

'Then why must you keep on about Dean and me? It can be very annoying, to say the least.'

'Truth always is, or don't you know that already?' he said quietly, his gaze steady and keenly observant.

'I don't think I'd call that the truth.' Her hand suddenly went to her head which was feeling heavy with an inexorable pain.

'Stop living a lie. You might learn of the truth then. I think you had better rest. Here,' he passed over to her a bottle, 'take these capsules regularly. It is a supply of iron,' he offered, before he turned to go, 'and don't strain your mind too much. No amount of treatment will take effect then,' he instructed quietly.

'You care?' she asked in an anxious tone.

'Care?' he appeared to be contemplating. Then nodded. 'Yes, but again, caring is different from loving,' he stated rather carelessly.

'That wasn't what I had asked!' she flung at him, her whole body shaking with rage. 'And, anyway, you need not answer. You'd think it mattered... it doesn't! Go... and give whatever you have that's yours to her. I bet she'll lap it all up. Go!' In her fury, she did not realise how close he had come to striking her.

'You had better rest now,' he advised coldly; his face expressionless.

'Is she downstairs waiting for you? My, how you must be longing to go down to her, but now that a husband has come into the picture, how difficult it must be for the both of you,' her tone was scornful as she began to laugh hysterically.

'Wild thoughts induced by a certain deplorable tendency to deliberately hurt, can in fact work against your own person. Be wise to remember that.' He walked out of the room, shutting the door behind him, and the room was suddenly struck by an alarming silence.

She felt suddenly alone as she looked around her dazedly. True, this feeling inside her was slowly destroying her. She was jealous of Marian yet she liked and admired her. And the very fact was now pricking at her sensitivity. She swallowed two capsules followed by a glass of water and she slid underneath the bedsheet, resting her cheek against the pillow, her mind active. She wanted to recuperate with much speed. There was so much that she had to do, so... much... so... and soon she fell into a dreamless slumber; an excellent device for treating restlessness, she thought before losing consciousness. When she did awake after about an hour, she sensed a hand caressing her unruly hair. She craned her neck to look up and met a pair of smiling eyes of devastating beauty.

'How do you feel now, my dear?' Marian bent to kiss the slightly feverish forehead, tenderly.

'Er, much better. Thank you.' She felt overwhelmed, seeing Marian there, so close to her, and so warmly enquiring after her health.

'Joseph was here too, to see you, but as you were asleep, he said he'd see you later,' she smiled warmly while conveying the message.

Delilah tried to arise into a sitting position, but her head still felt heavy. Marian's hand gently pulled her down again.

'Relax, Delilah. Your nerves, dear. I can actually sense the restlessness inside you, and I do believe your nerves are on edge. Relax...' she pressed the sides of Delilah's forehead with searching fingers, and succeeded in calming the upheaval in her with her soothing touch. 'Try to relax,' the equally soothing voice reiterated.

And it was then that Delilah felt inspired to confide in her aunt.

'Did you meet Dominic?' she asked, deliberately pausing before mentioning his name for effect.

She had noticed a strange light entering Marian's eyes, and then a soft laugh followed after that. But the expression soon turned grave once more as though the older woman was contemplating seriously on some matter of distinct relevance and importance.

The smile that she gave to Delilah was serenely lovely.

'I did, Delilah, but tell me what has made you so upset?' she asked ever so gently.

'Oh, nothing that would interest you,' Delilah retorted discouragingly.

Why was she behaving the way she did? It wasn't like her to use such a discouraging tone. Then why this urge to strip Marian of her cool demeanour?

'You are being very hostile.' Marian declared firmly, but her mouth was smiling, matching perfectly with the doe-like look in her eyes, almost unpretentious and portraying her vulnerability.

The woman's sincerity shook Delilah for a moment, but soon hardened up, once again throwing her a hostile look that was received with a vaguely understanding smile.

'Answer me!' she threw Marian a direct look, her gaze a shade too aggressive for comfort, although, the older woman remained unperturbed, though slightly bewildered. 'Do you love Dominic?

Marian did not appear to be taken aback. Instead, she smiled quietly as she answered Delilah soberly:

'How else would you feel towards someone who has in the past respected your need for total emotional detachment, and carried on a relationship with you, aware that what is not in his grasp belongs rightfully to another? He gains nothing, yet his understanding of your disposition puts a seal on a lasting friendship that would sustain durability for years to come.'

A new light entered Delilah's eyes as she posed a question which indicated her slowly receding apprehensive state.

'By that, can you be meaning that you've loved Uncle Joseph all along?'

'Yes,' Marian answered calmly.

'And Dominic... what about Dominic? Where does he fit into this scenario?' Delilah enquired breathlessly, a look of something close to agitation in her eyes not gone quite unnoticed.

'I love him for remaining by my side when I needed a friend the most... never demanding, always patient and attentive, ministering to my suffering health; a temporary relapse, though, but he had been present. It was like... like he had been rescuing a drowning man from himself. A man can sometimes be his own enemy, Delilah, but...'

she smiled warmly, her eyes gleaming with unspoken gratitude, 'Dominic with his support, his patience and understanding taught me to be my own best friend, instead. My observations about life then took a turn and I learned how to smile again. I began to recognise Dominic as a worthy man who had succeeded in renewing my trust in mankind.' She paused and watched her niece warmly. 'Believe me, dearest, it's an elevated feeling to learn that your grief, your suffering is understood and sentiments appreciated, and not denounced indifferently as a phase quite inconsequential altogether. And that can hurt so much more,' she had added thoughtfully, her eyes looking far into the distance.

For the first time, perhaps, Delilah felt that she loved a man of extraordinary strength of mind and purpose, with a rare capacity for human understanding, and her heart swelled with pride. She no longer experienced jealousy. She suddenly felt above such pettiness. But there were still so many more of those negative traits in her, she thought reflectively, that needed to be eliminated.

For just a moment she was too astonished to find her head resting on Marian's lap, with gentle fingers stroking her soft, unruly tresses as if savouring the sheer feel of it. And she discovered she actually liked it.

'Have you ever felt alone and rejected?' came a soft enquiry.

'Yes, Aunt Marian, but… but why do you ask? Why, has it been your experience, too?' Delilah asked bemusedly. She was slowly beginning to warm up to Marian's irresistible charm.

'Yes, that has been my experience, too, and then during such a phase, someone comes along. He lifts you from a feeling of acute despondency, making you aware of how precious your life really is, and explaining to you that in this very context lies the undeniable fact that you breathe to live and not the other way around. Also, the inclination should be to live by hope, with the hope of forever experiencing an era of perpetual contentment and even happiness sustaining infinitude. All this for self, then why to destroy self for what we live, struggle, dream, hope and grieve?' she sighed, turning sideways and in doing so presenting her exquisite profile to a rather attentive Delilah.

'Dominic made me realise life… my life in its correct perspective as to how every other individual should perceive it when his life's choices stand to be questioned by unfortunate circumstances. Dominic perhaps doesn't live by set values, but he lives his life that is measured to suit his very purpose for existence,' she went on in a state of preoccupation.

'And what is this purpose for his… existence?' Delilah intervened softly, curious to learn more about the man that meant everything to her by then.

Marian met those soft, enquiring eyes and smiled serenely.

'As I said, he believes in what he thinks; feelings and sentiments that he otherwise quite occasionally permits to be superseded by more pragmatic motivation. Hence, succeeding in leaving behind no scars from precipitous interpretations in a relationship, should certain feelings transcend all else.

I mean, the opposite party if any, can never feel deprived, as Dominic often chooses to remain detached emotionally, though not absolutely, but he makes no promises. Although, he may take and give back with equal ardour. And, quite often than not, his attitude and verbal exchanges in any situation, leave no doubt in a person's mind that he is beyond reach unless he chooses not to be,' Marian explained quietly and very patiently.

'Could this be owing to a secret inborn fear of commitments that he should mentally withdraw from involvements?' Delilah queried with mild curiosity.

'Probably not. However, it is perhaps with the view to keep misunderstandings at bay that he mostly assumes a detached attitude in relationships. And that is in fact attributed to his extreme sensitivity urging him to practice more caution; to be more careful. And that again is to his credit, don't you think?' Marian smiled warmly at her lovely niece who continued to watch her with something akin to awe.

'And isn't being over-cautious the root leading to all kinds of tensions? I do believe you said that he maintains a selfish attitude as he goes about life. That sounds contradictory,' she pointed out to her aunt.

'Hmm, being cautious and careful only with the view to avoiding misinterpretations, but not necessarily indulging in it as a habit formed, thereby, resulting in tensions like you have pointed out,' she made the clarifications, but her smile was far from discouraging. The enlightened exchange ensued with a smooth frequency, bringing to light many a revelation soon speeding Delilah to maturity. Yes, Marian was succeeding where all others had failed.

'You think he is capable of love?' Delilah asked in a small voice.

'If a man is capable of compassion and understanding; so also, is he capable of love... deep love. And Dominic as you know already is quite capable of showing compassion and understanding,' she said, then more gently, 'and yes, you must never judge a person based on his relationships with other people, Delilah. That would be a very big mistake. Particularly concerning more intimate relationships.'

'I don't understand,' Delilah said confusedly.

'We are mere mortals, Delilah, therefore, we are more likely to be led astray, and even then, some form relationships with a selected few, hoping for the ideal partner, friend or a lover if in any case the one chosen should be wanting in some manner, and for all you know, it could be quite an innocent quest born of inadequacy and insecurity quite often than not. And sometimes it could be the natural need to initiate more lasting friendships if mutual interests should be discovered. Allow a man space for freedom of thought and deed, and he is sure to return home to you, to your waiting arms. Doubts and suspicions even jealousy can, in fact, destroy your relationship and love if not nourished with good thoughts, can soon give way to contempt and hatred,' she explained patiently.

'How do you have all this detailed out? I mean, he can't have explained it so minutely.' Delilah's puzzlement was openly visible.

'Whatever I have said has been my personal observation, Delilah. Besides, if you can spare the time for love, so also you must spare some time for carefully studying and understanding the object of your love. Then can only a relationship blossom.'

'Only when a man's traits become a vivid reality can he face difficult situations with more patience and calm. You panic in a crisis and you have lost the battle and your man,' Marian countered with an incredible perception.

Delilah sat up suddenly, her mind alert and thirsting for facts.

'But what was it that has apparently been worrying you? You haven't yet taken me in your confidence, I think,' Marian said gently… reassuringly.

With a sudden spurt of spirit born of inadequacy, Delilah retorted, 'I love Dominic, but how is it I have failed to understand him better?'

'Hmm, have you ever given yourself the time to think about certain aspects in all seriousness, by that I mean, his part in your life, his attitude, his reaction to anything that has to do with you and him?' was her quiet rejoinder that resulted in bringing to life Delilah's dormant rationality.

'Well, I am afraid I was more occupied with trying to win his interest, instead of negating certain destructive traits. I let them grow so much that... oh, what's the use? Oh, you must know what I mean,' Delilah said helplessly. She had never mastered eloquence, so words came out with difficulty.

'You mean jealousy and gnawing doubts have been crowding your mind for too long to allow room for practical thinking?' Marian asked helpfully.

'Yes. Exactly,' Delilah put in grudgingly, her head lowered in shame and self-disgust, but Marian smiled upon her with much fondness.

'Such a frank admission I should think would help you in setting your priorities straight,' she interceded with conviction.

'I have wronged you too... oh, so often, Aunt Marian. Can you forgive me?' And there were suddenly tears in her eyes, and her lips trembled. Repentance was very much in evidence.

'I understand what you must have gone through, Delilah. And there is nothing to forgive. To feel possessive about someone you love is a universal trait and quite often difficult to control despite our better judgement.' She had risen from the bed, and her face at the moment looked serenely beautiful.

'You're wonderful, you know,' Delilah said in a whisper, eyes brilliant with tears.

Marian laughed, but the laugh was not unkind, and it was the most beautiful sound Delilah had ever heard.

'Then you can't be knowing I am a condemned woman and there is another word for it, only I can't utter it in your presence,' Marian interrupted gently.

'Anyone condemning you has to be ignoble and low in understanding. Surely what you do with your life is your concern only, and who is anyone to interfere in your private affairs? And this has always been my contention,' Delilah uttered the words vehemently.

'Delilah, to acknowledge life's many trials with a calm acceptance is like having won half the battle. And such condemnation overruled, haven't I still lived my life fully and free of guilt? So long as you don't permit anyone or even the judgemental system such as it is and has always been, to cramp your style, things can't be so difficult then. How often has it been told that life is not a bed of roses, Delilah? Yet live on, one must, and make the best of the worst should be your motto,' she stated quietly.

Delilah then lifted her head.

'What about fighting for rights?' she spread her hands expressively, 'for... for love, for certain gains in life? You can't mean one must accept defeat meekly... without putting up a fight!' There was shocked disbelief in her eyes.

With a sigh, Marian re-seated herself on the bed next to Delilah.

'I cannot argue about fighting for rights, dear. It is in fact a man's privilege. But love... fighting for love? Why love is far above all such endeavours. Once you strive to fight for love, it is then annihilated from its inestimable stance and is soon after relegated to the level of gains and losses. It would then soon lose its true valuation as it stands a class apart from worldly gains; untouched and unscarred. Something so indestructible and carrying such... such staying power cannot be tampered with for personal gains,' Marian protested this time, and for once bewilderment showed on her face.

Delilah's face suddenly fell in utter dismay.

'I mean I mustn't fight to win his love? I have got it all wrong, haven't I?'

'Love is earned, Delilah and not fought for,' she said very gently. 'You must first make yourself deserving of someone's love and the first step would be, is to be free of bitterness and lingering doubts.' Her forehead was creased into lines of worry when she noted Delilah's perplexity. 'Delilah... Delilah, oh, how can I make you understand?' She shook her head in dismay. 'You love Dominic. And it is natural that you want him to return your feelings, is that it?'

Delilah looked up perplexedly and nodded without saying anything.

'Well, then… give things time to develop and hope for favourable returns. Consider love as an investment and it shall be returned to you with interest. The time is not far, my dear, when you shall cease to complain, only be more patient. Now I must go, dearest. I have been with you for a considerable amount of time, I think.' Then consulting her gold wristwatch, 'My goodness! I have to go out and I am already late by fifteen minutes. We could talk later.'

'A moment, Aunt Marian,' she requested plaintively.

Marian paused at the door, but her stance remained patient and tolerant.

'It… it must have been a great trial while Uncle Joseph was away, wasn't it?'

At once Marian knew that Delilah was wanting to be reassured and she felt her heart reaching out to her, although her reply was placid and matter of fact.

'Indeed, it was, till I realised the strength of my love for him. And then acceptance of certain situations came naturally.'

'You mean, it did not matter that you might never see Uncle Joseph again?' Her eyes widened in surprise.

'Hope was there, though, I was no longer desperate. That I loved him was sufficient reason to cherish the life which was not devoid of memories of his, still vivid and alive, and, therefore, still had meaning. His memories and my life had to be preserved because hope lived on. Yes, I longed for him, but desperation,' she shrugged the thought away disdainfully.

'I schooled myself to be forever engaged in various activities and I permitted myself no time for brooding, although quite often my certain involvements have made me the target of controversy. Only, I alone know why and what it was that had made me the way I have been.' She looked sideways. 'I had my moments but they never lasted for long. Even in his absence, Joseph was present and that is why perhaps no other man could captivate me completely. And the void had persisted.' It was like she was talking to herself.

'And where does the Almighty enter into all this?' Delilah cut into her thoughts with an abruptness which was so typical of her.

Marian was for a moment nonplussed, but soon regained her composure and smiled yet again.

'Yes, He alone can help when all else fails.'

'Then He does grant His mortals with their heart's desires, does He not?' Delilah asked in all innocence, her face that of a lost child's.

Marian's smile was serene as she replied calmly. 'It is only for Him to decide what He should grant and what He must decline. Delilah, we are venturing into uncharted waters far too transcendental. However, His grants are always guaranteed to work, but I am told He expects patience. And as the subject is of a spiritual nature, it is moreover metaphysical in context, then faith should be summoned and it should be unshaken if petitions be granted. Now I must leave, child. I am already late for the appointment with the lawyer.' She again turned, but this time to wish her good luck with an accompanying smile that stole Delilah's heart all over again.

Much after when Marian had left, did Delilah recollect with renewed interest all that had transpired between her and Marian, and made a mental summary of it. Finally, she was beginning to see light. In the deep recesses of her mind, one thought persisted though; a single outstanding thought. Immersed in that thought she did not notice the door slowly opening and a tall figure walking in with a grace of an athlete. The thought persisted. Some people just never aged and that was because they forever remained young in spirit and good at heart. Was that the secret shared by Marian, Joseph and Sampson and many others like them? Evidently, they all three enjoyed good-looks, and a slow, tantalising smile took form on her lips. And she was already beginning to feel better; totally recuperated.

And it was then when her eyes registered the presence of Dominic entering the room and her smile lingered. And the thought that she had been entertaining for so long remained static in its conviction.

'Well, I did knock,' Joseph grinned, drawing further into the room. 'Dominic, you too here?' He enquired matter-of-factly.

'I didn't want to be branded Hitler; the heartless, so I came. How are you feeling now?' he directed the question to Delilah who gave him an enchanting smile.

'Considerably better now that you are here.' And she gazed at him with a disturbing directness.

Then shifting her gaze for a moment on Joseph, she quipped lightly: 'Aunt Marian was here just a while ago,' she informed Joseph with a teasing inflection in her voice.

'Well, my dear girl,' he began with, as he subsided into a chair that was sprawled on the other end of the room. 'So she was,' Joseph smiled, 'and I was beginning to miss her.' He glanced at her with a light of amusement entering his eyes.

'You will admit that talking with her can be an enthralling experience,' Delilah remarked appreciatively.

He stroked his chin reflectively. 'Hmm, I won't dispute over that for fear of being called a liar.'

Delilah laughed at his mock seriousness.

He then turned serious all of sudden, watching her concernedly.

'You must be back on your feet and really fast. I'm told you're a good dancer.' His eyebrow quirked in a question-mark.

'I believe I am,' she laughed then, 'but you shall be the second in my list of partners.' And lifting her eyes to Dominic she said with some intentness, 'Dominic would, of course be the first in the queue or there will be hell to pay,' she said deliberately, but it was evident that she was silently laughing, and her smile was more in the nature of mockery. How she wanted to pull him down on the bed and have him make wild love to her, and that brought a blush to her cheeks.

'You sure you don't need a check-up?' Joseph looked really worried.

'It won't be necessary, now that I have you both such charming men here,' she put in suavely, and watching Dominic's frown deepening and again looking at Joseph, her smile very much in evidence, she said, 'but, Uncle Joseph, you have forgotten your stethoscope, I think,' she added, her smile provocative.

'And very conveniently too,' he threw her a sly glance as he stood up. 'I gave up my practice a long time ago.'

Delilah blushed crimson.

'Uncle!' she admonished gently, though her lips were parted in a sweet smile.

'I found I could not resist pretty women er, sorry... pretty patients.'

'Pretty women, Joseph, often have the makings of irresistible patients,' Dominic drawled with lazy interest.

Joseph quirked an eyebrow. 'Interested?'

Delilah could feel the strong palpitation of her heart. For just the briefest second Dominic glanced in her direction before once again reverting his attention to Joseph.

'I am extremely selective and so few possess appeal,' was Dominic's brief rejoinder.

'You will not make an easy conquest, then?' Delilah intervened quietly.

'Meaning?' he sounded curt.

She smiled as she replied in an indulgent tone, 'You are so fastidious, Dominic, so…so hard to please.'

'The Madame is absolutely right, Dominic,' Joseph agreed good-humouredly. 'Not just any beautiful woman will do for you.'

'So true. Not any woman would do, however beautiful,' he smiled wryly, but his eyes had been fixed on Delilah all the time with a message unfathomable. 'Are you coming, Joseph? The appointment is for five. We have very little time.'

Joseph shrugged his shoulders. 'Very well then. Let's go.'

Joseph briefly waved in Delilah's direction before moving to the door.

'Can you wait for me downstairs? I will follow you in a minute,' Dominic requested calmly.

'Sure,' Joseph nodded in Delilah's direction. 'By tomorrow, I want to see you out of that bed.'

'Doctor's orders?' Delilah joked, while she was beginning to feel far too overwhelmed in Dominic's presence.

'Doctor and a denounced chauvinist? Why, you have to be kidding,' he grinned as he casually left the room, and leaving Delilah in a state of confusion.

'What could he have meant by that?'

'Oh, it's a story that had been circulated when he was in the forces,' Dominic explained in a dry tone. 'On one occasion…' he started with, but was gently interrupted.

'Dominic, you needn't explain now. I mean, it isn't really important.'

'All right, we could leave it for a later date. In the meantime, how do you feel now? Are those prescriptions helping?'

'I'm heading towards a quick recovery. No complaints so far.' Her smile was quiet as she continued to feast her eyes on him.

'That's good news,' he stopped, then continued in a different tone that sounded hollow to his own ears. 'Marian was here, I heard.'

'She is indeed deserving of admiration. Moreover, she is like the river that clearly reflects the face of truth,' her voice sounded as though coming from a distance.

'But you're a mystery, Delilah, that yet needs to be unravelled. I only pray the truth you carry inside you should invariably be mirrored in your eyes,' he had spoken with a quiet intonation.

'Every man is mystery in himself, Dominic. Each has his own reservations and each follows his own convictions, and what he believes to be correct. And it is perhaps only in this respect that we are no different from each other, for who would not wish to follow the dictates of his own mind if granted such a liberty?'

'You have a point there, young lady,' he said, as he made his way to leave when her voice stopped him in his tracks.

'Is it a point taken, then?'

'Compelled to, as it leads to logical explanation why people behave so righteously at times, myself included.' His smile, though slight was genuine. 'Nevertheless, talking of mysteries again... you, my temptress, are definitely a mystery that would be worth unravelling and I don't doubt the unravelled be worth beholding.'

Their eyes met at that moment, but only for a minute before he turned and strode out of the room.

Her smile was perfunctory as she slid out of her bed, meaning to exercise her legs. She still felt lethargic, but she knew it was nothing to do with her weak constitution. It was strictly the result of her mental lassitude, although, the iron capsules were proving to be extremely helpful.

A wisp of gradually receding musk cologne reached her senses, alerting it to instant thoughts of Dominic, yet again. It was so typical of a man, she thought, to practice cajolery; luring a woman to believe in her powers of attraction, until such a time when he should think it expedient to drift into the background and leave a woman more confused and insecure. She refused to allow herself to bathe in masculine attention. But then it was all so superficial. Their every word, their every gesture manoeuvred to suit their own ends, trapping a woman into a web of deceit, and leaving her confidence to degenerate for fresh conquests.

She strode out into the veranda, enjoying the soft flow of cool breeze, wrapping her in a cloak of increasing vigour.

She looked around her, not missing anything and yet strange, but true that everything that she feasted her eyes on carried significance, as it all associated in some way or the other with the human race; mankind in particular of which Dominic was one, and because he mattered, she would not be indifferent to all that was made for him, for mankind, for a better existence.

The vast spread of land so rich in various produce, she noticed was heading for full maturity. She looked up to see how the glow across the vast sky was feeding life into the breathing organic plenitude down below and embracing the earth with its warmth and unparalleled radiance. How it bathed the whole expanse of the wide plateau in its liberal spread, and for the moment, Delilah lost in such enchantment forgot the oncoming of the temporary sheet of darkness, which now inevitably lay far beyond sunrise. Her eyes enthusiastically focused on the mountainous ranges rising one behind the other against the all-engulfing frame of mingling clouds and still dormant sunrise. How beautiful it all was… how great and powerful… He who created such sublime beauty, who controlled this all, and how miraculous the love that made her susceptible to all things alive and so splendid a spread. And lending the issue some relevance she contemplated just how many had time for nature's extreme possibilities, what it had to offer, standing independent, unsupported; it's strength and capacity for endurance against all natural calamities.

And suddenly it struck her how foolish man was, with his indifference, depriving himself of true solace and mental peace; and instead chasing through life succumbing to make-believe world of empty fun and gaiety. With a lack of insight, he managed to turn the rare gift of life into a superfluous existence when he could easily savour every glorious truth which is within his reach and grasp; if realised and properly understood.

She expelled a sigh, allowing her hands to be raised above her head. So much undiscovered lay ready to be exploited, so much goodness in man; so much soundness of character that needed to be developed, but man only had time for poor substitutes.

He remained ignorant of the truth; its staying power, its sustenance and life's many trials that go hand in hand with it, tutoring a man to develop strength and endurance if permitted. Alas! And this way, she imagined, sufferings would never cease, as man's essence; his inner self should resignedly give up the struggle for reaching out to his invisible God.

'And it isn't as if the journey be interminable to seek the eternal truth,' Delilah murmured to herself. 'It's the briefest I'd say. Begin to feel love for your fellowmen and complain not when agonies should follow. Those are mere clouds from behind which stars shall someday emerge.' She clenched her fists in concentration. 'Oh, I wish I could remember who had said that.' Her mind was momentarily startled into attention when her shoulders came into contact with something hard and warm.

'They are only my hands, Delilah,' Sampson chuckled softly, turning her around to face him. 'Taxing your brain?' he mused, ruffling her hair fondly. 'Come, let us go inside. There… your mother too has joined us. Now, isn't that flattering?' he pinched his wife's cheek, then twinkled at Delilah who was smiling warmly at both of them.

'Nowadays, she follows me wherever I go. She finds me irresistible, I think.'

'Sampson! Must you tease me so?' Selena circled her arms around her daughter and planted a kiss on her forehead. 'How does my sweetheart feel now?'

'Oh, Mama, I feel good. Papa, can you tell me who had said, "Behind every cloud, there is a silver lining?"'

'He was a sage whose name I cannot remember now, but it should suffice that it is indicative of the essence behind the eternal truth,' his slight smile denoted understanding, and Delilah responded to it secured in the knowledge of his having overheard what she had uttered, quite unaware of another presence in the room.

'You two at it again?' Selena laughed, humour lighting up her face.

'It's just a matter of time, dear,' Sampson added quietly in reference to what Delilah and he had been briefly discussing.

'He is right, Delilah. There have been quite a few examples in our family. Take Joseph's, Marian's and Anna's examples. Take my example, dearest. I found my star in Sampson.'

'Now, that's what I call inspiration.'

'Sampson!' Selena admonished him gently, but her lips were smiling as he pulled her to his chest and kissed his wife on the tip of her nose. Delilah continued to smile. She would she knew never again be blind to life's many possibilities.

Hours after, when Bertha entered the room, it was to find Delilah resting in bed. Stepping forward she pulled the blanket a little, to cover Delilah's exposed feet that had grown icy cold. She quietly moved to leave the room, eyeing her wristwatch keenly. Jarrod, she knew, would be coming to pick her up in half an hour. She still had to get ready. She had almost reached the door when Delilah's eyes flickered open.

'What's the time, Bertha?'

Bertha had turned with a smile as she strode back into the room. She gently helped Delilah into the cushion-backed chair.

'It's a quarter past seven. By the way, there is a letter from Joan. She is returning home the following Friday.

'Oh, I know that,' Delilah said absently, making herself more comfortable in the chair, 'Mother read out the letter to me. It will be good to have her back. And,' she looked excited as she remembered something suddenly, 'Anna is pregnant, Bertha. I just remembered,' she chuckled wickedly. 'What fun if she has to give birth to twins?'

Bertha laughed, not able to hide her amusement.

'I'd like to wish that upon you. How would you feel, then? Er, once you get married, of course.'

All laughter was swept from Delilah's face.

'I wonder if I'll ever get married,' she said in a lost voice, her mouth drooping slightly.

'Marriage isn't everything.' Bertha said quickly, knowing how she felt about Dominic.

'I want very much to be a mother someday, Bertha.' She lifted her eyes towards Bertha who felt a stab in her breasts when she noticed those eyes filling up with tears. She couldn't resist gathering her up in her arms.

'Of course, you do, you idiot. And what's more, you will one day be a mother. Don't be such a poker-head!' her own eyes filled up.

The sudden sound of footsteps across the hallway pulled them apart, giving them adequate time to rid their eyes of tears and regain surface composure. 'I... I think probably Jarrod...' then the words trailed off.

A clear sound of hearty laughter rang in the long corridor, soon followed by another and yet another.

'Oh Papa, how about sharing the joke with us?' Bertha ran to Joseph who stood in the doorway with spread out arms.

He turned his head and glanced amusedly at a quietly smiling Dominic, while his hold on Bertha tightened.

'You think it would be the wisest decision?' Joseph slanted Dominic a glance; a secretive smile lighting up the handsome features.

Dominic's smile was crooked.

'It's difficult to tell.' Dominic shrugged carelessly. 'How a woman would react to it is unknown to me,' his eyes were suddenly fixed on a quiet Delilah, 'and they are two in number. That makes it all the more difficult,' he remarked in a quiet tone, thrusting his hand in his pockets.

'Ah, now,' Joseph acknowledged the fact with an exasperated sigh, 'I think we better skip it,' he nodded vehemently. 'Hardly a joke for ladies.'

'Papa, could I use your car today? Jarrod's car is punctured.' Bertha peeped at him from under the curve of his shoulder, her eyes carrying an earnest plea in them.

'Unfortunately, no, my darling. Your mother and I are going out for dinner.'

'You may take mine, Bertha,' Dominic intervened quietly.

Delilah's face which had fallen brightened up suddenly.

'B... But are you sure you won't need it yourself?'

'Not likely to. I'm staying in, tonight,' he said in a crisp tone, his eyes once more settling on Delilah before he turned on his heel and strode out of the room, and down to his study.

'Is something wrong, Papa? I mean, he sounded very abrupt. He's not usually like that,' Bertha asked worriedly.

'Obviously, there's something that's worrying him. Surprisingly even the lecture at the university didn't go so well. It's not like Dominic,' he too sounded really worried over the matter.

'You mean he was assigned to give a lecture at the university? Dominic?' Bertha smiled pertly, her mood changing.

'You can believe that, child,' Joseph smiled back. 'You're quite forgetting, he was a professor once for a short while, and that he holds an outstanding degree in advanced Psychiatry.' He then glanced at Delilah significantly.

'Delilah, make sure Dominic has something for dinner. He has had nothing since morning, and even then, over breakfast he had just a cup of tea with plain toast.'

'I'll try my best, Uncle Joseph, although, I myself can't think what's got into him.' Delilah couldn't have known that she had gone pale.

'And, Bertha, my girl, go and see if Sampson is in his room. Selena…' he called out as she suddenly appeared on the scene followed by a vision of a woman that was Marian, and momentarily holding everyone's attention in the room.

Everyone seemed to be spellbound. What a contrast the sisters were and yet Selena had only to smile to turn into an even more captivating a woman. Marian had stepped forward, and with natural ease brought the atmosphere back to normal again.

'There now…' she began with a faintly exasperated look, 'I thought as much. You're not ready for our night out. Know something,' her scowl was slight, though, as she turned to face a smiling Selena who dropped into the chair.

'We ought to leave these two gentlemen behind,' Marian suggested calmly.

Sampson too had joined them in the room, and he too was not dressed for the occasion.

But upon noticing Joseph's stunned expression, Marian couldn't suppress a smile as she moved further into the room, and approached where Delilah was lounging in the chair, watching the scene before her, rather fondly. Marian impulsively bent to kiss Delilah on her cheek.

'Your cheek is cold, darling. Do warm-up,' she whispered, as her hand was pressed lightly against Delilah's other cheek. She straightened up when a cheerful, masculine voice just then reached her:

'Marian, I think we should be making a move. I know we are a little late, but Joseph and I won't take long to get into our evening attire, and besides, we are to pick another gentleman on our way to the party,' Sampson suggested patiently, and although still in casual clothes, he had never looked more handsome, and Marian was for a moment disturbed. She was secretly amazed to discover how alike the two brothers looked, and just as good-looking.

'On second thoughts, why don't the two of you follow us ladies, later? This arrangement, I think would be even better,' she informed Joseph, and then turning to Selena she said unhurriedly, 'I do believe you forgot to give me the bracelet.'

'I… oh, yes. I'll have to…' Selena started to leave the room to hurry down the corridor to her own private chambers, but she was stopped by Marian.

'Oh, you can forget it now,' Marian smiled cheerfully, 'you had better hurry instead. I do believe our dear spouses would rather go alone, so let them. Little time wasted, the better for it. I can already see someone here getting impatient,' and adding reminiscently, 'Sampson is so like his redoubtable son, I must confess,' she added, but instead her conspiratorial smile was received by Delilah who watched on with a smile one of warm indulgence.

Bertha was beginning to show irritation. And now her watch had stopped. 'That's just what I needed to turn my evening into a…'

'Bertha, Jarrod is here, dear,' Marian informed from the corridor that she was already crossing in a great hurry.

She hardly had time to greet the young man waiting in the hallway as she descended the staircase. Bertha had soon after followed her mother, throwing Delilah a flying kiss, as she ran down the stairs.

Downstairs, she greeted Jarrod with mock displeasure. Marian looked on briefly with some interest, her eyes all the time straying towards the staircase.

'I'd like to know what time it is,' Bertha demanded with a slight frown.

'Hmm, let's see,' Jarrod calmly consulted his watch, pulling up his sleeve a little. He lifted his head. 'There is enough time for you to get dressed,' and his voice, though pleasant, brooked no argument. His eyes were moving over her with some disapproval.

At that moment Bertha recalled once telling Delilah how much Jarrod and she had yet to learn about each other before plunging into marriage. And how right she had been. She knew so little about Jarrod, but she had to confess the little that she was learning about him was acceptable enough.

She discovered she was not averse to the way he managed her sometimes without actually making his domination obvious.

With a quick look at him, she once again made her way upstairs, almost dashing into her father.

'Take care, child,' Joseph cautioned her.

'I ought to have dressed up a long time ago,' she murmured impatiently.

'Save your breath. He is not here to point out your errors,' Joseph smiled rather impishly at his daughter.

'I know, Papa,' she breathed. 'You better hurry. Mama is waiting for you down there, and boy... she can really get impatient. So, watch out,' she added with some spirit, her smile attractively crooked as she rushed up the remaining stairs.

At the reminder that his wife was probably waiting in the hall for him, Joseph began to consult his watch and then threw a wink at his daughter who had paused just briefly before continuing on her journey to her room. At that moment Dominic emerged from his study, his car keys dangling from his fingers as he strode briskly towards where Marian and Jarrod were standing in the hallway, and waiting for the other couple to join them.

Halfway, Dominic was met by the housekeeper. He paused briefly. 'Sir, would you now like your dinner to be served?'

'Er, no. I'll have it later,' he said flippantly, and as a quick afterthought, he added, 'What about Miss Delilah? Has she had hers yet?'

'No, sir. She has instead stated the wish to join you at the table for dinner.'

'Oh well, you may go now. I shall see you about dinner later,' he dismissed the matter and the housekeeper absently, as he approached his uncle. But it was to Jarrod that he spoke, 'Here, Jarrod, Bertha thinks you might need this.' The key landed on Jarrod's open palm. And then with a brief nod, Dominic turned to go.

'Wait a minute Mr Redford. I won't be needing this. I have brought my own car.'

'But,' Dominic turned around, exasperation, though mildly, written all over his face.

'She did say something about your car not being in a working order.' He took back the keys forwarded to him with an awkwardness not gone unnoticed.

'I have a spare car, Mr Redford,' Jarrod supplied calmly and without sounding pompous.

'Hmm, have a good time, Jarrod,' so saying, Dominic strode towards the staircase when he was stopped by Joseph.

'Care to act as my moral support?' he said, eyeing Marian significantly.

Dominic briefly glanced in Marian's direction before turning back to Joseph again. A smile evident in his eyes as he said with a touch of wry humour, 'The lioness seems dormant for the time being, methinks. Her smile is placid, Joseph, though misleading. Never can tell with a woman, especially a woman as beautiful as she,' he glanced again at Marian who was politely attending to what Jarrod was conveying to her.

Joseph too followed Dominic's glance and nodded briefly.

'You may be right,' he said with a grin and excusing himself he walked to where his wife was standing.

Dominic resumed his journey upstairs without once turning back.

'Joseph,' Marian turned to him impatiently, 'I think we must make a move.'

And just then Sampson and Selena joined them and said their goodbyes to Jarrod, as they all four finally left the place.

Minutes ticked by, stretching into an hour. Dominic had completed his paperwork that had evidently been pending. In the privacy of his room, he stretched his hands behind his head, his fingers intermingling into one another while he allowed his head to rest against the wooden writing table. He experienced fatigue, his neck ached, and so did his fingers that had been busy for some time, and at a stretch.

A polite knock made him raise his head as he called out to the person to enter. The house-keeper discreetly opened the door.

'Sir…about…' she started with, but was sharply interrupted.

'Not again, Mrs Ralex. I told you when I want dinner to be served, I shall myself inform you. Now leave me please.'

'Pardon me, but that wasn't what I came to tell you,' she corrected his assumption patiently, and by now quite accustomed to his change of moods. He watched her with a bored expression on his face that looked a shade too strained.

'Miss Delilah would like you to join her down in the library.'

For a moment he appeared to be digesting that bit of information before rising from his chair leisurely, and flexing the muscles of his shoulders. 'Tell Miss Delilah, I'll be there shortly.'

In the library, Delilah occupied herself by reading a book, her mind relaxed and refreshed after the half-an-hour nap she had taken. Suddenly the door flung open without any preamble.

'What's up?' the deep, abrupt voice startled her for a minute, but soon enough she gathered up the scattered composure as she threw him a warm smile.

'I gather you wanted me?' he threw at her, and brisk steps brought him further into the library.

Delilah put her head to one side as she joked:

'And I do believe you came here to clear your doubts,' she said, with a hint of mockery.

His eyes narrowed, before he turned his back to her to stare out of the window.

'Come to the point, Delly,' he ordered without turning around.

'I told you once before I don't like being called by that... that ridiculous name,' she reminded him, and the sudden change in the voice carried a definite hint of the old fire and spirit, making him turn around, and a new interest entered his eyes.

His smile, though, was derisive, as he remarked caustically, 'So, the shrew is not yet tamed?' his eyebrows elevated sardonically.

'I don't take very lightly to be being ridiculed.' Her stance as she sat straight, indicated cold dignity poised for a veiled onslaught in defence of her vulnerable disposition.

'That's more like it, I must confess,' he nodded approvingly. 'You're finally recovering.'

'You don't sound too happy about it,' she remarked in a note of acute dismay.

'I'm happier than you can imagine. Besides, I like it so much more when you exhibit some spirit. And for the past few days, your quietude and resigned attitude had in fact disappointed me. And you seemed like a stranger. And I find it difficult to handle strangers,' he explained, now turning to face her with yet another sardonic smile.

She strove hard to keep the antagonism at bay.

'We are straying from the main purpose for you being here, Dominic,' she sketched out the words with easy confidence, the gaze that she directed at him; unwavering.

He threw her a sideways glance as he rested his elbow indolently against the mantlepiece.

'Yes, I'm anxious to know what's it all about; the purpose for calling me here.' He waited with a deceptive calm, his eyes not straying from her face.

Shedding the cloak of embarrassment, she began assessing his taste in clothes first, and not finding them in any way wanting in elegance. The grey pullover and the faded denim jeans, completed by the suede shoes, were casual so to speak yet extremely becoming on him. And she had to keep reminding herself that the man was beyond her reach, and that reminder would she knew keep her away from fantasising.

Dominic expelled a low whistle as she crossed one leg over the other, her change in position only enhancing her petite, seductive frame.

She looked up with a starched hauteur in response to the indication of a typical masculine appraisal of her.

'Don't blame me for showing such interest,' he shrugged carelessly, his eyes once again settling on her lovely, shapely legs. 'The brevity of your skirt makes me want to do more than just stare,' his voice with a hint of drawl gave away his apparent interest in her appearance.

'You haven't had anything since morning,' she remarked, trying hard to divert his attention from her for the moment.

'And so?' he watched her with hooded lids.

'I'd like to suggest you have something to eat. We could have dinner together, Dominic,' she added very patiently, trying to keep her calm. 'Please,' she appealed upon seeing his closed expression, 'don't push aside the suggestion.'

'I'd like to know why you are so concerned. It isn't as though... you love me,' he commented testily, his irascibility confusing her, and at that moment, she experienced a heaviness in her heart.

How she longed to tell him that she loved him. But should she confess openly about her feelings, she feared it could be a failing on her part. He was probably baiting her like most men liked doing.

'I care enough to feel concerned for you, Dominic,' she picked her words carefully. 'No woman likes to be made a laughing stock and her love be made a subject of mockery.'

'Caring isn't loving, Delilah,' he reiterated, as once before he had said the very same thing, she distinctly remembered. 'You had better drop the idea of persuading me to eat.' He made as if to retreat from the room, 'You must be hungry. You go ahead.' Then suddenly he swirled around, throwing her a glance that was one of restless fury, 'But for God's sake don't use me as an excuse to go on a hunger-strike! It won't impress me,' his voice sounded hard and uncompromising, but Delilah had not heard it all just to sit back and listen to him hurling insults at her.

Her seething rage built her strength for conducting a necessary retaliation. And then she gave vent to all that pent up fury, even as she rose from the chair to confront him with a fury of inexhaustible strength.

'You... you think you can have your say and turn heel and run? How about staying back and listening to what I have to tell you in response to your... your scathing comments? I can say they are in fact more in the nature of spite than anything else,' she flung at him, her breasts heaving.

He turned sideways and glanced at her with narrowed eyes.

'You'll listen, Dominic Redford, if it's the very last thing you do.' She had turned feverish, her face flushed and looking vibrantly beautiful. Her voice was not raised, but the command in it was unmistakable. 'Now then, using you for going on a hunger strike! It would be the very height of ridicule should I execute such means of stealing the show, of capturing your attention, and trying to impress you,' her voice had begun to sound more forceful, tempered by the sure evidence of sarcasm.

'Words! What are words to you? A gratuitous flow of unsymmetrical thinking, specially rendered to stab at a woman's vulnerability and... and,' she caught her chest in pain, coughing before continuing with some difficulty, 'and... and gloating over her pain, and...' she faltered, but she was suddenly caught firmly by her shoulders, as unrestrained tears ran down her flushed cheeks. She shrugged off his hands, pushing him away with vehemence.

'Delilah, darling, calm down. I didn't mean to... look, please forgive me...'

'I said let go of me. I'm finished with the entire male species. You heard me? But... but I am not among those women who keep silent. I'll fight every inch of the way for the women's right to command a man's respect, his realisation of a woman's depth, you heard me? The depth that is intensified, solidified with time. Feelings... love, yes, love, Dominic, that only a woman can feel and take pride in; pledge to honour, love; the glorious image of truth, the completeness and purity of it defying all dogma, all code of conduct preached by society. And why is this so that a man initially seeks a woman out for love, attention, her companionship, substituting for mental and physical solace, and... and,' she regally pointed a finger at him, vehemently shrugging away his hand, 'and you... you dare mock a woman for what she has to offer you, for what is expected of her by you! Y...you. Oh, I feel sorry for you,' she laughed, almost on the verge of hysteria as she slipped on the carpeted floor, but her head raised proudly, and her fingers still pointing at him contemptuously. 'Yes, what a tragedy! I pity you, Dominic. I pity all men blind to love, blind to all that a woman has to offer him with such total magnanimity,' her voice sounded breathless and words articulated in a low, weak tone.

She strove to rise up to her full height, and Dominic in a very much subdued state of mind came forward, stretching his hand out once again towards her. Her tear-filled eyes now watching him with defiance, she proudly let her hand be taken in his for just once, but this time her smile was slow and even a bit remorseful, almost melancholic. Nevertheless, she surprisingly seemed glad to accept the support of the man, for she truly loved him, and wanted him to know of it.

Her eyes met his as she finally stood up, now facing him squarely and proudly. There was now wisdom in her eyes and unshed tears in his that carried the distinctive look of an injured man, but gradually the expression changed to one of silent rapture as he continued to stare into those eyes of such remarkable beauty. They were the eyes of a woman who had finally understood love.

This time gentle hands pushed back unruly hair from the forehead beaded with perspiration. Then those hands leisurely came down to rest on the shoulders of delicate structure. His fingers tightened around those shoulders a little before they slackened upon noticing how fragile she had turned in her current condition. His eyes smiled down at her.

Her passion had rendered him speechless and still not aware that her passionate outburst had as always been only the manifestation of love that had crowned her existence over the years. For perhaps the first time, he was seeing her in her complete woman's guise. The woman had matured and he discovered that he loved her for giving voice to the call of passion.

With the same answering passion, he grabbed her closer to him and buried his face in her hair, and she let him. The frustrations had obviously died out, and passion temporarily subdued, and instead, she experienced tranquillity in his presence. For the first time in those few minutes, she looked truly relaxed and self-assured.

'How about dining together?' Dominic asked in a tender whisper.

'That was the original idea.' She threw him a dazzling smile, her eyes journeying over him with silent adoration.

'And a perfectly good idea it is, but perhaps you can think of something more promising after that routine session over the dinner table to serve as a dessert,' his smile was infectious. He helped her back into the chair and straightened up, looking down at her relentlessly, adoringly, like he was seeing her for the first time.

'I had better go ring for Mrs Ralex. That is, to serve us dinner.'

She waited, expecting him to move which he didn't, for he continued to look down at her, and his eyes carried a strange light.

'You're not gone yet,' she pointed out softly, and meeting those eyes bashfully for just once.

'And for what you are to be blamed,' his voice was ever so soft and matching the warmth in his eyes.

She grew serious again upon noticing the look in his eyes that closely resembled love.

'Dominic?'

'Hmm?' he had hitched up one leg on the small table lying opposite to her.

'Please don't allow yourself to get carried away by the unchecked passion with which I spoke, and permit your mind to be influenced. I... I wouldn't want it to be a momentary recognition of love's magnitude only for the mind to retreat into oblivion once again.' she pleaded in a voice of a woman distraught by lingering doubts.

'A mind that functions in favour of self-interest would rarely succumb to exhortation manoeuvred by others. However, in the face of the admission of truth, bearing such profundity, I should find it difficult to efface all that my mind has registered with such clarity.'

She looked up suddenly, her gaze levelled with a question in them, but finally verbalised when she asked quietly while enjoying a steady rapport with composure, 'And what has your mind registered?'

He had his back towards her as he replied with equally admirable composure.

'Love, Delilah. The love that is coupled with a woman; the indispensable backbone of a man.' He then turned around, his eyes never leaving her beautiful, radiant face, 'And without which a man is spiritually crippled. This, lovely one, is the overall registration of the structural truth securely assembled in the deep recesses of my mind and… heart.'

'I dare to believe it, Dominic?' Her eyes were that of a wounded deer.

Dominic smiled, his eyes lighting up with love.

'You mustn't deny yourself the right to believe in what is the actual truth,' he spoke ever so gently, and pulled her up to his side, his arms lovingly holding her in a warm embrace.

Her face raised to his, and the look in her eyes enigmatic, she said: 'I can foresee storms, Dominic.'

'No live emotion can be passive. Its magnitude, Delilah, is such that it vibrates in rhythm to the palpitation of two linked hearts merging into a force, and quite often receiving a jolt upon experiencing a tremor of doubts and swaying convictions that what you otherwise interpret as… storms.'

'You speak of love?' she asked hesitantly, and the look that she gave him was innocently expectant.

He nodded patiently, pulling her even more closer to him.

'The love that a woman feels, Dominic?' her tone still apprehensive.

He bent to plant a kiss on her feverish forehead.

'I speak of love that you feel for me, Delilah,' he whispered, his lips slowly journeying to meet hers in a long, passionate kiss.

'And, sweet woman, I speak of the love that I willingly give unto you.'

Her lips were sealed by his in a kiss surpassing the remnants of the passion for physical desire, and instead, to revel in a rapport of mind and soul.

THE END

www.ingramcontent.com/pod-product-compliance
Lightning Source LLC
LaVergne TN
LVHW061539070526
838199LV00077B/6835